Gideon's Heart

by

Faith V. Smith

Third Book in
Bound By Blood,
The Legends

This is a work of fiction. Names, characters, places, and incidents either are the product of the author's imagination or are used fictitiously, and any resemblance to actual persons living or dead, business establishments, events, or locales, is entirely coincidental.

Gideon's Heart: Bound by Blood, The Legends, Book Three

Contact Information: info@thewildrosepress.com

Cover Art by *Tamra Westberry*

Cover Model is *Evan Scott*
www.platinumcoast.biz/evan.htm
Mr. Romance 2003 2nd Runner-up/Contestant's Choice

The Wild Rose Press
PO Box 708
Adams Basin, NY 14410-0706
Visit us at www.thewildrosepress.com

Publishing History
First Black Rose Edition, 2011
Print ISBN 1-60154-934-2

Published in the United States of America

"Please..."

"Everything's going to be okay. I know I keep telling you that, but you have to trust me. I'm going to take you where you'll be safe."

Eyes the size of saucers stared back. Their lavender hue deepened. A shiver inched up his spine. He'd seen eyes that color before. They'd belonged to Gabriella, a woman—no, make that vampire—who tried to kill Zacke and Miranda in a fit of rage and jealousy.

He leaned down and placed one arm beneath the woman's shoulders and one under her knees. He barely registered her slight weight. Her silver-blond hair fell over his arm and swung loose. The color and texture reminded him of moonbeams on a calm lake. She was nothing like Gabriella.

He brought her closer into his chest in an effort to warm her cold body. She tilted her head back. Her gaze looked calmer. Her lips parted. "Where are you taking me?"

Gideon wished he could listen to her velvet tone all night. That wasn't an option. She needed warmth, food, and some rest.

He cleared his suddenly hoarse throat. "I'm taking you to my house."

Panic filled her gaze once more. "Don't worry, you'll be as safe with me as you would be in your mother's arms."

The soft sigh she gave made him want to beat his chest. He just hoped he remembered he was playing the part of dear old mom.

Dedication

To my Rick, who will forever be my angel in Heaven.
To Amanda, my daughter,
who slaves to keep things going so I can write.
To Feisty, my little dog who went to Rainbow Bridge
to join her daddy on November 11th, 2010.
I'll miss the sound of your little paws.
To Callie Lynn Wolfe, thank you for all you've done
to make this series possible.
To Tamra Westberry who made my cover come alive.
You are awesome!
Also, a big thank you
to the Reading and Copyediting Department
and Nan Swanson
who always fixes my galley mistakes.
To Maureen Sevilla,
thank you for convincing me to change the villain.
It made all the difference in the world.
To Maryln Claussen, this one's for you!
Thank you for loving my vamps and their ladies!
And to God be the glory. I could not do what I do
without knowing He watches over me.

Acknowledgments

As with any book I write, I know I will miss someone who needs to be praised. So please accept my apologies if I missed adding your name.

There is one name that does need to be mentioned, and that is Evan Scott. I first met Evan at a Romantic Times Booklovers Convention. He was the perfect southern gentleman, and so kind.

Evan was also Mr. Romance 2003 2nd Runner-up/Contestant's Choice

Through the years of our friendship, he has been so supportive. I want to thank him now for being the perfect "Gideon" on my cover.

As most of my readers know, Gideon is a gentleman, southern to the bone, handsome, and has a huge heart. All of these attributes are shared by Evan.

Evan went out of his way to do a photo shoot for me. He used his own gun, and what a gun it is. In Evan's own words...

"I only shoot a Colt 45-caliber ACP (Model 1911A). By today's standards, it's a bit of a dinosaur but a very powerful round. Many agencies have gone to newer high-tech pistols with high-capacity magazines. However, if you hit your target the first time, you don't need all the extra rounds. And nobody gets up after being hit by a 45."

Evan is not only handsome but also extremely intelligent. Check out the Bio on his website: http://www.platinumcoast.biz/evan/ESbiocredits.htm

Thank you, Evan, so much, for giving your time. As an author I am grateful: you made my hero literally walk out of the pages of my book. Love to you and Tamara!

Chapter One

The smell of blood lingered in his nostrils, as he
stalked his prey. After centuries of searching he'd
finally find her. The one he was forbidden to have,
the one who looked upon him with open revulsion,
but this time he would take what he wanted. He
crept closer. So close he could feel her emotions, he
could read her thoughts.

****

Hopelessness sucked at her limbs like a morass
of mud. It reminded her of the bogs back in Scotland
where she'd lived and died. Life or death for
Katheryne Alastair held no meaning. She had spent
a century looking for goodness among humanity and
then for her own kind.

Now, in an alley deep within Savannah's Red
Light district, she had come to the end of her hope
and existence. If there were any vampires in this
area, they had hidden their identities deep. She had
followed a trail of what ifs to discover the detective
she sought, Zacke Kensington, was just a mortal
husband and father.

The second vampire, Miles Dunbar, in question
turned out to be nothing more than a Good
Samaritan married to a physician. And finally, the
last of her anticipated brethren, Hawk Sherwood,
was a History professor. All three men walked in
daylight, and although some of the ancient vampires
could, she had never heard of children being sired
from a vampire—mortal mating.

With the addition of non-existent morality in
this district, as well as the other cities she had

1

visited or lived in since her immortal creation, she decided she'd had enough.

Her body was weak from lack of nourishment. Yes, she could have fed from any of the vagrants or prostitutes living and working in the area, but why? She would only be draining what little life force they had left. The blank stares of the homeless brought her closer to her own frustration with life.

Better she end it now than to wait on an obsessive mortal to stake her. Of course, the stake wouldn't kill her but it would hurt like fire. Losing her heart and her head, if they'd done their homework, would be the way to send her from earthly realms for good.

Yes, dying by her own hand would be best.

Katheryne moved further back into the alley and leaned against the cold bricks of the wall. She shivered with anticipation of the near-dawn, and would enjoy the blend of pink, purple, red, and orange as the sun awoke and moved slowly toward the skyline. Once again, she would delight in the sheer pleasure of a newborn day before she met death and her judgment when the fiery planet reached its zenith.

****

Gideon Hawks sidestepped a drunk and waved off an advancing streetwalker. His quarry was of a different kind. A rash of sexual assaults in the Red Light district had his captain up in arms. The last victim was a rich socialite slumming for the thrill. Her daddy reamed the mayor a new one, and the mayor's angst exploded down through the chain of command. With threats of replacement, nights spent walking a beat, and crew cuts for all detectives, he and Zacke, his partner for over a decade had split up to search for any potential victims. And hopefully catch the perpetrator before he struck again.

His gaze swept the last of his appointed route

before he checked his watch. Just a few minutes more and he could head back to the station. A quick notation of the night's activities, and he'd be off for an entire three days. Yes! It'd been a long time coming. And it'd only cost him a box of donuts in payment to the sergeant in charge of time off and well worth it in Gideon's opinion. The first thing on his to do list was kicking back with a six-pack, a new CD, and then after a long nap, he'd hunt up a date for the annual policeman's ball.

He didn't normally do the tux scene, but after being best man in Zacke's wedding and an usher in Miles nuptials, not to mention his brief stint as a bachelor for the Children's Charity Auction, he kinda liked how he looked in one. Of course, his opinion didn't matter a hill of beans. It was what the babes thought that mattered.

He turned to meander back down the alley but a soft whimper caused him to pause. It sounded like a kitten. He retraced his steps but only saw the same row of cardboard boxes lining the alley. Winter had arrived early this year, just in time for Halloween and the nights had grown colder. He pitied the homeless trying to keep warm in their makeshift shelters.

Again he heard the whimper. Definitely a weaker imitation of the first cry. Something or someone was in pain. Gideon hated abuse of any kind. In this hellhole, it usually stemmed from an irate pimp taking out a slow night's cut on a poor working girl.

But, occasionally it was a child who'd been beaten. It didn't matter to Gideon why a parent might chastise a child; he couldn't abide the various ways the discipline might be meted out.

The cry came again. Who or what it was needed his help—*now*. He picked up his pace and skirted the last cardboard home. Something rustled on the

3

pavement beside his booted feet. He hoped it wasn't a rat. He hated those things. Almost as much as he hated spiders. Those eight-legged monsters gave him the creeps.

Gideon scanned the area. Nothing jumped out at him but a more detailed survey turned up a flash of color against the alley wall. He moved forward and eased his gun out of his shoulder holster.

It never hurt to be careful. His mama use to say, it might walk like a duck and quack like a duck, but that don't make it a duck.

He inched closer to the purple fabric fanning across the filthy pavement. His gaze followed the material and found the face of an angel.

An angel who wasn't breathing. He holstered his gun and dropped to his knees. His hand shook as he laid it against her neck. No pulse. His brain tried to remember the steps of C.P.R.

Think man. Hell, why couldn't he think?

Gideon inhaled and exhaled, almost strangling on his own breath. Okay, he could do this—he had to do this.

He placed one hand under her neck, tilted her head back, and pulled her chin forward. He checked her airway and then pinched the slender bridge of her nose. Again, he inhaled before placing his mouth over her blue tinged lips. He exhaled twice and watched her chest for movement.

Nothing!

A firm but gentle count of fifteen and he repeated the procedure. The sixth time awarded him a faint rise of her chest.

Thank God.

He sat on the pavement, and checked the pulse in her neck and found what he sought. A slow but continuous beating made Gideon want to jump for joy. It was faint but there. He would have passed out too in surprise if his limbs weren't cramped with cold. His gaze stayed glued to her porcelain features as he pulled out his cell phone to call his partner.

Lashes black as a funnel cloud flickered. His breath hitched when a second later they did it again. A third movement and they stayed open. Lavender eyes gazed at him in confusion.

"It's okay. I'm a cop. You're going to be all right." His words didn't help. She tried to scoot away from him. Her slender body shook with the effort. Gideon's heart ached at the fear now centered in her gaze.

"I won't hurt you. I promise. But you need help. Let me help you." He allowed his words to penetrate the rapidly retreating darkness of the night. He slowly stretched his hand out. He held his breath. Would she take it?

Yes!

He caught the fragile hand she lifted into his own trembling grasp. He wanted to shout halleluiah. "Hang on just a minute. I'm going to call for help. We'll get you to the hospital and have a doctor—"

"No." Although soft, that one word held a world of meaning. Terror, distress, and hopelessness also played out in her frantic attempt to snatch her hand free.

"Hey, take it easy. I won't call an ambulance, I swear. Okay? Just let me call my partner." Gideon loosened his grip and allowed his wounded angel to ease her hand away. He flipped open his cell phone, but continued to keep his gaze pinned to hers. He hoped to convey he wouldn't break his promise. He punched in a number.

"Zacke, I've got a victim. At least I think she is. She wasn't breathing when I found her but she is now. I don't know if she was sexually assaulted or not. She's scared to death and doesn't want me to take her to the hospital. What can we do?"

He listened for a moment. "Yep, I know that's

what I should do, but... Look, I'll take care of this if you log me out at the station. Thanks, Zacke, I owe you one."

Gideon clicked off his phone and managed a grim smile. What he planned to do went against all regulations. He could lose his shield. He shifted his weight and climbed to his feet.

"Please, just leave me here." Her voice a veritable whisper of sound that hurt his heart.

"I can't do that. You could die." The thought of her actually dying caused a stab of pain deep inside his chest.

"Please..."

"Everything's going to be okay. I know I keep telling you that, but you have to trust me. I'm going to take you where you'll be safe."

Eyes the size of saucers stared back. Their lavender hue deepened. A shiver inched up his spine. He'd seen eyes that color before. They'd belonged to Gabriella, a woman—no, make that vampire—who tried to kill Zacke and Miranda in a fit of rage and jealousy.

He leaned down and placed one arm beneath the woman's shoulders and one under her knees. He barely registered her slight weight. Her silver-blond hair fell over his arm and swung loose. The color and texture reminded him of moonbeams on a calm lake. She was nothing like Gabriella.

He brought her closer into his chest in an effort to warm her cold body. She tilted her head back. Her gaze looked calmer. Her lips parted. "Where are you taking me?"

Gideon wished he could listen to her velvet tone all night. That wasn't an option. She needed warmth, food, and some rest.

He cleared his suddenly hoarse throat. "I'm taking you to my house."

Panic filled her gaze once more. "Don't worry,

you'll be as safe with me as you would be in your mother's arms."

The soft sigh she gave made him want to beat his chest. He just hoped he remembered he was playing the part of dear old mom.

****

"Damn." Marcel Charmant's incisors cut into his bottom lip. If not for the interfering policeman, Katheryne would have been his, ripe for the taking. He would have consoled her and given her a reason for living. Now, he would have to wait, for killing the man as he wanted would bring him too close to the authorities. However, someone would pay for keeping him from his love. His nostrils flared as he scented a woman approaching. This time when he fed, he would not only quench his thirst but leave the policeman something to occupy his mind. Then Marcel would reclaim his property.

Chapter Two

Katheryne awoke to the horrific sounds of whistling and snorting. She peered around the small space and found the annoying source of discomfort. The man who had rescued her lay sprawled on what looked to be a sofa. An assortment of clothes and bed linens covering the furniture made it impossible to tell.

Nor could she tell what time of the day it was— shades covered the only two windows in the room. By her internal clock, it felt like she'd slept a long time. Thank the higher power that she'd lived long enough in death she didn't have to feed every night.

Somehow, she didn't think her knight in shining armor would understand or appreciate why she needed a pint of blood. Katheryne sat up and slid back against the bed's headboard. A bed that dominated most of the room's space.

Although she'd lived most of her mortal and immortal years in the sixteenth century, some things had not changed. Men valued a status symbol of their prowess.

The owner of this particular symbol stirred and stretched on his improvised bed. He grunted in his sleep as his arm connected with a table sitting in front of the sofa. The man, she didn't know what else to call him, looked like he could use a shave, and his shoulder length blond hair with its darker streaks stood out against the white pillow wadded under his cheek. His nose looked like it had been broken once or twice, and his lips were pulled into a tight line.

Handsome, although not in a classical way.

Katheryne didn't mind. Actions were more important than looks, and his actions spoke volumes to her heart and misplaced soul.

Maybe if someone had shown her kindness earlier in her life, she wouldn't be a fanged monster.

"Ouch!"

She watched in fascination as the man looked up from his new resting place on the floor. A rapidly reddening spot marred his forehead. He lifted his upper body and reached for the couch. Whoosh! An avalanche of bed covers and clothing showered down on top of him.

She giggled aloud at the muffled mumbling coming from underneath the small mountain. The clothing shook as if alive and then the man's head popped up, followed by his shoulders, and then the rest of his body.

"Found that funny, did you?"

The humor in his tone canceled out the scowl on his face. She fought her additional laughter and lost.

"Can't say I blame you. I must have sounded like a ton of bricks when I hit the floor. I hope I didn't wake you."

He stood up and stretched. A short-sleeved, white shirt and some type of short pants, maybe underclothing, hugged his frame. Last night—no, early that morning, she hadn't paid any attention to his muscular build. His kind eyes, the color of rich chocolate, and tentative smiles had captured her attention. Now, though, she could see he was above average height and in good shape. He'd said something about being a cop. Although, she'd only been in this century a brief time, she had done some research at one of the libraries to find out how things worked in this day and time. If she remembered correctly, a cop was a shortened form for policeman, much like the constable in the village where she'd lived as a child.

"I forgot to ask. How are you feeling? Do you have any idea what made you sick? Were you attacked? Do you have family I can call?"

She watched and listened, enthralled as the questions spewed from his mouth like a geyser of water. His tone was almost a drawl. How had she missed that earlier?

He advanced toward the bed. Katheryne couldn't move any further back. She really shouldn't be frightened. He had shown her nothing but kindness, and it wasn't as if she couldn't protect herself.

He perched on the edge of the bed and grinned. "Guess I have a case of run-on-mouth. Why don't we start over and I ask one question at a time, okay?"

She gave him a smile of her own. "I'm feeling much better now. Thank you for your kindness."

The pink tinting of his bronzed cheeks endeared him even more to Katheryne. She knew the new millennium had cast off many of the morals that encompassed the centuries she'd lived through. And to find someone, especially a man, who blushed was totally unexpected.

She supposed she could have lived out her immortal life, moving from one place to another to prevent mortals from questioning why she didn't age, or she could have traveled forward to a new century. Instead, she'd chosen to sleep decades at a time. She'd been fearful of what she might do to a mortal, and of men. That particular gender had not treated her kindly, but then neither had the women of her kind. So, she had gone to ground, awakened, and been determined to find more of her own kind. Maybe she'd find kinder souls in this century full of strange devices and birds of metal. The library books and papers explained most of what she had missed but there were still things she needed to learn.

"There's no need to thank me. I was only doing my job." If possible, his blush deepened. "I mean, I uh, would have done it for any person in need."

"Well, I thank you anyway. I'll be happy to answer the rest of your questions, but first, what is your name?"

"Oh, I'm sorry. I'm Gideon Hawks."

"Nice to meet you, Gideon. I'm Katheryne Alastair."

"Wow, that's a pretty name and a mouthful. How about I call you Kat?"

"Cat? As in a four-legged creature?"

Gideon's laughter made her giggle again.

"No. Kat as in short for Katheryne. Did I pronounce it right?"

"Yes, you did, but I like Kat, too."

"Great, so Kat, do you know why you got sick?"

"It was probably due to hunger." Katheryne's hands trembled. She couldn't believe she'd said that.

"Oh, man, I should have thought of that. How long has it been since you've eaten? It has to have been awhile. You weren't breathing when I found you. Did you pass out?"

Katheryne didn't know what to say. She couldn't tell him she hadn't been breathing because she was asleep. That her heartbeat would be non-existent to a mortal's eyes unless they knew what they were looking for. She couldn't tell him what she was or could she? Did he believe in vampires or would he have her locked up in an asylum?

"Yes, I did faint, but I'm feeling much better now."

"I don't really have much here to eat, but I could call out for a pizza."

Pizza? It had to be edible but Katheryne wasn't sure she wanted to try it. She could eat some mortal foods but it'd been a long time in-between meals for her—even the liquid kind.

"Thanks, but I'm not hungry. Maybe..." She didn't want to hurt his feelings, "A glass of wine?"

"Wine? Darn it. I've only got beer."

A few moments later, she found an ice cold can in her hand and an expectant Gideon waiting on her to say something.

"It's different."

"Great, now maybe we can get back to my earlier questions."

"I wasn't attacked, and I don't have any family here or anywhere else for that matter."

"You're an orphan?"

Katheryne would have laughed if not for Gideon's compassionate expression. She'd been an orphan for centuries. The death of her parents had torn her life apart. Lady Katheryne Alastair, daughter of a Scottish laird and an English lady had lost all when her parents died in a tragic accident. An English uncle took control of the estate and later cast her out of her childhood home. Penniless, she lived day to day. She'd stolen what she could to eat and slept where she dropped after a day of evading men. Men who wanted to sell her body or keep it for their own perverted habits.

Months went by until one day she'd been lucky enough to find a job. While at her employer's home, she caught the attention of a woman who wanted her services as a maid. It wasn't until much later she discovered the woman was a monster.

A creature without a soul. That same creature made Katheryne a servant and then in a fit of jealous rage she'd transformed her into a creature. Then one day, the lady simply disappeared.

Someone may have killed her, but she doubted it. Gabriella had been vicious. Nightly parties resulted in men's mutilations after she satisfied her carnal appetites. Sometimes she changed them into vampires but for the most part, she'd laughed as they begged for their lives and then lapped the blood pouring from their wounds.

"You okay? You got awful quiet on me. I didn't mean to bring back bad memories."

"It's all right. I've grown use to it over the years."

"Well, don't worry about a thing. You can stay here until you get back on your feet. I've got friends who'd be happy to help you find a job."

Katheryne set the half-empty can on the table by the bed. A lifetime and death behind her, and she'd never found a man who actually seemed to care. How could she convey what his offer meant? Her mistress of evil wouldn't have hesitated in bedding the man, but Katheryne didn't play those types of games. When she took a man to her bed, it would be because she loved him not because of gratitude.

"Thank you. Now, why don't you tell me about yourself."

"There's not a lot to tell. I'm a cop, I told you that before. I work nights and when not on the job sometimes I get together with friends."

"Are your friends cops also?"

Gideon eased his body further onto the bed and propped on one elbow. "Not all of them, but Zacke is, and he's my partner. His wife is a doctor. They have twins—a boy and girl. Through Zacke, I met Miles and Hawk. Neither of them are cops but they are okay guys. Miles is married, but Hawk's still single. I got to know them better when they helped me and Zacke out on a case."

"A case?"

"Yes. We had a killer running loose and Zacke asked Miles and Hawk to help find her."

"The killer was a woman?

"Yeah, a real vicious woman." Gideon's brows drew together. "I don't suppose you believe in vampires?"

Katheryne's heart stalled. Why would he ask

her that? "Well, there are a lot of strange things in the world."

"I agree and this woman took the cake for being strange and vicious. She killed without batting an eyelash." He fidgeted with the bedspread. "She almost killed Zacke. She kidnapped his wife and used her as bait. My partner fought and killed her, but the wounds she left him with were fatal or should have been. It's only by a miracle of God he survived Gabriella's attack."

Katheryne shook her head in an effort to dislodge the appalling truth. The woman who had changed her and reaped such havoc on this man's friends was the same. His partner killed Gabriella. And as much as she feared his answer, she had to ask.

"What is your partner's last name?"

"Kensington, why?"

Blood moved sluggishly through Katheryne's veins before stopping altogether. The man she'd sought to find when she first came to this century was a vampire killer. Oh Lord, what on earth was she going to do? She couldn't stay here, not now. Gideon despised vampires, his partner killed them, and it sounded as if his other friends felt the same way. She had to leave.

Katheryne made an effort to get off the bed but a shrilling noise stopped her.

Gideon bounded off the bed and headed toward the door. "Be right back. It's probably Zacke and Miranda. I called them before I crashed this morning."

The rapidly beating organ in her chest rebelled before slowing to thunderous thuds. The vampire hunter was here.

The door opened and a man slightly taller than Gideon with hair black as soot and a woman with hair the color of copper advanced into the room.

They spoke a few words to Gideon before turning toward her.

"Hi, I'm Miranda." The woman's words were followed by a smile but Katheryne didn't care. She'd been stalked before and several narrow escapes had taught her to trust no one. She hadn't until today—now look at the mess she was in.

The man held out his hand, "I'm—"

She didn't allow the man to finish his introduction. She moved off the bed, stumbled across the room, and ran out the door.

She launched her body into the night sky and allowed the wind to do most of her flying. Tears flooded her eyes. She was right back where she'd started. Without hope, she might as well be dead. Something she planned to rectify come sunrise.

****

Marcel watched as Katheryne ran from the man's home. Her vault toward the heavens nothing short of elegant. He wondered who had sired her. Not that it mattered; he wanted her by his side for all eternity. Gabriella had been jealous of his interest in the le petite chat, and kept Katheryne hidden when he visited except for twice when he'd caught her unaware. But Gabriella was dead, and nothing and no one would prevent him from attaining the treasure he sought.

Chapter Three

Gideon raced after Katheryne. What had spooked her? The street outside his apartment was empty. Where had she gone and why? She'd been fine before Zacke and Miranda arrived.

He retraced his steps and closed the door. "I don't understand it. Why would she leave?"

Zacke crossed to the one chair Gideon owned, a ladder-back that had seen better days and drew Miranda down onto his lap. "Uh, hem, I hate to say it, Gideon, but you know your guest could be in trouble."

"I know she's in trouble. She's got no where to stay, and it's gonna be even colder tonight."

"That's not what I meant. You found her on the streets and at a time, most people would be at home in the bed. She could be a—"

"Don't say that. You're wrong! Katheryne is not a prostitute. She's just down on her luck."

Zacke stayed silent, but Miranda eased off his lap and crossed to Gideon. "Hon, I know that you want to believe that and you could be right. But, Gideon, your track record with women isn't the greatest. You've been known to fall for anything in a skirt batting her eyelashes at you. Could you be mistaken? You know if she knew you were a cop, she could be scamming you."

Gideon allowed Miranda's hand to stay on his arm. Could he be wrong? Katheryne seemed so nice and needful. He couldn't imagine her as a woman prowling the streets for a john or someone trying to find a mark and score. Had he been on the job so long he'd lost his instinct?

"Possibly, but she wasn't breathing when I found her. She couldn't fake that."

"No, that's kinda hard to fake, but there are drugs that can slow your heart rate down to where it's impossible to hear without a stethoscope."

Gideon looked down into Miranda's sympathetic but earnest face. "Sure, and she just knew I would be the one finding her. Besides, I don't care one way or the other. I just need to—"

"Gideon if you're in between women, I'm sure Miranda can fix you up. Maybe with one of the nurses at the hospital, or what about the new clerk at the station?"

"No! I don't want to be fixed up. This is different."

Gideon watched Zacke and Miranda exchange looks. Yeah, he knew what they were thinking. He'd said that before and not so far in the past. But this time *was* different. For the first time since Maddie, a younger cousin, someone really needed his help.

"Look guys, thanks for coming by. I hate that you couldn't check Katheryne over for any problems, Miranda, but—"

"It's okay. Maybe next time."

He walked them to the door and hugged Miranda, then exchanged a brief smile with Zacke. "I'll see you when I get back to work on Monday."

"Yep. I'll be there. After I got back to the station this morning, I found out I have the next three days off, also. Guess no one wanted to work with me."

Gideon couldn't prevent a chuckle from escaping. Even after shedding his vampire heritage, Zacke was still hell on wheels as a partner and on a partner.

"Yeah, well, I'm a tough act to follow." His remarks garnered an answering chuckle from Zacke and a delightful peal of laughter from Miranda.

He ushered them out the door with threats of *don't be late for work next week* echoing in his too quiet apartment. He moved to his CD player and popped in a country western tune. The fast and riveting sounds of *Bullets In The Gun* by Toby Keith didn't help.

Odd, but he missed Katheryne.

****

Katheryne landed silently on the sidewalk near a deserted building. Her desperate flight earlier only emphasized how taut her nerves were strung. She had soared the skies over Savannah until the wind picked up. Its punishing force caught her unaware, almost plummeting her to the ground. Thoughts on where she would die, and her distress over Gideon had caused her inattentiveness.

For just a brief moment, she'd thought her life had turned around. Possibly, just maybe, she might have found a reason to live. Gideon's unselfish act of help and his offer of temporary refuge had lightened her heart. Now—knowing his dearest friends killed her kind made anything between them impossible.

For her there was no future. Although, vampires were refuted to not feel pain and shouldn't feel the elements, Katheryne did. She hurt deep down in her bones with a cold that snapped the brittle thread of life's hope.

She glanced around but found no mortal traffic on the street or near her. This was just as good of a place as any to wait for the sun to take her lonely life and miserable soul.

She made her way to the end of the street and into an alley. The overhang from rooftops blocked out the weak moonlight and made the dark area even blacker. This would do. Facing the east as it did, the sun's rays would creep forward until they blasted her in a fiery release.

She rubbed her arms and pulled the sleeves of

her gown down over her wrists. A useless gesture, but it made her feel better—more human. The wall against her back held the cold of the night as she prepared her final resting place. A few scraps of cloth, a bit of cardboard, and a nice piece of plastic would cushion and shield her from human eyes until the sun rose.

Katheryne pulled the plastic up to her chin and rested her head on her arm. It was too early for the pull of her immortal sleep, but she closed her eyes anyway.

The nightmare began the same way.

Gabriella snarled with blood-flecked fangs. "So my little slave wants to party with my lover?"

Katheryne tried to get away from the vicious tear of her claws. "No Lady Sanspree, I only answered the door. I don't want anything to do with Monsieur Charmant."

Gabriella turned her gaze toward her lover. "So did she promise to warm your bed or did you proposition her, Marcel?"

"Much to my chagrin, you interrupted us before I could ask her, Gabriella." Marcel flicked his fingers, as if dismissing the incident, the ring he wore on his hand glowed in the candlelight. A fleur de lis set center in the ruby stone.

"Well, I'm not sure I believe you, but if you're so desperate to taste Katheryne, then I would prefer you do it in front of me."

Katheryne twisted her body trying to escape— she knew what Gabriella meant. She did not want Marcel to touch her, let alone take her blood.

"I would like that, would you care to join me afterward in your bed chambers?" The Frenchman's leering smile turned her stomach. Bile burned her belly as she prayed Gabriella only taunted her lover.

"Yes, I would. Now, only a taste, and then after this if I catch you sniffing around Katheryne, you will be banned from not only my bed but my home."

The next few minutes were terrifying and painful, but she'd lived through them. Not so when months later Marcel caught her alone again. After Gabriella tossed him out, she'd turned on Katheryne.

Katheryne's heart stalled when Gabriella's claw-tipped hand grabbed her throat. She couldn't escape the choking grip. She opened her mouth to beg for mercy but before she could get the words out, she felt a shard of fire attack her flesh. The next moments were a blur of pain and horror. She awoke to darkness. A darkness she only realized later would be the total existence of her life.

Her whimpers of disbelief and a terrifying hunger crawled from her abdomen to her throat—their release turned into an explosion of screams threatening to burst her eardrums.

Katheryne jerked awake—the remnants of her nightmare fresh in her mind. She shook her head to dislodge the sounds of her ghastly cries. They still echoed, almost as if they had found substance in the night air.

A grunt and low cry of pain filtered to her ears. Katheryne threw off her covering and followed the next groan.

A few streets over she spotted three men in a scuffle. One man held another in his grip while the third pummeled the captive's midsection with fists.

A blow to his face propelled his head back. The streetlight illuminated features she recognized.

Gideon! They were attacking the one man who had shown her kindness.

Another drive to Gideon's jaw caused him to slump in the man's arms. A second and third round of fists and his captor released him. His body collapsed to the hard pavement.

The man who administered the blows pulled out

a gun and aimed it at Gideon. Katheryne felt her incisors stretch. Rage assaulted her—a desire to kill enveloped her senses.

She snarled.

The men looked up.

She opened her mouth.

They screamed.

She flew across the alley.

They ran.

Katheryne started after them but a groan at her feet stopped her from giving chase.

Gideon lay on his side. She dropped to the alley floor and touched the bruise already darkening his chin. His eyelids were puffy, and a similar purple tinge spread below his lower lashes.

His top and bottom lips were split open. The slow oozing of blood caught her attention. Reawakened hunger, fired by her rage, knotted her stomach.

No! She would not sip from this man's blood. She would take him home and then return to the alley. Her plans had not changed. Katheryne would destroy the creature she had become.

Although her longevity as a vampire equaled centuries, most of them had been spent in slumber. Her talents as a creature were still new to her. She'd never had the inclination to hone them. But, she desperately needed to get Gideon back to his house.

Katheryne placed her hand gently on his face. She didn't know what to say but uttered a prayer that he would sleep.

She opened her eyes and much to her surprise, his chest rose and fell in a pattern of rest. Good! Now, should she try to heal his injuries? If successful, wouldn't he question why his face bore no marks of the fight? Could she wipe his memory clean of the assault? Did she have the right?

Her claws scored a groove into her free palm.

Why hadn't she learned more of the traits of a vampire? Why had she taken the easy way out by sleeping most of her immortal life away?

Stop it, Katheryne! She wasn't helping Gideon or herself by the questions or guilt. She needed to see he got help. She supposed she could carry him back to his house. Immortals did have supernatural strength, but what if someone saw her? She didn't want to answer questions. She couldn't give them any answers. None they would believe anyway.

Only one solution came to mind. She would have to fly him home.

Katheryne stood, bent, and lifted the still sleeping Gideon into her arms. She allowed herself a brief moment of pleasure. It'd been centuries since she'd willfully held another person within her arms. The last time had been a child lost on the streets of Edinburgh. Katheryne returned her safely to her parents and wished then, as she did now, for what she couldn't have.

She prayed the night wind would not pummel her precious cargo. She pitched herself skyward and gripped Gideon tighter. She'd never tried flying with a passenger before.

A moment later, she spied his apartment building. She landed cautiously on the street right in front of his door.

She used one hand to hold him to her, thank God for her abilities, and then with the other turned the doorknob—locked! Of course he would safeguard his home against intruders.

Katheryne kept her hand on the knob and concentrated. A faint click rewarded her ears. She opened the door and then moved to the bed, depositing her precious burden on the mattress. She placed a pillow under his head.

Now, what? He wasn't moving. Maybe she had put him under too deep or could it be from his injuries?

Katheryne paced up and down the space at the side of the bed. What could she do now? Who could she call?

Her heart knew the answer but her mind screamed no. She feared Gideon's friends. They could kill her. Her steps faltered. So what? She planned to die anyway. What did it matter how? At least she could help him.

Think! How had he called his partner? Bits and pieces of the night before came back to her. She gingerly eased her hand inside his jacket. She felt for the small square she remembered. Nothing. Neither did she find it in his shirt pocket. That left his pants. She braced herself for a more intimate search. Yes, it was ridiculous, but she had been an innocent when transformed and kept to herself ever since.

Her hands glided to his waist and prepared to move to his pants pockets but she found that journey would not be necessary. The item she sought was attached to his belt.

She unclipped it with much effort and frustration. She turned it over. There had to be a way to open it. She smoothed her fingers around the edges and felt a slight lip at the bottom of the box. She pushed and the lid popped up.

Numbers danced before her eyes. Which one had he pushed? Katheryne closed her eyes. A moment later, she pressed the first button at the top. She put the box to her ear. A ringing captured her attention.

"This had better be an emergency, Gideon." The gruff and extremely irritated voice barked beside her ear, causing Katheryne to almost drop the instrument.

"Gideon?"

"Hello?"

"Who is this?"

"I'm Katheryne, you met me earlier tonight. Your friend is hurt. He needs help."

"Where is he?" The detective's tone was sharp.

"I brought him home." Katheryne cast a glance at Gideon.

"Stay there. I'm on my way."

A shrill tone replaced the voice.

Katheryne closed the box, placed it on the bedside table and sat down on the bed. She rested a hand on Gideon's forehead. He didn't move. She couldn't be sure if that was good or bad. Hopefully, she wouldn't have to wait long to find out.

After an eternity, or so it felt like, the door opened and then slammed back against the wall.

Chapter Four

Gideon's partner and his wife cleared the threshold in a frantic lurch.

The woman moved to the bed opposite of Katheryne. She opened a black bag and pulled out a tube with a disk on the end, and placed it on Gideon's chest.

The man stared for a moment at Gideon's face. "What happened? Were you involved and what in the hell was he doing out?"

Katheryne cringed inside at his harsh words. She knew Zacke was upset and frightened but so was she. His words struck her to the core. He didn't have to say it out loud. He blamed her for Gideon being hurt.

"Zacke, go easy. You're scaring Katheryne."

Miranda's soft words, as she opened Gideon's shirt to examine the bruises beginning to show, seemed to soothe the man.

He raked a hand through his hair before he gave Katheryne a slight smile.

"Look, I'm sorry. Gideon is more than a partner to me. He's family—can you understand that?"

"Yes, I can." Katheryne gave him a smile of her own. "It's been a long while, but I do know what it means to have someone you care for injured. It's frightening, and I know you have questions." She took what courage she had and approached the man. "I will gladly tell you what I saw."

Zacke took the hand Katheryne offered.

"Thank you."

****

A while later Gideon stirred on the bed. His movement galvanized reactions on Katheryne's part by moving closer to the bed, as well as from Zacke and Miranda.

"Gideon, how are you feeling?" Miranda's voice trembled.

"Can you tell me what happened?" Zacke's tone was gruff as he asked the question.

"Ugh! What hit me?"

"We were hoping you could tell us. Katheryne said you were jumped by two men." Zacke's gaze turned toward her before looking back down at the man on the bed.

Gideon's voice grew a bit stronger. "Katheryne? Is she here?"

Katheryne eased down on the side of the bed. "Yes, Gideon. I'm here too."

The hand he reached out to her trembled slightly, but his grip was strong as well as gentle. "I'm glad you're here. I went out to find you but ran into a bit of trouble."

"Do you remember what happened?" Katheryne prayed he had not witnessed her appalling act of terror. She still couldn't believe she'd lost control that way. It had never happened before, and she hoped it wouldn't again.

"I was on my way to the alley where I first found you when I got hit from behind. I stumbled, almost fell, and some guy jerked me to my feet and then the other one used me for a punching bag. Ouch! I reckon laughing is out for awhile, huh, Miranda?"

"Yes. I would also suggest you don't go prowling around the streets without backup."

Katheryne noticed Miranda's harsh words were at odds with the concerned look in her blue eyes.

"Hey, my backup is Zacke, remember? If he'd been with me, it could have been him. It's not like he's still a—" Gideon looked like he wanted to swallow his tongue. "Anyway, I'll be fine. Thanks for riding to the rescue, Zacke."

Zacke's previous stern expression changed into a look of chagrin. "Katheryne deserves your thanks, not me, Gideon."

"Katheryne?" Gideon turned his head and his gaze settled on her. What could she tell him? Certainly not the truth.

"I found you after the men left. I brought you back here."

"How? Did you call a taxi?"

Lord help her, what was a taxi? Think Katheryne, think. Her mind delved through some of the facts she learned at the library. A way of transportation.

"Yes, I called a taxi."

"How did you pay the fare?"

"Uh, I uh—."

"Gideon, leave the poor girl alone. You should be thanking her—not giving her the third degree."

Gideon's face flushed pink in the spots that weren't occupied by his bruises.

"I'm sorry, Katheryne. I owe you one."

"No, remember, you took care of me. I say that makes us even." A frisson of electricity shot between their joined hands. She'd never felt the like before. Gideon looked equally astonished.

She would love to explore the feeling but her internal clock signaled dawn was approaching fast. She had to get out of there and find shelter. Her plans to end her life would have to wait for now. She wouldn't feel right if she didn't keep an eye on Gideon until his injuries healed.

She gently freed her hand from his grip. "I hate to go, but I have an appointment."

"At six in the morning?"

"Actually, the appointment is at eight. I need to get ready for it." Lord she hated lying to him.

"For a job?" Gideon's tone implied happiness for her. She didn't feel happy. She'd told more lies in the last several hours than she ever had in all her years.

"I'm hoping. So I really must go."

Katheryne nodded to Zacke and Miranda and crossed to the door. She reached out to grip the handle.

"Wait!"

What heart Katheryne had completely stopped. God in heaven—had she given herself away? Did they know she was a vampire?"

She slowly turned back. Would a stake through the heart hurt as much as she thought it would?

"Katheryne, before you leave, why don't you let Miranda check you over?" Gideon's tone was gentle.

"I'm fine." Her words sounded as breathless as she felt. Relief beat a frantic wave of release through her suddenly fluid limbs.

"It won't take but a moment. Miranda's really a good doctor."

"I'm sure she is, but I don't want to take up any more of her time. Besides, she's here to take care of you."

"Nonsense, Katheryne. I'll be happy to take a quick look."

Miranda moved to her side and gently tugged Katheryne to the bed. "Just sit right here. I'll check your vitals and then you can go, okay?"

She wasn't sure what vitals were, but what choice did she have?

"Thank you." She sat on the edge of the bed as Miranda took out the instrument she had used on Gideon. She placed it around her neck but didn't insert the little ends into her ears. Instead, she caught Katheryne's hand and held it. As to why, she wasn't sure.

Miranda sought a spot right above Katheryne's wrist. She looked at the clock on her wrist. That wasn't what it was called, she knew that but couldn't think of the right word.

Miranda moved her fingers to another spot and looked again at the numbers on the glass face.

Finally, she released Katheryne's hand. Next, she placed the silver disk on Miranda's chest and listened. Her concentrated expression changed to puzzlement. Just a moment more and she stopped.

"Everything seems to be fine." Miranda's words seemed cheerful enough but her features had grown a bit pale.

"Uh, thanks. I'll just see myself out. Good night."

Katheryne didn't waste time looking at Zacke again or even glancing at Gideon. She moved to the door, pulled it open, and then shut it behind her.

For the second time in less than twenty-hours, she left the warmth of a home behind. Life wasn't fair—she didn't expect it to be. She just wished life after death didn't have to be so painful.

****

A few hours later, after returning home, Zacke cornered Miranda. "Okay, you want to tell me what's going on? What happened back at Gideon's?

Miranda wondered if she could sidetrack Zacke. Probably not. Should she tell him her suspicions? It might set him off. Even though he'd been a vampire when she met him, his heart had been pure gold. Would he understand about Katheryne?

"You were there. What do you think happened?"

"I think you're stalling, Miranda. What aren't you telling me? You were fine until you examined, Katheryne. Is there something wrong with her?" Zacke raised an eyebrow.

"No. Her vitals were fine." And they were...

"Then why did you look as if you wanted to faint?"

"I swear, Zacke. You're like a dog with a bone. I'm not one of your suspects. I will not allow you to interrogate me."

Miranda eased around Zacke and strived for a *don't mess with me walk.*

"Oh no you don't. I'm not falling for that woman, hear me roar crap." Zacke caught her arm in a gentle but uncompromising grip. "Now spill it."

"Fine, you want the truth. Katheryne isn't mortal. From what I remember about your make-up, she's a vampire."

Zacke did some blanching of his own. "Are you sure?"

"As sure as I can be without running blood tests."

"We have to tell Gideon."

"No, we don't!" Miranda was prepared for a fight.

"Miranda."

"Don't Miranda me. Remember, I fell in love with a vampire. Gideon is already halfway there." She stared into Zacke's blue eyes, praying he'd consider how much his best friend wanted love.

"How can you be so sure?"

Miranda resisted the urge to wallop Zacke upside the head. "Listen to what he's not saying, Zacke. He's not saying how hot she is. He's not saying all the normal things he would about a woman who's grabbed his interest. And there lies your answer. He thinks Katheryne is different. He acts like he wants to protect her. Not something he's ever offered to do for one of his love interests."

"Well, maybe he feels sorry for her."

"Yeah and maybe pigs fly."

Zacke's sigh ruffled Miranda's bangs. "Okay, so what do we do?"

"We, my darling, do nothing. This is between Gideon and Katheryne. From what I see, she's scared spitless of us and maybe even him."

"Scared? She's a vampire!" Her husband

sounded astonished as well as puzzled. Men!

"Yes, and if you bothered to look beyond that fact, she had to have been transformed at a very young age. Who knows what she's been through. You hated what you were. You were changed against your will, why not Katheryne? I say we wait and see."

"And if she hurts Gideon?"

Miranda linked her arm through Zacke's and tugged him toward the stairs. "Then we'll pick up the pieces. Now, do you want to spend the rest of the night hashing this out, or do you want to come upstairs with me?"

Zacke's answer was a quick scoop and run. At least his mind was now on something else.

****

His plan to bring Katheryne out of hiding had been successful. His plan to capture her, however, a failure. The two idiots he'd sent to flush her out, by attacking the cop, had run like rabbits. Of course they would have been frightened by her fangs and claws. He'd been a bit surprised to see the docile maiden he'd known before turning into a veritable monster as she flew at them in rage. He wanted to scream in frustration but it wouldn't help. Marcel could have done the job himself, even gone to the policeman's home, but he'd read how he and the other policeman had been instrumental in killing Gabriella. He'd prefer not to accost them personally at this time. He would think of another way to get Katheryne alone. If he had to kill her new friend, as well as his friends to do so, then he would.

Chapter Five

"I'll be right there!" Gideon rinsed the soap out of his eyes and off his body. He shut off the taps, slung back the shower curtain, and grabbed a towel. A couple of swipes, one to his upper body and one to his lower completed his drying act. He secured the towel around his waist with one hand and headed for the door—damp footprints marking his passage.

Whoever was ringing the doorbell had better make it quick. He had to get to work. It couldn't be Zacke; he'd just use the key Gideon kept hidden, and they'd talked earlier. Zacke had queried if Gideon felt well enough to come to work. And it better not be a salesman. The last one had tried his patience to the max. Like he had time to try out a vacuum.

Gideon looked out the peephole. Katheryne! He almost lost his grip on the towel. He inhaled and waited ten seconds before letting his breath out. He had to let her in—he couldn't leave her on the doorstep. But, he also needed to put on some clothes.

He decided to compromise, and slid the bolt back and undid the chain. He cracked the door a few inches and stuck his head out. "Katheryne, hi. I wasn't expecting company. Come on in." Gideon motioned with his free hand.

Katheryne stepped over the threshold and moved further into the apartment. "Did I come at a bad time?"

"Naw, I was just getting ready for work. Take a load off. I'll be back in a few."

Katheryne's brows drew together, and her eyes held a bit of confusion.

"Sorry." Gideon grabbed the jeans, T-shirt, and briefs off the chair. "Guess you noticed I'm not the best housekeeper in the world. Have a seat, please."

Once his guest took him up on his invitation, he turned and padded back to the bathroom. The clothes he snared held in front of him, anchoring the towel. Once inside, he yanked on his briefs and then struggled to pull the denim over his wet legs.

Finally! He closed the button and zipped. His reaction to Katheryne hindered the metal teeth from a smooth glide. He shouldn't feel this way. She didn't need him sniffing up her skirts. The woman needed a friend. Someone to help her. Beer and Bourbon—he wanted to help her. He wanted to be her friend. Hell that was a lie; he wanted to be more than a friend to Katheryne—if she'd let him.

Gideon pulled the shirt over his head and yanked it down with such force he almost ripped the neck. Katheryne was off limits—for now. She would have to call the shots when she was ready for something more.

He pulled a comb through his hair before turning off the light and then opened the door.

Katheryne hadn't moved a muscle. She still perched on the edge of the chair. Her dress, he assumed she had no other, was a bit frayed. Her beautiful hair hung loose and looked weather tossed. Her eyes bored a hole through the cracked linoleum floor.

"Sorry, it took me so long. Can I get you something to drink?"

Her head jerked up. Her gaze uncertain and a bit alarmed. Lord, was she scared of him? She shouldn't be. He wouldn't allow Katheryne to be frightened. Not of him—not of anything.

Gideon crossed the few feet separating them and squatted by the chair. "Kat, you know, I'd never hurt you. I mean physically or otherwise, right?"

"Of course, I know that."

"Then why do you act like you're petrified?" He hoped she'd answer him truthfully.

The small hand that caught his squeezed gently.

"Gideon, I'm not used to being with a man by myself. I mean without there being others around."

"You were here just a few nights ago. You weren't acting this way then."

"A few nights ago, I was not myself and you didn't come to the door dressed in just a towel."

Gideon could have whooped for joy. Katheryne's reticence was due to his dress or rather undress. "My apologies, Kat. I guess I'm just not used to a beautiful woman lighting on my door step."

Katheryne's silver blond locks contrasted nicely with the pink now adorning her cheeks. He resisted the urge to trace the path of color with his finger.

"I'm not beautiful."

"Little darling, you should look in a mirror more often. You'd make some of those famous magazine models green with jealousy."

Katheryne's lips parted. The pink curvature delighted Gideon to no end. The surprise in her lavender gaze made him want to take her in his arms and kiss her innocent invitation.

He shouldn't! He wouldn't! Damn it! He couldn't help himself!

Gideon caught Katheryne's hands in his, stood up, and pulled her against him. He eased his arms around her waist and clutched her tighter. His head dipped, and he captured her lips with his own.

His first taste of heaven almost brought him to his knees. Never had he experienced such sweetness in a kiss. He wanted to taste more of Katheryne. He teased her lips with his tongue. She trembled. A gentle and forward assault gave him access to the nectar beyond. An exploration of her mouth culminated in a tentative flick of Katheryne's tongue.

Gideon lost it. He countered with an invasive rush of testosterone. His rod swelled when their tongues dueled in a sweet dance of desire. He deepened the kiss. His arousal lengthened. He grasped her shoulders. His hands moved downward following the slope of her breasts, which were a perfect fit. A quick flick of his thumbs over desire-hardened peaks sent his lust into over drive.

Katheryne's whimper ripped into his eardrums like a freight train into a car. What was he thinking? Another minute, and he'd have her backed up against the bed—then flat on her back. His hands slipped away from fiery temptation down to Katheryne's waist. He released her mouth and opened his eyes. Lavender spheres gazed up at him. Gideon could pick out surprise, confusion, and what he hoped was disappointment in her gaze.

"Kat—"

A soft knock on the door prevented him from issuing a second apology of the night. Gideon reached out and caressed Katheryne's cheek. The now almost neon pink of her skin taunted him to take her back into his arms.

"Gideon?"

The voice wasn't Katheryne's but a second unexpected visitor.

"Hang on, Miranda. I'll be right there." His hand dropped to his side. He crossed to the door and unbolted the chain before pulling the door open.

"Miranda, to what do I owe the pleasure?"

"Hi Gideon. Sorry to just drop in, but I wanted to check your injuries before you went back to work. I also wanted to see if you knew where I could find Katheryne."

Miranda stepped into the apartment, looked around, and squealed. "Katheryne!" She moved across the room and clasped Katheryne's hands.

"I'm so happy to see you. What luck finding you here. I was hoping we could have a chat."

Katheryne resisted the urge to shake her head. Miranda's enthusiasm was a bit overwhelming, but it gave her a warm feeling inside. However, not the same type of feeling Gideon's kiss had left her with. The marauding, fiery blast had done things to her insides that she'd never dreamed of. Her lips still burned, her limbs felt like a newborn babe's, and the spot between her thighs pooled with liquid.

"Katheryne?"

Kat pulled her thoughts back from Gideon and his touch.

"It's nice to see you too, Miranda."

Miranda tugged her over to Gideon's unmade bed. She tossed the covers up, raised an eyebrow at Gideon, and then smiled when he shook his head.

Katheryne wasn't completely sure what their silent conversation was about, but she could guess. At least Miranda knew Kat hadn't just come from Gideon's bed. Her cheeks heated again at that scenario.

"Sit for a minute. I have some ideas I want to run by you."

Once they were both seated, Miranda took a deep breath. "Please don't think I'm trying to interfere, I want to help. I can't help but notice you seem to have just this one dress. I would love to get you into some more comfortable clothes."

Kat applauded Miranda's tact in not mentioning the visual facts that her dress had seen better and cleaner days.

"I also want to help you find a job. That is, if you will allow me to, if your appointment the other day didn't work out."

Katheryne didn't allow the tears burning her eyes to fall. She'd given up any hope when she landed in this century of finding one soul who was kind. Instead, she'd found two. Three, if you counted the reticent Detective Kensington. Should she take Miranda up on her offers? Was she wrong in trusting someone whose husband had killed a vampire?

Gabriella was better off dead. The world would be a better place for that slaying, but Katheryne feared for her own life if they uncovered her origin. She had made up her mind to end her existence, but the assault on Gideon had sent her waffling back and forth with the decision.

Now, after tasting her first kiss, she wasn't sure she wanted to die. What she wanted might never be possible, but she would take what comfort she could get for as long as it lasted.

With that decision firmly fixed in her mind and heart, she turned to Miranda. "I would love to have your help. Just tell me when and where you want to start."

****

Katheryne swished the wet mop head over the floor. She finished cleaning the corridor before dumping the mop back into the water bucket. She stretched just a bit. Her muscles weren't sore, but she'd seen other employees at the hospital do the same thing. She wanted to fit in. The job was menial but she could handle that. Her job as a maid to Gabriella had included many such tasks.

The fact that Miranda cared enough to follow through on her ideas meant the world to Katheryne. Not ten minutes after she gave her consent, Miranda herded her to her car.

The experience had been a bit overwhelming but exhilarating as well. She could probably get use to that type of transportation. It was easier than walking everywhere and it was less strenuous than trying to fly in inclement weather. Maybe Miranda would teach her to drive a car? The possibilities were endless and exciting. That is if she could do it without alerting anyone to her status as a vampire.

So far, no one had questioned her about her background. She'd been at the job for four nights now. Miranda's offer of board in her and the detective's home, until she got her feet back under her, had been most appreciative—although declined.

Fear aside, Katheryne didn't want to explain why she needed to be alone. She'd found her own place. An abandon building with a basement. A sturdy lock she pilfered from a box of junk left for city crews to pick up had given her a sense of security. Blankets and a pillow from the same source had completed her décor.

Yes, life was looking up for Katheryne. In a few days, she would get her first ever paycheck. She wasn't sure how Miranda had pulled it off but she was grateful. Her new friend had explained something about a social security number and ID.

Somehow, she had both now. She wanted to ask Miranda how it came about but decided against it—blessings shouldn't be questioned.

The only fly in her, otherwise lovely, ointment was the fact she hadn't been able to procure any blood. The scarcity of her diet staple hadn't mattered before now.

She hadn't planned on living long enough to feed. However, her self-inflicted starvation couldn't continue. Her daily immortal sleep was becoming harder to wake up from. Dizzy spells caught her unaware at times and were becoming a nuisance. A nuisance that needed to be resolved before she saw Gideon again. She'd avoided him except for a few moments here and there while she was working. She didn't trust herself around him, not now.

As much as it sickened Katheryne, she would have to find a blood source and soon.

She caught the handle of the mop and started pushing the bucket back in the direction she had come. The dirty water swirled in a brown and gray pattern. Katheryne closed her eyes but still saw the murky outline. She shook her head to get rid of the image.

A mistake—waves of obsidian took over. Katheryne's grasp on the handle splintered the wood. Her body hit the floor. It looked as if her newfound luck had run out. Dying was no longer a choice but a certainty.

****

Gideon leaned over the woman's body in the alley. He checked for a pulse but didn't find one. The situation reminded him of the night he found Katheryne. The difference being, this woman really was dead. He'd known it was a long shot that she'd survived the assault. The knife protruding from her chest had sealed her fate.

It looked as if whoever had been targeting prostitutes with rape had escalated to murder. Yes, he knew the scuttlebutt around the station. Some of the men didn't figure a prostitute could be raped.

Gideon disagreed. If a woman said no, then no matter what her lifestyle, she shouldn't have to put up with force.

Footsteps sounded behind him. Gideon whirled and pointed his weapon.

"Whoa, Gideon. It's me."

"Zacke! Next time give a man a bit more warning." He slid his gun back into his shoulder holster.

"Stop complaining. At least now you hear my footsteps." His partner grinned.

"Yep, that's a good thing. Not like the old days when you could pop in and out at will."

Zacke moved closer. "Damn, why did he have to kill her?"

Gideon reached down and picked up the woman's purse before answering. "I don't know. This is what, the sixth assault? The perpetrator is stepping out of his mode of operation."

"Yeah and that's not good."

Gideon called in for the coroner. Dr. D wouldn't like being called out at this time of the night, but nothing else for it. At least the murder wasn't as gruesome as the ones they'd all witnessed when Gabriella had been on the prowl.

He ended his phone call and looked down. The victim's eyes stared up at him in a haunting and agonizing plea. Heavy makeup framed a face that shouldn't have looked old but did. The woman's ID put her age at eighteen. Much too young to live the life she had or to die.

Amber Brown might not be missed but she would be mourned. He and Zacke would make sure of that. And if it was the last thing he did, he would make her killer rue the day he was born.

"You okay?"

Zacke's question pulled Gideon back from the threshold of anger he almost crossed. "Sure, just want to find the son-of-a-biscuit eater before he rapes or kills again."

"We're on the same page, partner."

Sirens sounded in the night.

"Hopefully Dr. D can find something that will help us."

"I hope so, Zacke."

The men waited as the sirens drew closer. "I saw Miranda a few nights ago." Gideon offered.

"Yeah, she told me she dropped by your place. She also told me that Katheryne was with you."

Gideon took note of Zacke's frown. "I take it you weren't thrilled with that idea, since you didn't mention it until now. You disapprove of Katheryne?"

"It's not that I disapprove, Gideon, but you still know next to nothing about her."

"Zacke, we've been friends and partners a long

time. I've been through some things with you that I never thought possible. But, in this case, your concern is appreciated but not needed. I like Katheryne." Gideon gritted his teeth.

Zacke plowed a hand through his hair. "I know you like her, so does Miranda. I just want you to be careful."

"Sure, I can do that. Now, why don't we wrap this up? I know Katheryne's working tonight. I want to stop by for a few minutes. I'm seriously thinking of asking her to the policeman's ball, even if I have to dress up in that torture suit you call a tux."

****

His bloodied hands clenched into fists as he listened to the detectives' conversation. Mortals were clueless. Too bad they weren't aware of what type of creature watched them. If they were, they would be frightened and beg for mercy just like the woman he'd killed tonight. When he'd laughed at her pleas, she'd spit in his face. For that, he not only killed her after taking a bit of blood but also left his brand on her flesh. It would be interesting to see if these backwoods policemen would even know if the symbol was part of France's heritage, and if they would assume their killer was French.

Chapter Six

Katheryne plummeted back into consciousness with a sated feeling. She opened her eyes and almost screamed. A strange device was attached to her arm. She wanted it off. Her fingers trembled as she tentatively touched the cool surface. Its long thin shape reminded her of a snake she'd surprised in a meadow several lifetimes ago. She wrapped her hand around it and readied herself to yank it away from her skin.

"Don't!"

Katheryne's hand fell. It coincided with the frightened jerk her body made. Her gaze found the one issuing the order.

"Miranda?"

"Katheryne, I'm sorry. I shouldn't have yelled. I just didn't want you to pull out your IV."

Her confusion at what Miranda was talking about must have shown.

"That's right, you've probably never heard of an IV tube. It's okay. It won't hurt you. In fact, it should take care of the reason you collapsed."

Miranda sounded as if she knew what she was talking about, but there was no way she could know Katheryne had passed out from blood starvation.

Katheryne moistened her dry lips before trying to speak.

Maybe she could bluff her way out. "Why do you think I don't know what an IV is?"

Miranda moved to the bedside. Her lips smiled slightly but her gaze remained concerned. She caught Katheryne's free hand in a light grasp.

"Because, I know you weren't born in this century or the last one. I know what you are, Katheryne."

"I don't know what you're talking about, Miranda." She snatched her hand away. "You speak foolishness."

"No, I speak from experience. You're a vampire, Katheryne. No ifs, ands, or buts."

Katheryne could feel her eyes go wide. Her blood froze in her veins. What on earth could she do? Miranda had shown herself to be a friend. Could she trust her or was it a trap?

"All right, let's say I am a vampire if there were such a thing. What of it? You can't kill me here. Or even have your husband do it."

Miranda's mouth dropped open. "Katheryne, did you hit your head when you passed out?"

Had she? Maybe this was just a dream or a nightmare?

"I don't think so. But, then you're the doctor, you tell me."

"No, you didn't. It's a figure of speech." Miranda again took possession of Katheryne's hand. "Why on earth would you think I would want to kill you?"

"Well, your husband has killed vampires before. Gideon told me." She hated her words carried the fear she felt in them.

"Yes, but only in self-defense. Gabriella was a monster. And her death didn't come cheap for Zacke. He almost died." Miranda's eyes held a bit of moisture within their depths.

"I don't understand. Why would a mortal attempt such a thing?"

"A mortal? You thought Zacke was a mortal. I mean, he is a mortal but he wasn't then."

Katheryne's mind reeled. She might not have hit her head but her world felt upside down. Confusion warred with curiosity.

"What was he then?"

Miranda's laughter sounded a bit hollow and her gaze held more than a bit of sorrow. "Zacke was a vampire. Gabriella transformed him back in the early sixteenth century."

"So what happened after that?" She barely got her question out over the shock of learning the detective had been one of her kind. Not only that, Gabriella had changed them both.

"Kat, may I borrow Gideon's nickname for you?"

Katheryne nodded her head.

"Zacke suffered horribly with his immortal birthright. He hated Gabriella with a passion. Zacke's not an evil man, nor was he an evil vampire. He only went after Gabby, my nickname for her, when she started killing innocents here in Savannah."

"I can't believe he actually killed her. She was so powerful."

"You knew Gabriella?"

"Oh yes. I knew her. She transformed me as well."

Miranda's already magnolia complexion turned paler. "Oh no... I don't know what to say, except...I'm so sorry."

Katheryne raised one shoulder in a mock shrug. "It wasn't your doing, Miranda. At least Gabriella is dead. I never really knew what happened to her. She left Scotland not long after she turned me."

This time when Miranda squeezed her hand, Katheryne returned the gesture.

"You said Zacke is no longer a vampire?"

"That's right. He's been a mortal for the last few years."

"Did you know he was a vampire when you married him?" She waited with inhaled breath for Miranda's answer.

"Yes. After Gabriella almost killed me in the

morgue right here at the hospital, and Zacke was almost killed by one of her henchmen, he told me. I decided I would rather live with him as he was than without him."

"So, how did he become a mortal?"

"A miracle. That's all I know. Zacke never did tell me the exact details of what happened the night he died a second time. His wounds from the battle that took Gabriella's life were horrendous. I'd given him up for dead, but he survived the attack. Not only survived it, he also regained his mortality and soul."

"I didn't know that was possible."

"Looking back it seems like something out of a book or a dream. I guess I didn't question it at the time, because I was too happy."

Katheryne digested all Miranda told her. Maybe Zacke knew some other vampires. A clan that she could at least meet. Creatures of her own kind that were not evil.

"I don't suppose there are other vampires here in Savannah. I ask because prior to coming to this century I heard there were. Instead I discovered one was a detective." She shared a smile with Miranda.

"The other two rumors turned out to be bogus as well. One a college professor and the other a do-gooder."

Miranda's laughter started as a giggle but escalated into full-blown hoots of amusement. Katheryne couldn't imagine what was so funny. Finally, Miranda wiped her eyes and took a deep breath. When she let it out, she again patted Katheryne's hand.

"Kat, forgive me, I just couldn't help myself. When you called Miles a do-gooder I lost it."

Katheryne's mind whirled with questions. "Are you saying that you know this man?"

"Of course. Miles is a friend of Zacke's. He and

Hawk Sherwood, the professor, helped Zacke hunt Gabriella." Miranda stood up and stretched across the bed to check the IV.

"They were there when Gabriella died and when I almost lost Zacke."

"Miranda, are you telling me they were or still are vampires."

"They still have their fangs and claws if that's what you mean." Miranda's cheeks reddened. "My apologies again. I didn't mean to..."

"It's all right. You answered my question. And to answer your unspoken one, I do have fangs and claws but until recently I'd never used them."

She responded to Miranda's arched brow. "The night Gideon was injured, I frightened the men away. Then I flew him home."

"Wow, it's hard looking at you to think you could frighten a gnat let alone grown men."

Katheryne laughed, and not just a giggle, for the first time in an eternity. "You should have seen them run. They were like mice scampering away from a cat's fury."

Her amusement suddenly fled. "Miranda, I scared myself. You have to understand. Gabriella transformed me and left not long afterward. She taught me nothing about being a vampire. I literally almost died. That sounds strange. I did die but I didn't know how to take care of myself. That first night I took blood from a stray dog. Just enough to survive. That's all I've been doing is just surviving. I went to ground for years at a time. I'd resurface and find myself in a more decadent time period than before."

"Katheryne, it's not your fault. Gabriella was a monster. What you need is to learn what you can and can't do."

"Is that possible?"

"Yes, I'm sure Miles and his wife, Hope, as well

as Hawk would be more than happy to teach you."

Joy streamed its way through her veins. Finally, she would be able to really live. To know her limitations and to be amongst people she didn't have to fear. She would be able to stay here and maybe explore a relationship with Gideon.

Katheryne's joy dissipated like bubbles in champagne.

Gideon. He would never understand what she was. He would despise her.

"Katheryne, what's wrong? Your face lit up for one moment and now you look like it's the end of the world."

"For me, it is, Miranda. If I'm not mistaken, Gideon is also a friend of Miles and Hawk."

"Yes, but what does that have to do with anything?"

"I can't learn from them. Gideon would find out." Her words rang with despair.

"You don't want Gideon to know you're a vampire?"

"No! He would despise me. I heard it in his voice when he told me about Gabriella's attacks here in Savannah and on Zacke, how much he hated her. He would hate me."

"Nonsense! You're nothing like Gabriella, although your eye color does remind me of her."

"I'm a vampire just like her. I was in her employ. Although I didn't kill for her, I watched her maim and torture her victims before she slaughtered them."

"Were you a vampire then?"

"No, but still, I didn't try to stop her."

Miranda's face creased in a frown. "Honey, you couldn't have stopped her if you'd been transformed. Zacke had years of honing his skills before that final showdown."

"But, I didn't even try."

"And you should be thankful you didn't. You would be dead now. Somehow, I think that would upset Gideon."

Would her death upset him? Gideon did seem to like her. The kiss they had shared had been totally unexpected but it had made her want so much more from him and life. Could she share her legacy of death with him? Would he understand that she was nothing like Gabriella? Or would the fact that she had fangs and claws send him running away?

"Maybe you are right. He might care if I'm dead, but I can't take a chance on him finding out about me. Not now. I need more time."

"You want to make sure he cares for you before you spring it on him?"

"Yes." Katheryne fiddled with the coverlet.

"Well, that's what Zacke did. He was scared spitless even after all we'd been through together. But thankfully, I realized that he wasn't a monster. I knew that all along, but the thought of him being the same type of creature in makeup as Gabriella terrified me."

Katheryne knew Miranda's words were spoken to comfort. Somehow, they didn't quite reach their goal. Just the thought of Gideon thinking about her in the same context of Gabriella frightened her to pieces. She didn't want him to know she was a product of that monster.

"Any suggestions as to what I should do now?"

"Yes. First off, we introduce you to Hope, Miles' wife. Miles transformed her into a vampire after her throat was cut. They have a little girl almost two years old. Then the boys will teach you what you need to know, and we'll keep it a secret—for now." Miranda smiled before continuing.

"You do know you will have to tell Gideon sooner or later what you are. I mean, if you are falling in love with him like I suspect he is with you, then honesty is the best thing."

Katheryne's heart thundered in her chest. "Yes, I know I will have to tell him. I just want a little more time before my heart is broken."

****

Gideon didn't make it to the hospital to see Katheryne. Zacke waylaid him right after they filed their report for the night's shift. He gave him some cockamamie story about Katheryne being too busy to chat, according to Miranda, and that Miranda needed his advice on giving a party for Kat. Like he'd be any help. He was still mystified when he dropped by Zacke's.

"So, Gideon, what do you think?" Miranda asked.

He pulled his mind back from where he wanted to be to the here and now. "Sounds fine. Just let me know what day and time, and I'll pick Katheryne up."

"It's tonight, eight sharp. And actually, Katheryne will already be here. I asked her to stay with us for a while. I hope that's okay."

Miranda's gaze held concern and wariness. What was she hiding and what did it have to do with him and Katheryne? It could be as simple as her trying to match make. She'd done it before, but he'd made it perfectly clear already to Miranda and Zacke that he really liked Katheryne. So there'd be no need for them to do a fix up. Maybe they were playing the other side of the fence. The party could be a way of trying to throw a monkey wrench in the works.

"Hey, Kat's her own woman. I don't have any holds on her. If she wants to stay with you guys, fine by me. Now, if there's nothing else, I need to get on home."

"Gideon, I think you are—."

"Misunderstanding? There's   nothing   to

misunderstand, Miranda. Katheryne wants to stay here. Probably better that way anyhow. I didn't want her living on the streets, and she didn't really act like she wanted to stay with me."

He knew his tone sounded grumpy and jealous. But, he didn't really give a rat's ass. Maybe he'd read more into the kiss he and Katheryne had shared than it warranted. Maybe he'd frightened her. Whatever the reason, she'd made it perfectly clear by accepting Miranda's invitation that she'd rather be anywhere than with him.

"Oh, I'm sure that's not the case, Gideon. She could just be shy, and she might not feel comfortable living with a man. She might be worried about how it would look. I felt the same way."

"Well, you certainly changed your mind about staying with Zacke after Gabriella attacked you. Guess you had a change of heart about the proprieties."

"Gideon!" Zacke's tone was low but deadly.

"I'm sorry, Miranda. I know you had no choice. Katheryne did. I mean I'm hardly at home, but she would have been safe with me. Guess it rankles she didn't trust me enough."

"I think you're wrong. Katheryne just needs some time to get things sorted out and all." Miranda's words fell upon deaf ears.

"Yeah, maybe you're right." Gideon moved toward the door. "Again, I'm sorry. I was out of line with my comments. I love you like you were my sister. Just chalk it up to a bad night on the streets."

Miranda followed him to the door while Zacke stood back—a frown still evident on his face.

"I'll talk to you guys later, okay?" Gideon leaned over and kissed Miranda's forehead. He welcomed the hand that caught and squeezed his.

"Night."

Once out on the street, Gideon resisted the urge

to kick the mailbox at the curb. No need in landing himself in jail for a federal offense. He'd already stepped into hot water with Zacke. If he could, he'd yank his tongue out and toss it in the nearest garbage can. For that's what he'd been spouting—garbage.

He'd hurt Miranda with his words. Something he'd never have done if he weren't so eaten up by uncertainty. Kat wasn't his—maybe in the future if he prayed hard enough, but for the moment, she was her own woman. Able to make her own decisions and by her choice she'd shown him she did need time. Problem was, when it came to patience, he got left off the list.

He climbed into his truck, the true love of his life, and slammed the door. At least, he'd get to see Katheryne tonight. The dinner party started at eight, and if he got there early, he might get a chance to talk to her by himself.

****

"He didn't take it very well about me staying here." Katheryne leaned against the kitchen doorway. She still felt a bit shaky despite the two bags of plasma Miranda had pumped into her.

"No, but, Gideon will get over it. He's just hurt."

"That was the last thing I wanted to do." Her hands clenched into fists.

"He's lucky, I didn't hurt him after his remark to Miranda." Zacke's words did nothing to help Katheryne's peace of mind. Not only had she hurt Gideon, she'd caused strife between him and his partner.

"Sssh, Zacke. You know Gideon didn't mean it. He looked almost as upset as you did at his comments.

"Maybe this wasn't such a great idea. I can go back to my place."

"No, Katheryne." Zacke moved to stand by her

side. "I know what it feels like to live alone. I know what it feels like to fear someone will find out what you are. Here, you'll be safe. Think about it and remember if you don't stay with us, Miranda will kill me."

The grin he sent her way caused a flutter of warmth to bud inside her heart. "Thank you. I promise I'll be a good houseguest."

Miranda twined her arm through Katheryne's. "Now, I think you need to go back to bed. Get some sleep, as if you have a choice, and then when you get up, we'll find something for you to wear tonight."

"What about work tonight?"

"I think we need to find you something else to do. I'll square it with the hospital. And in the meantime, you can learn what you need to about being a vampire." Miranda tugged Katheryne toward the stairs.

A few minutes later, tucked into a darkened bedroom, Katheryne examined the night's events. She never dreamed in her wildest imaginings that her search for kindred creatures would net her such a bounty of friends.

Zacke was right, she felt safe. For the first time since her parents died, she felt like she had a family. Not that she wanted to claim Gideon as such. His touch made her crave more than a brother's kinship. Yes, she wanted more but after seeing how upset he had been, Katheryne wondered if she could even count on his friendship.

The drag of sleep's chains pulled tight around her. Katheryne rested her cheek on her hand and gave herself to immortal slumber.

****

Finally, Marcel had tracked down Katheryne's whereabouts. Taking her blood so long ago had allowed him to follow the trail she'd left, after leaving the dilapidated building where she slept. But the little Kat moved fast through the night crowds on the street, and with the combined mix of several blood types, her entrancing scent had fizzled out. He'd gone back to her sleeping place and waited.

It was now almost dawn, and she had not returned.

He needed to feed.

Chapter Seven

"They're here!" Miranda's excited shriek caused Katheryne's fangs to ache. This was a bad idea. A totally horrendous idea. She had no business meeting these people. How could she trust them? True, they were vampires but not all vampires were nice.

Gabriella had proven that point, not to mention Marcel.

A hand settled lightly on her shoulder. The weight so soft she didn't even think about jumping out of her skin.

"It'll be okay, Katheryne." Zacke's tone matched his touch.

She looked up into his cobalt blue eyes. "How can you be so sure?"

"Miles and Hawk are good men. You can trust them with your life. They guarded my back when I was a mortal warrior and then as an immortal. You have nothing to fear from them. They will do all they can to help you, as will Hope."

"Thank you, Zacke."

The low rumble from the front of the house grew louder. "I guess we should go."

"Yes, we probably should." Katheryne heard the amusement in his words. She answered it with a slight smile.

"Oh, and Katheryne?"

"Yes?"

"You can also trust Gideon."

Before she could form a reply, a barrage of people surrounded them.

"Kat, meet Miles and Hope and Hawk."

She could feel her eyes grow larger. The men were extremely tall. Their bodies were muscular and their faces were handsome. The woman, who snuggled close in one of the men's arms, was beautiful. Hair the color of midnight with silver streaked though the long length.

Katheryne felt Zacke's hand tighten just a bit on her shoulder. "Okay, give the woman some room. You're crowding her and probably scaring her to death."

His words had the desired effect. The trio moved back a bit, and Miranda moved forward. "Katheryne, I'm sorry. I'm just so excited."

"It's fine. I'm not used to a lot of people. It's been a while."

"Of course you aren't, you poor thing. Next time, just throw something at us, and we'll stop." The vampiress' voice was lyrical as she continued.

"I'm Hope, and the man who looks like he swallowed a post hole digger is my husband, Miles."

"A what?"

"Sorry, it's a tool that you dig holes with."

"Hope!"

"Can it, big guy. I'm not scared of your fangs and claws."

Katheryne felt as if she'd fallen down a hole like *Alice in Wonderland*. A book she'd found way back when and enjoyed.

The big guy moved forward, picked Hope up under the arms, and set her back away from Katheryne. He then knelt on one knee. His jade gaze even with her own.

"Katheryne, ignore these imbeciles, including my wife. I'm totally harmless. And I'm at your disposal. I'll be happy to teach you anything you want or need to know about being a vampire."

"Okay, that's enough, Miles. Leave her alone."

Hawk reached down and pulled Miles to his feet. "Don't hog the new lady vamp. We're both supposed to help her."

Katheryne couldn't believe the laughter that escaped her lips. The situation was more ludicrous than funny, but the eye rolling and raised eyebrows going on behind the men had turned a tense moment into something Katheryne had missed—fun.

"Thank you. I appreciate all of you making me welcome. I just hope—"

"Yo, where is everybody?"

Katheryne could feel the blood pulsing through her veins.

Gideon was here.

Now what? How should she behave? What if someone told him what she was?

She started to back up but Zacke's hand steadied her. He may no longer be a vampire, but he seemed to be able to read her thoughts. The other two men grinned and caught her by the hands.

"Come on little one, it's too late to run. Besides the mortal isn't that scary." Miles voice held laughter and commiseration.

"Don't worry, Katheryne, we'll keep your secret. Everything will be all right. Besides if it doesn't work out with Gideon, there's always me."

Hawk's teasing brought her comfort. She only hoped all three of her new protectors knew what they were talking about. The scowl on Gideon's face as he approached did nothing to reassure her of that fact.

****

Gideon stopped in his tracks. Miles and Hawk flanked Katheryne as she exited the kitchen. Zacke brought up the rear. Miranda and Hope stood to the side. The women's gazes held amusement.

He didn't find a damn thing funny about Miles and Hawk being glued to Kat's side.

Nor did he care for the close surveillance his partner had on Katheryne either.

He ignored everyone but the one person he really wanted to see. The green film of jealousy abated enough that he got a clear picture. The long dress he'd been accustomed to seeing Katheryne wear had vanished—replaced by a knee length black skirt and boots. The lavender sweater covering her torso sharpened the color of her eyes and contrasted softly with her silver blond hair. The moon kissed tresses fell downward and caressed the slight mounds pressing against material he envied.

Kat's lips were parted and painted a pale pink— just a slightly deeper shade than the naked lips he'd kissed, in what seemed, an eternity ago.

Gideon moved forward, pulled Kat's hands from Miles' and Hawk's, and took them captive in his own. He tugged her gently away from the group. The sounds of muted laughter reached his ears but he tuned it out. He forgave the fact that she had refused his offer of a home. He forgot anything and everything but the lure of the woman before him.

He drew her into his arms and pressed his lips against hers in a gentle but possessive kiss. The kiss, which instigated from undeserved jealousy toward men he trusted turned into a sensuous explosion when Kat opened to him. He pulled her closer. The soft curves of her lower body became a cradle for his rock-hard erection. He deepened his kiss.

Total silence finally pricked his awareness. He opened his eyes to the passion filled gaze of Katheryne. He blinked and tried to shake off the vestige of lust. The soft woman he held in his arms now felt like a statue.

Her cheeks glowed a bright pink and a slightly desperate appeal radiated in her gaze. He loosened his grip. His arms fell to his sides. He felt heat sting his own face as he turned and met shock and stunned expressions.

Gideon was still trying to scramble his wits together when Miranda snapped into control. "Okay, everyone. Dinner's going to get cold. Let's move it to the dining room.

For the life of him, he couldn't look at Kat. She must hate him for turning the evening into a sexual spectacle. Her probably first real dinner party and he'd ruined it. Someone should kick his butt to the curb. He glanced at the men who ignored Miranda's order. It looked as if he was fixing to get that thought in spades.

"Are you out of your mind?" Hawk's question exploded into the silence.

"Where do you come off mauling Katheryne in my home?" Zacke's blue eyes were glacial.

"Good Lord, Gideon, even for a redneck, that was crass." Miles' condemnation hurt the most for he was usually the most affable of the men facing him now.

The trio, of possibly his ex-friends, escorted him outside. He could have thrown off Zacke's punishing grip but the vampire boys were a different matter. He'd seen them both in action when protecting people they cared about. And for some reason they had taken Katheryne under their wing.

Once the front door closed, none-too-gently, Gideon decided it might be best to apologize before things got out of hand. "Look, I know, you're right. All of you! I just don't know what happened. I only planned to give her a peck on the lips. Something went wrong."

"Yeah, like your lower half kicked into overdrive."

"That about says it all, Miles." Gideon agreed.

"Well, I'm thinking it's a bit more than lust driving our friend to embarrassment."

"I think you're right, Hawk." Zacke released the grip he had on Gideon's shirt. "But, you still need to apologize to Katheryne. She looked mortified when you finally stopped the lip lock."

"I am, I mean I will apologize. Dammit. I can't believe I did it. It's like my mind went totally haywire."

"Yeah, well, love has a way of making us all look like a donkey's ass." Miles' commiseration as he spoke helped soothe Gideon's self-angst.

"I was that transparent, huh?" Gideon could feel his cheeks grow hotter.

"Like a piece of glass. But if it's any comfort, Katheryne wasn't fighting you off." Hawk grinned, showing his incisors.

Gideon's heart tripled its beat. Could she possibly feel the same way he did? Maybe after all the fruitless searching and one-night stands, he'd finally found the one woman who could love his unworthy hide. Or maybe not after tonight's blunder.

"Don't beat yourself up over it, Gideon. It takes a good woman, and Katheryne seems to be just that, to make a man out of any of us."

"I'd really appreciate it if you would quit reading my mind, Miles. It's downright bad mannered, not to mention embarrassing."

Instead of the quick retort of defense he expected, laughter greeted his ears. Again, he found nothing hilarious about the situation. Just 'cause the trio thought Kat might care about him, didn't make it so.

"Well, if there ain't nothing else, I think we might better join the women."

"I agree. Miranda's been cooking all day. If we don't get in there, she's gonna have my head." Zacke slapped Gideon on the back.

"Yeah, and Hope told me if I didn't behave I'd

have to sleep downstairs in the basement again." Miles green gaze looked a bit dismal.

"Glad I don't have a woman calling the shots." Hawk's chuckle didn't quite reach his amber eyes.

Gideon laughed at their combined expressions of horror.

"I wouldn't laugh if I were you, mortal. Just wait, your time's coming. And from what I've seen of Katheryne, she's got a few surprises up her sleeve too." Hawk seemed happy to rub in that fact.

"Hawk, I couldn't have said it better myself. Women, no matter what their size, when crossed resort to the nasty habit of using their fangs and claws."

Gideon snorted. "Not Katheryne, Miles. She's one of the sweetest women I've ever met."

Zacke hooted with laughter. "Come on partner, you need to eat. Lack of food has done a number on your brain. Besides, you're going to need all the strength you can get. Being in love, even for a bit, is wonderful, but it's the morning afters you have to watch out for."

Gideon groaned as he and the rest of the men entered the house to join the women.

Chapter Eight

Katheryne hid her claws beneath the tablecloth. She wished she could crawl under the material and hide herself. How could she face Gideon after her wanton display? Never had she fallen so deeply and so completely. Miranda, Zacke, and their guests had faded into thin air when Gideon's lips had captured hers. She'd felt the bulge of his desire pressing against her tummy. This kiss had made the one in his apartment suitable for a child's play.

At least Miranda and Hope hadn't chastised her. They both looked as if they wanted to say something, but she appreciated their tact.

The men were still secluded on the front porch. Their combined exit had caused all three women to jump, but then Miranda and Hope exchanged grins. Kat couldn't find one thing comical about the evening so far.

The click of the front door interrupted her self-loathing. The gentle noise caressed her sensitive hearing with a warning.

It was time to pay the piper.

"Are we in the doghouse?" Zacke voiced his question as he stuck his head around the kitchen door. The other men stood at his back.

Miranda's laughter broke the chain of tension encasing Katheryne. She drew a deep breath and then promptly lost it when the men almost fell into the kitchen. The other men took a seat leaving Gideon looking a bit discomfited.

Instead of dropping her gaze to her lap like she wanted to do, Katheryne took pity on the man. "I believe you're supposed to sit here." She patted the wood seat next to her.

"Uh, yeah, guess I am."

Katheryne applauded the reticence of the others. Maybe the evening wouldn't be so bad after all.

Miranda said grace and then bounced up to grab platters of food off the counter. "I hope ya'll are hungry. I've got steaks cooked well and some rare, as well as baked potatoes." She set the steak platter down. Miles and Hawk reached for ones marked with a red toothpick. Hawk cut into his without a by your leave.

Red juice pooled onto the white china plate.

When the platter reached Gideon he pushed the last rare steak aside. His face screwed into a grimace. He forked his offering onto the plate in front of him and then held the platter for Katheryne.

She took the last red-tipped steak and placed it gingerly on her plate. Cutlery rattled and elbows bent as the rest of the steaks were spoken for. Gideon picked up a bottle of steak sauce and slathered his meat.

Miranda's quick lesson in modern day foods had been a blessing. At least now, she had the knowledge to not pour something detestable on her own food. Another platter appeared at her side. Katheryne took a baked potato and then spooned a dollop of butter on top. It might make her sick later but it looked and smelled wonderful.

Silence reigned for a few moments before Miranda once again took to her feet. "Attention everyone. In honor of Kat being from Scotland, I made a Blood Pudding."

"Miranda, where did you find the recipe?" Miles asked.

"On the Internet, but I had a really hard time finding three quarts of pig's blood to go in the mixture."

"Yuck!" Gideon rolled his eyes and waved away the tureen of pudding.

Hope shook her head without making a comment, but Zacke took a small portion. As soon as he relinquished the Scottish fare, Miles and Hawk grabbed for it at the same time.

"Uh, when you two gentlemen are finished, maybe you could offer Katheryne a bite?"

Katheryne glanced away from the food combatants. Miranda's slight wink caught her by surprise. Bless her heart; their hostess had known all along what she was doing.

She mouthed a silent thank you. Hawk offered her the bowl and she took an ample portion.

"Gideon, are you sure you don't want to try this?" Katheryne asked.

"Uh, thanks but I think I'll pass."

"Ah, come on and have some. You might like it." Hawk's teasing turned his eyes into shards of amber as he held up the tureen.

Gideon's tone took on an edge. "I said no, Hawk."

Miles opened his mouth, probably in an attempt to antagonize Gideon, but Hope rapped him on the hand.

"Ouch! Woman, how many times have I told you not to hit me?"

"Behave and I won't."

Katheryne dared a glance toward the end of the table. Hawk looked in danger of spitting out a mouthful of pudding. She turned her head to the other end of the table, careful not to look at Gideon.

Miranda looked like she wanted to throw something. Zacke finished the last of his pudding and reclined against the back of his chair, a smile on his face.

Katheryne laid her spoon back down. "Miranda,

I just want to say how much I appreciate you giving me this lovely dinner. Everyone has been so sweet and kind."

Magically faces cleared. Gideon reached out and touched her hand. She returned his light caress and caught Miranda's eye.

The wink she gave her new friend was returned.

A brief while later, Katheryne helped the women clear the table while the men adjourned to the den. "So, Kat, what did you think of your first dinner party?"

"I think it was fun, Hope. A bit different than the ones I remember from when I was mortal but I enjoyed myself."

"We didn't put you off with our dinner antics?"

"No, Miranda you didn't. And the food was lovely."

"Whew, I'm glad. I haven't had to cook much for non-mortals since Zacke was changed back, and Miles got married. Hawk usually comes by, maybe once a week, after a late class."

"Well, I think everything turned out great."

"Uh, hum, what about the before dinner appetizer?"

Katheryne had to think for a moment before she realized what Miranda meant. She could feel the heat diffusing her cheeks. "Well, it was splendid."

"Splendid? You can do better than that, Kat. On a scale of one to ten what would you rate it?"

Katheryne giggled. "An eleven."

"That a girl. That's what we wanted to know." Hope's laughter spilled out and Miranda joined in.

The kitchen filled with rib-hurting guffaws that grew louder.

****

Later after the women rejoined them, Gideon waited for a break in the conversation. "Hey ya'll, it's been fun but I've gotta go."

He crossed the room, tugged Katheryne out from under the noses of the women, and made for the door. "Miranda, thanks for dinner. Catch ya'll later."

The door closed on a barrage of comments, one in particular. "How rude!"

He avoided looking at Katheryne until they had cleared the porch steps. Finally he turned and looked down.

Amethyst eyes opened wide held what looked like surprise and nervousness. Lord, did she think he was going to jump her again? And why wouldn't she? The thought had been on his mind and in his crotch ever since he'd kissed her earlier. Still, he didn't want to scare her off.

"Kat, look, I uh, need to apologize for before. I should never have kissed you. Wait, that's not what I meant. I wanted to kiss you. I just shouldn't have done it in front of the zoo crew."

Gideon looked everywhere but at Kat. His explanation had sounded like a bunch of bull. He wouldn't blame her if she told him to take a hike or worse. The words go to hell came to mind, but what he heard was totally unexpected.

Katheryne's giggles grew louder. Gideon's head pivoted back and down. The little minx laughed harder.

"Kat?"

He caught her shoulders with his hands. He could feel her entire body shaking with amusement. "Katheryne, what's so funny?"

She caught her bottom lip with her teeth. A pinprick of blood dotted the silken surface. A second later, the tip of her tongue caught it. Lust shot straight to his groin. The intense arousal kicked like a mule. One moment he had Katheryne by the shoulders, the next, he had her airborne. He caught her gasp in his mouth. His lips crushed hers and then opened the portal he craved. His tongue sought and trapped hers in a desperate effort to swallow her whole.

Katheryne's arms encircled his neck. Gideon's hands trailed downward and grazed the hem of her sweater. His fingers raised the barrier and caressed the cool and sleek skin beneath. His mind lost all connection to caution. He tore his mouth away from the warmth of her lips.

"Wrap your legs around my waist and hold on."

He moved the short distance to his pickup truck, one-handed the catch on the tailgate and eased it down. A second later, he sat his precious and extremely seductive armful down.

"Now, where were we?" His whisper was hoarse.

The question went unanswered as he again sought the heat of her mouth. Her tongue parried his thrust. His erection pushed painfully against the zipper of his jeans. His body leaned closer, desperate to climb into the flame of lust Katheryne generated.

His hands caught her neck; anchoring her body to his. Katheryne's hands slid down to lightly score his back with her nails. Once again, he slid his hands under the barrier of her sweater. His fingers grazed the crested tips of her breasts.

Katheryne's low moan turned the flames of lust higher.

Gideon's right hand moved and started its own search—pushing the material covering her upper legs aside. Nylon caressed his fingers as they traveled a path up her thigh.

The woman in his arms pulled her lips away. He felt their absence like a lost pup needing its mama. The protest on his lips died when her teeth scraped along the side of his throat. Below his waist, his southern rising grew harder.

He resisted the urge to buck against her center. He did pull her closer. Now, his aching arousal begged to bury itself deep within her core.

Katheryne squirmed and he fought the claws of desire. A light sensation of pain radiated from his neck. She must have bitten him. Before he could react Zacke's front door open.

"Easy, Kat, we've got company."

Gideon's hand trembled as he caressed Kat's face. Her lashes flicked once before he glimpsed the deepening purple of her gaze. Her lips were swollen and looked a cherry red. He wanted to wipe the sheen of moisture from them with his tongue but now wasn't the time.

"Come on hon, I'll walk you back inside." Her body trembled as he gently tugged her forward. He allowed himself a brief moment of pleasure and pain as he slid her body down his before setting her feet on the pavement. Gideon draped an arm over Katheryne's shoulders and walked to meet the incensed trio of men.

"What—."

"Don't! What just happened is between me and Katheryne. It's none of your business. Although, I will take into consideration your concern, Zacke. I care for Kat. I hope she cares for me. Now, if you have anything to say, say it now. Say it to me and put it to rest."

"Why you son-of—."

"Miles!"

Miles turned to Hope, who had followed him onto the porch, whispered something in her ear before addressing Gideon again.

"I don't give a mortal's ass in hell. You've got no right to maul her in public."

"Hold that thought." Gideon pulled Kat closer and looked down at her. She looked a bit put out, and he'd love to apologize again, but it would have to wait. He needed to take care of the problem at hand first.

"Go on inside, babe." He dropped a kiss on Kat's

lips and waited until she as well as Hope, who placed an arm over Kat's shoulders, were inside before speaking his mind.

"Well, as I recall not one of you three men or bats gave a fig's butt if you kissed your women in public. What's more, at the time, two of you were vampires hitting on mortal women. At least I'm a mortal man trying to spark a mortal woman."

Miles incisors disappeared back in his mouth. Zacke opened his mouth but no words came out. Miranda, who now stood on the porch, caught his hand and squeezed it. She looked troubled. Hawk stood silent. His gaze issued what looked to be a warning and concern.

"If it helps your sense of decency, and call me old-fashioned, but I do plan to court Kat, if she'll let me."

When the group remained silent he continued. "Good, now since the parties of the first part agree, I'm going to say goodnight. Ya'll all have been brothers to me, and I don't want to end the evening fighting with you again."

Gideon turned and walked back to his truck. Not a sound followed until the roar of his truck's engine broke the silence of the night.

****

"Say, mister, are you interested or not? I don't have all night."

The young blonde prostitute moved closer to Marcel. She never saw the knife enter her chest, but he enjoyed the look of shock on her face as she realized what he'd done. He pulled the weapon out.

Blood gushed forth onto his hands, bathing them in a hot tide of pleasure. He wiped the blade on a towel he'd begun to carry for that purpose.

The woman slid down the brick wall of the alley. Her eyes began to glaze over in death.

He suckled a bit of her blood and then took a

lighter from his pocket. He liked new inventions and this one served him well as he took off his ring, heated the stone, and then pressed it into the woman's flesh.

Chapter Nine

"Katheryne, if you have a few moments, we'd like to talk to you."

Katheryne looked at Miranda and Zacke who'd spoken before raising an eyebrow at the three vampires standing in the hallway outside her bedroom.

She'd awakened before sunset and relived every wonderful moment of Gideon's lovemaking. His touch gentled her fractured soul, and the fire in his fingers scorched the inside of her body. Nothing she'd ever experienced prepared her for the emotions he invoked, not to mention the sensual desire intensified by the warm delectable taste of Gideon's blood. She had not planned on biting him. She'd never bitten anyone. But, she couldn't seem to help herself.

Her surrogate family hadn't been thrilled with her being outside with Gideon. Their frowns and attitude toward him proved this, but she wasn't allowed the chance to ask them why last night.

Suddenly, Zacke had to go into work. Miles and Hope took off as if shot out of a speeding carriage, citing they needed to get home to the baby, and Hawk mumbled something about having papers to grade. When she'd turned to Miranda, the good doctor said she had to check on the twins, but she failed to reappear for the rest of the evening.

Finally, she'd grabbed a book from the library and read until almost sunrise.

"I'll be right out." Katheryne gently but firmly closed the door in her host's faces. She pulled on undergarments and a pair of the denim jeans Miranda had given her, before yanking on a T-shirt. She then ran a brush through her hair and cleaned her teeth.

Whatever they wanted to talk to her about sounded important, and she needed to, at least, look as if she was awake. A moment later, she stood in the kitchen. Miranda handed her a cup of chocolate, mixed with what looked like blood, before motioning for her to sit down. She did so and the rest of the entourage followed suit.

"Katheryne…" Zacke cleared his throat and then started again. "We, uh, wanted to talk to you about last night…"

The detective's words trailed off again as he shot a panicked look toward his wife before turning back to her.

It's about the uh…"

"To hell with being gentle, Zacke, she needs to know." Miles harsh words caused Katheryne to jump. His green eyes almost glowed as he stared a hole right through her. What on earth was wrong with the kiss she and Gideon had shared? Why were they all staring at her like she'd committed a carnal sin.

"I don't understand. What is it you're trying to tell me? What did I do?" She hated the way her words came out in a rush of panic. But what if they were upset enough to turn her out? Where would she go?

"No one is going to throw you out, Katheryne." Hawk placed a hand on her shoulder. "We just need to make sure you realize you can't go around biting people."

"You're all upset because I bit Gideon?"

Nods and a couple of yes's from Miranda and Hope followed her question.

"I thought it was acceptable to take blood from,

a, umm..."

"Soulmate?"

"Yes Hope."

Hope smiled for the first time since the conversation started. "Honey, it is okay, but Gideon is mortal. You have to be careful about taking his blood."

Kat could feel her brows forming a frown, not to mention the headache now pulsing in the center of her forehead.

"Gabriella took blood all the time." She held up her hand to forestall all the comments she was sure to come. "What I mean is not just when she transformed someone, but when she took a lover."

"Were her lovers mortals?" Miles' question caused her to frown more. Were they? The more she thought about it...

"No, not all of them. And it's the ones who weren't that disappeared." Horror dotted her arms in goosebumps. "Oh no. You think I would bite Gideon and hurt him?"

"No sweetie, at least not on purpose." Hope crouched down by Katheryne's chair. "I think you led a very sheltered existence. Although, how you managed to maintain your innocence with that monster Gabriella as your sire beats all the odds. Thank God you did though."

Kat took the hand Hope held out and squeezed it lightly as she surveyed the others.

"I think what you need is an education in what you can and can't do. If indeed Gideon is your soulmate, and I for one am beginning to think he is, then you want to make sure you don't hurt him or even alert him to what you are until you're ready to tell him your story." Hope's gaze held Katheryne's.

"Yes, I would like that." Tears stung the back of her eyes as she realized the ramifications of what could have happened last night. So involved with the erotic sensation of tasting Gideon's blood, she wondered if she would have stopped if they had not been interrupted.

"Good, and it wouldn't hurt if you got a bit of education. Gideon is a great guy, but he never has any money. If ya'll do end up together, it will take both of you to make ends meet."

Miranda's smile helped a bit to dull the ache of her error but what type of education did she have in mind?

"What can I do? I've never really worked before, except as a companion and then at the hospital."

"What about computers? Would you be interested in learning how to work one?" Hawk's question held a hopeful note. If she remembered correctly, he was what the others called a computer geek.

"Yes, if you think I can." Katheryne squeezed Hope's hand once more before addressing the entire group.

"I appreciate everything you are doing for me. I never really had friends. My uncle, who took over my parents' estate, kept me away from most of the visitors at home. It was only when he needed a hostess that I even mingled with people other than the servants. And nothing changed after he tossed me out. Gabriella also kept me in the background."

"I'm not surprised." Miles snort drew her attention.

"She would not welcome the competition when it came to the men in her life." Zacke's words were followed by a slight smile.

"Okay, enough talk about that woman. We need to talk to Kat about how to handle her hormones and her taste for blood." Miranda's words, although matter of fact, brought an involuntary heat to Kat's face.

"Well, I guess now is as good a time as any."

Katheryne prayed she was a fast learner.

****

Gideon rolled out of bed and stumbled to the bathroom. He'd slept a grand total of four hours—spending the time after he left Kat the night before in a great deal of thought. Not to mention tossing and turning once he hit the sheets.

And the lust he felt every time he thought of their aborted lovemaking didn't help either. Another reason he couldn't sleep worth a damn. Hard to stretch out on your belly when one vital organ was saluting the ceiling.

And the way the evening had ended left a rancid taste in his mouth, not to mention a hurt place in his heart. Gideon turned on the taps and sluiced water over his face before brushing his teeth.

The men he'd come to admire and respect as well as care about like brothers had played dirty. No way had he mauled Kat, although it did get a bit more out of hand than he'd planned. Still, their love life had been their own, and he deserved the same consideration. Maybe he was pushing a bit hard, but there was something special about Katheryne. Yeah, he'd thought that about a lot of women, but he'd bet his badge Kat was different.

So what, maybe he wasn't a big bad vampire or an ex-fanged creature, but he didn't need the trio overshadowing him like he was a snot nose, randy kid. His mama raised him right, and he knew how to treat a lady, and that was exactly what Kat was, but boy could she kiss.

Gideon smoothed shaving cream on his face and then grimaced as he cut himself. He finished the job and then cleaned off the left over mess. He ripped a piece of toilet paper off the roll and slapped it to the nick under his lip and then turned his face from side to side to make sure he'd gotten all the stubble. A small red blotch caught his attention. It was low on his neck, almost to his collarbone. He swiped at the dried blood. Funny, he didn't remember cutting himself there.

He shrugged his shoulders, and pulled the shower curtain back. Fifteen minutes later, he dumped his wallet into his jeans, clipped his badge to his belt, and slid the .45 into its holster. A leather jacket, that had seen better days but was comfortable, went on next. Now, he was ready to face the night and if lucky, he'd have time to stop by and see Kat at the hospital before he headed to the station.

****

No, he didn't plan to apologize, but he did want her to know that he meant what he said. He cared about her and when the time was right—he prayed it would be—he wanted more.

Gideon locked the door behind him as he left and then climbed into his pickup truck. Kat's background didn't bother him, but he felt like it did her. He wanted her to be certain of what she wanted and to have more opportunities to find out if he was one of the things she did want in her life.

Sure, he was probably shooting himself in the foot, but he'd seen enough relationships break apart because of resentment, and even though Kat acted like she cared about him too, he didn't want her to confuse lust and the need for a permanent home with the scary emotion of love.

The engine caught, rumbled, and then skipped before settling into the loud purr he loved. He turned into the street and headed for Zacke's.

Ten minutes later, he pulled into the Kensington's driveway. His partner and Miranda lived in a better neighborhood than Gideon did, a circumstance that would need to change if he took a wife.

He smiled as he cut the engine and exited the

truck. Life had indeed changed for him when his best buddy and then Miles took wives. He'd envied the loving relationship they each had with their soulmates, and had begun to wish for someone to come home to after work also. The writing appeared on the wall when he met Katheryne. No other woman in his history of love 'em and leave 'em had ever jumpstarted his heart as she had. The innocence in her beautiful lavender gaze, the way she'd trusted him almost from the moment he found her in the alley, and then the soft kisses, turning into passionate and lust inducing flames made him want to protect and keep her safe forever.

However, the guys were right, he needed to be careful of Kat's feelings, but dammit, he wanted her like there was no tomorrow. Gideon chuckled out loud. If he had his way, they would be together for all their tomorrows, until they were both old and gray. Thank God he didn't have to worry about some of the problems Zacke and Miles went through. Being vampires and then Miles having to turn Hope after her business manager sliced her throat was something out of a nightmare for all concerned.

Yep, he was glad he didn't have that problem. The most trouble he and Kat would see would be the ordinary trials of finances, disagreements, etc. With both of them being mortal, it was a certainty they would have children one day, or at least he hoped she wanted to be a mom. He sure as hell wanted to be a dad when the time arrived. He shook his head. Was he moving too fast? They had not even gone on a first date yet. Should he listen to his friends? Slow it down a bit? Gideon didn't want to. Part of him was afraid she might find someone else, someone better than him. No, she was different.

Gideon hunched his shoulders against the chill in the wind and rang the doorbell. A moment later, he stood face to face with Miranda.

"Hi Miranda, can I come in?"

"What a surprise, I wasn't expecting anyone this late. The kids are in bed." Miranda made no effort to open the screen door she kept locked.

"Well, I didn't come by to see the twins, I wanted to see Kat." As he waited, the slight smile on her lips disappeared. She half-turned toward the living area, and then faced forward again.

"Kat's not available, Gideon. Maybe you could come back tomorrow night?"

Miranda's words knocked the hope right out of his heart. Kat must regret what happened the night before. Why? She seemed fine when he'd left her. Dammit, what had he been thinking? They'd just met and he'd rushed her like a rookie cop with his first suspect. "Miranda, would you ask Kat if she would talk to me for just a few moments?"

Again, she turned toward the interior of the house and then turned back. "I'm sorry, she said not tonight."

A sigh escaped in a rush of hurt, frustration, and resentment. They were trying to keep Kat from him, and whatever they'd discussed after he left last night had to be the reason.

Miranda's gaze was filled with what could have been regret, but it didn't keep her from closing the door in his face.

Gideon stood there for a moment before swinging around and walking back to his truck. He resisted the urge to kick a tire. The treads were old and he didn't relish walking to the station if one of them blew. What the hell had just happened? Miranda, a woman he'd risked his life for, had refused him entry to what he called his second home. Kat refused to speak to him. He revved the motor and then in a juvenile show of frustration he burned rubber out of the driveway.

The short ride to the station didn't take away

any of his hurt or his fast escalating temper. Did they think he wasn't good enough for Kat? Was that why they were making him play odd man out?

Zacke was already in his office when Gideon rounded the bullpen into the hub of activity. His partner waved him in, and then motioned for him to be quiet. Gideon waited for Zacke to finish his phone conversation. A moment later, he did, and the blue of Zacke's eyes, although no longer a vampire color, literally glowed with ire.

"What in the hell do you mean going by my house and upsetting, Miranda?"

Chapter Ten

"That's better, just try a bit harder to block your thoughts." Katheryne heard Miles' words but she couldn't concentrate. Gideon's arrival and subsequent departure stuck in her head. She didn't like turning him away, but Miranda as well as Hope and Miles and Hawk thought it was for the best.

She needed to learn the vampiric skills she'd never bothered with before. The ability to fly had surprised her, but she'd seen Gabriella do it numerous times. She'd gotten lucky unlocking Gideon's door the night he was attacked.

Her new mentors told her why she should not take Gideon's blood, not even a small portion, even if in the throes of passion. That it should be something he offered, not something she took without permission.

"Katheryne, I can read you loud and clear. You have to focus!" Miles' disgruntled tone pulled her away from thoughts of Gideon.

"I'm sorry. I just…"

"I know, but you have to—"

"Give it a rest for a minute, Miles. Kat needs to get her application filled out for school." Hawk's tone although calm brooked no argument from his vampire brother in arms.

"Sorry, Kat. I know I'm pushing you, I just…Nevermind, we'll try again tomorrow night." Miles smiled and then caught his wife around the waist. "Ready to go home?"

"Yeah, by now Samantha will be driving the babysitter nuts." Hope's gaze danced with amusement.

"Good thing we pay her over the top. Sammie's a handful even when she's not practicing her skills." Miles looked the part of a proud papa, and Katheryne's heart ached for what she would probably never have. Even if Gideon accepted what she was, and even if Miranda and Zacke had managed to have children, it didn't mean she could. It was rare that a mortal and vampire could mate and have offspring. And the fact two of those couples did was just a miracle.

"I told you, her name is not Sammie." Hope's half-hearted admonishment met with a kiss from her husband.

"And I told you, she loves being called Sammie." Miles smirked.

"Only because you spoil her rotten, Miles."

"Hey, I'm not the only one, her uncles do the same thing."

"Yes, and when the twins as well as Samantha cry when they don't get their own way, then you men are going to be taking care of them while we sleep." Miranda's words held no ire, but the look she exchanged with Hope spoke of a firm commitment to stick together.

Miles and Hope said their goodbyes and then Miranda went up to bed. She had to be at the hospital early, and Kat promised to watch the twins until their nanny arrived.

"Come on over here, Kat." Hawk waved her over to the silver square sitting in the center of the coffee table. She knew Miranda had an office upstairs, but the busy doctor also liked to work downstairs so she could see the twins at play once she arrived home from work.

"Now, sit here, and I'll explain how you start the computer, this one is called a laptop. You should probably be learning on a desktop but the elements are pretty much the same to get started."

Kat processed what Hawk told her and then a few minutes later, he seemed satisfied with her progress. "Okay, now we fill out your application for school."

"I still don't see how I can go. I'm not even from this century. I have no credentials."

Hawk lightly rubbed Kat's tense shoulder. "You let me worry about that, I will get you all the background info you need. You already have an ID set up, and if you're really good, I'll throw in a credit card."

Katheryne felt her eyes go wide. She knew what that was; the small plastic card was something Miranda had used when she took her shopping for clothes. Hawk noticed the smile that climbed on her lips.

"Okay, one credit card thrown in. Now, you rest, and I'll take care of the rest of what you need for entrance to Savannah U."

Kat was glad to leave him to it. She wanted—no needed time to think about Gideon, and how she could put to rights what happened tonight and the night before. She'd heard the hurt in his voice, and the slight anger. She didn't want that. She might never have him as her own, but she would not allow him to think she sent him away because she didn't care.

He had shown her kindness, and if she wasn't mistaken given her a piece of his heart. Yes, he'd said he'd planned to court her, she'd heard that much after entering the house last night, and she loved how old-fashioned he seemed, but it could have something to do with the compromising situation they'd found themselves in. She wanted to know more, to know he did care.

Kat smiled slightly at Hawk and then transported to her room. Another skill she had learned. Actually, it was better than flying for her. Not as much chance of someone seeing her, unless she popped in right in front of them.

The room she'd been given as her own was nice. It felt good to be away from the elements, to actually have a chance to start a new life. Although, she wasn't sure she could learn computers half as much as Hawk thought she could, it touched her to think there were people that believed in her.

She threw herself down on top of the comforter. What could she tell Gideon? And if he forgave her then what? Where would their relationship lead? And if it did lead somewhere how would he face the fact she was going to outlive him several lifetimes over?

Kat closed her eyes against the grim questions. Maybe she should just pick up and leave. No, her heart screamed. She didn't want to go. For the first time since she'd lost her parent's, she felt like she belonged.

****

"Let's get one thing straight, Zacke. You're my partner, not my keeper. I didn't say a damn thing to upset Miranda." Gideon kept his stance straight as he faced Zacke who'd stood up and rounded the desk when he'd entered.

"Back off, Gideon. I'm not in the mood." Zacke's growl sounded as lethal as the look Gideon gave his out-of-line friend.

"Instead of placing blame on me, why don't you tell me why the hell you and the fang pack are keeping Kat away from me?"

Zacke blew out a breath of air, and then motioned for Gideon to take a seat. He did the same.

"Look, we're not trying to keep her away from you. She...she...she needs some guidance." The detective's blue gaze darkened, and Gideon wondered if Zacke was lying to him for the first time in their history of partnership.

"Okay, let's say I believe that, why can't I guide her?" Gideon couched his question in a polite tone, although he still felt the urge to beat the crap out of his partner. A partner that suddenly found it hard to look him in the eyes.

"Miranda thinks working at the hospital is too much for Katheryne, and she needs to learn how to make a living. Do you know anything about computers?"

When Gideon shook his head, Zacke continued. "Neither do I but Hawk does, and he is willing to help Katheryne."

Zacke's explanation seemed reasonable enough, but Gideon wasn't sure he liked the idea of Hawk teaching Kat anything. He didn't like the only other bachelor in their group eyeing his woman.

"Well, she can learn what she wants, but I don't want anything forced on her."

Zacke blew out another breath of air. "Then don't you think she deserves to make her own decisions—including whether or not she wants you in her life?"

Gideon slumped back in the chair. Had he stopped her from doing what she wanted? Did he feel it was his right because he'd plucked her out of that alley while at the point of death? Did Kat feel beholden to him because he'd found her?

"Look Gideon, all I'm saying is slow things down. You've always jumped in with both feet whether it was the next woman in your life or fighting crime. Take some time. If Kat truly is the one for you, then you both need to spend time together just chilling out."

As much as he hated to admit it, Zacke was right. He'd rushed things and more importantly rushed Kat.

Gideon stood up and held his hand out to Zacke.

"You're right. Thanks bro." After they shook hands, Gideon pulled the ball cap down a bit closer on his forehead. "I've got tomorrow night off, I think I'll ask Kat out on a real date, and if that works out, maybe the police's man's ball like I'd planned."

Zacke grinned. "I think that's a good—" A buzz from the desk phone interrupted him. "Kensington here." His grin disappeared as Gideon watched. A second later, he hung up.

"Another woman's been murdered." Zacke's visage remained grim as he yanked a jacket off the back of his chair. "Over in the red-light district."

"You think it's the same guy that killed the first woman"

Gideon hoped not. He prayed it was a coincidence, but...

"Yeah. The MO is the same. Looks like we may have a serial killer."

Damn. No woman deserved to be sliced up like the first woman had been. The ME said she'd had cuts on her thighs as well as a brand on her chest. Something Dr. D had only found after cleaning off all the blood. Only someone with a serious mental problem or a SOB who just got his kicks from hurting others could be responsible for both crimes.

"I take it we're primary on this one too?" Gideon hoped so; he'd love to catch the killer.

"As of right now we are. So you want to ride with me?" Zacke's hopeful expression made Gideon want to laugh. His partner hated the pick-up truck with a passion.

"Sure, why not. We can pick up some tacos on the way. I didn't have time to eat after I got up."

Zacke grimaced as in pain. Oh yeah, the mere thought of someone dropping food particles in his convertible made the man sick.

****

Several minutes later and without the tacos,

Gideon had taken pity on Zacke, they arrived at the crime scene. A small group of scantily clad women stood right next to the yellow crime scene tape. Some of them were crying, others cursing, but the overall mood was one of despair. If it could happen to one of them, it could happen to another and another.

"Detective Kensington!" A fragile looking redhead clutched Zacke's arm.

"Yes?" Polite was Zacke's middle name. It didn't matter how tired he was he always behaved like a lord of old.

"You don't know me, but your wife, Dr. Miranda took care of one of my kids when he fell and broke his leg. She's a good woman, and from what I hear you and..." Her voice faded for a moment as she gave Gideon a look. "Your partner and you are both good men. Please find this animal. Lord, I don't like working the streets, but most of us don't have anybody to help. We've got to work to feed our kids."

Her green eyes filled with tears for a moment before the dead hopeless look returned to her gaze.

"We will." Zacke nodded to the woman and then ducked under the yellow tape.

Gideon pulled a card out of his pocket, penciled in the name of a help-center on the back, and handed the woman the card with a bill attached. "Here, they'll help. Tell them I sent you."

The woman took the offering, and her less than clean hand pressed his. "God bless you."

Gideon nodded and followed Zacke to the victim's body.

"You gave her the last of your money until payday didn't you?"

His cheeks burned but he merely said, "Yeah." Payday was at least a week off, but Gideon had bought groceries and beer, so he was okay. If he got in a bind, he could pull it out of savings, but he really would rather not do that. For the last decade, most of his money was put into different interest bearing accounts and some stocks. He didn't want to touch his stash. He planned to use that money to buy a house some day. His little hole in the wall was okay for one, he'd moved there after he got out of the police academy. The purchase price had been extremely low, but he couldn't really have anyone over. Yes, he'd told Kat she could live there but at the time he just wanted her to have a place to stay until she found something else.

"Gideon, you with me?"

Again his cheeks burned. He needed to concentrate on the task at hand. "Yeah, so what's the story?"

Dr. D, their medical examiner answered Gideon. "Poor girl. Looks like she put up quite a fight, considering the defensive wounds on her hands. Probably thought she could get away." The ME shook his head. "She's been dead about twenty-four hours from her liver temp."

"What about DNA from the killer? Any luck?"

"No, he must be wearing gloves. Not even a bit of what we need to even run a database." Dr. D pulled back the sheet and then looked at Gideon and Zacke. "We've worked a lot of murder cases together, and this one reminds me of the vampire kill—"

"What?" Both Gideon and Zacke blurted out the question at the same time.

"Look, I've been doing this a long time. I see a lot of things, and it's just my theory about what happened over four years ago. Besides, I have no way of proving it." The ME looked at both men and then motioned for the attendants to come get the body.

"You'll have my report on your desk in the morning."

"Thanks," Gideon responded as Zacke took a closer look at the body.

Gideon looked away. He remembered the mass of wounds Gabriella had left on her victims before Zacke killed her, and he didn't want to see something worse. His imagination already worked overtime when he slept.

"You ready?" Zacke's tone sounded disgusted and angry at the same time. His partner had a cast iron stomach and his history as a vampire had allowed him to see many horrors of the past and present day.

"Yeah, but I think I've lost my appetite."

"I know what you mean." Not a good thing if Zacke lost his taste for food after getting it back. "Okay, where to?" Gideon asked as he waded through the milling crowd of policemen, medical personnel, and then the crowd outside the crime scene.

"The station," Zacke responded as he hit the unlock button on his key chain. "I want to go over the other murder."

And a few minutes later that's what they did. "I don't understand it. We've had a red-light district here since as far back as I can remember. Why pick on the women now?"

"I don't know. Maybe a disgruntled john?" Zacke riffled through the papers on his desk and then pulled one out. "Isn't this close to where you found Katheryne?"

Gideon took the photo. "Yeah it is." His tone was matter-of-fact, but his insides seethed at the thought the killer could have mistaken Kat as a lady of the night.

"I think we need to go back and look at that alley. Although we had some assaults, the murders didn't start until after you found Katheryne.

He drummed his fingers on Zacke's desk. "You don't really think this has anything to do with Kat, do you?"

"There's nothing to tie her in to it—" He held up his hand against the protest dying to escape Gideon's lips. "Not as a suspect, of course not. But there's something nagging at me, and I can't put my finger on it."

"Okay, well then let's do it. The morning I found her I wasn't thinking of it as a crime scene, so maybe there's something there that might help." Gideon's breath escaped as he sighed. "I hope we can come up with something. This ain't right, Zacke. I know prostitution's against the law, but Lord if there were better laws to help some of these women find jobs, they wouldn't be on the streets."

Zacke nodded his head. "I'm with you partner. It's not right they have to pay for their livelihoods with their lives."

"Well then we need to catch the SOB and soon."

****

Katheryne awoke sometime before dawn. She hadn't planned to fall asleep, but years of conditioning herself to act almost mortal in order to blend in were hard to dismiss.

She knew Zacke would be getting off work soon, which meant Gideon would also be heading home. She could go see him, but probably shouldn't. Someone might see her fly if she used that means of travel, and although she'd teleported easily enough inside the house, she wasn't sure about attempting it over a distance—at least not yet.

Now wide awake and knowing she would stay that way past dawn, she headed for the library downstairs.

She'd grab a couple more of the romance books Miranda kept on hand, then snatch a bag of blood in the cold box they called a refrigerator. Good thing, they kept the blood on hand for their vampire friends. She didn't relish stealing the fluid from a poor animal or asking Miranda for a blood transfusion.

She pushed the kitchen door open and then stopped.

Zacke as well as *Gideon* sat at the table.

Chapter Eleven

Kat felt the rush of heat warming her face. If she'd known she would run into anyone she'd have thrown on a robe.

Gideon's stare kept her rooted on the threshold. She tugged at the hem of the nightshirt she wore. It was shorter than what she'd worn as a mortal, and came barely to her knees. At least the neck was round and hid her breasts from view.

"Hi, I didn't know anyone was here. I just came down for something to drink." She shot Zacke an almost desperate look. She didn't know what to do now with Gideon being there.

"There's some *fresh cranberry juice* in a pitcher. Just help yourself." Kat smiled at Zacke, tried to smile at Gideon whose stare made her want to do all kinds of things. The topmost being to kiss him, but the more tempting option was to run back upstairs. She'd turned him away the night before. Would he even talk to her? He hadn't said a word as of yet. Should she speak first?

"Thanks Zacke. Hi, Gideon." Well so much for thinking about it, her lips just seemed to spew out her greeting.

"Morning, Kat." He gave her another slow and definitely arousing scan.

Her feet felt like molasses as she walked to the cabinet, took down a glass, only to hear a quick intake of breath from Gideon. She almost dropped the glass as she tugged on the shirt she knew had ridden up well past decency's sake.

"Sorry. I'll just get my juice and leave so you can

finish your conversation." Katheryne did just that and her feet almost flew toward the door and freedom.

"Kat?"

Gideon's voice stopped her in her tracks. She slowly turned to face the man she was coming to truly care about.

"Yes?"

"I'd like to talk to you for a minute, if that's okay." His words tentative as if he was afraid she'd say no.

"All right. Here or..."

Gideon gave Zacke a brief look and then nodded toward the living room behind Kat. "In there, if you don't mind."

Instead of answering, she nodded her head and backed her way out of the kitchen as Gideon stood and followed.

Kat took a seat on one of the chairs. She tucked her feet under her, and pulled the shirt down to cover as much of her legs as she could. She took a big sip of her drink and sat the glass on the side table.

Gideon took a seat on the wide and cushiony couch. He rested his elbows on his knees and steepled his fingers together.

"Look, Kat, I want to apologize for the other night." His brown eyes looked shadowed.

She hated she'd put that look in them. She'd much rather see them laughing or filled with passion after he kissed her senseless.

"Gideon, you did not do anything wrong. I was as much a part of what happened, if not more so, than you were." Kat grabbed her glass and drank down almost all the mixture of blood and juice.

"Kat—"

"No, listen, it wasn't what you did, it's about me. I just needed what Hope calls down time. I..."

Gideon moved closer to the end of the sofa and

caught one of her hands. She welcomed the masculine combination of gentleness and hardness as his calloused fingers caressed a pattern of sensual bliss.

"It's okay. I think I was probably rushing you, or so Zacke said. Maybe we could start with a simple date." His gaze was wary but hopeful.

From what the wives told her, a date was a way of getting together for dinner, etc. Katheryne liked that idea. Maybe she would somehow find the courage to tell him what she was if they took it slowly.

"I would very much like that." Her words were a mere whisper, but Gideon's smile proved he'd heard her loud and clear. His caress turned into a light press of her hand before he sat back on the sofa.

"Great, but it'll have to be one day next week if that's okay, I'm kinda short—"

"I think I can help you out there, Gideon." Zacke spoke from the kitchen doorway. So intent on watching Gideon, Kat had forgotten one of the rules Miles taught her. To always be on alert. She'd have to try harder.

"Uh, thanks partner. I'll owe you." Gideon's grin did strange things to her insides. Was this what falling in love was all about? And was she falling for Gideon?

"I'll remind you. Now, let's finish our conversation." Zacke dipped his head toward Kat, and then returned to the kitchen.

"I guess I need to get in there. What if I pick you up about seven tonight? Or is that too soon?" He stood to his feet and then leaned down toward Kat.

"Yes, that would be nice." Kat wished she could say more, but the excitement of having her first date ever and with Gideon positively clogged her throat.

"Ditto. See you tonight, beautiful." He dropped a light kiss on her lips and then he was gone.

Kat waited all of two seconds before she finished her drink and then teleported to her room. Giddy with hope and then fraught with dread if and when she told Gideon her secret, she decided she would lie down. She had just a bit of time before she needed to watch the twins. The pull of the rising sun didn't normally affect her, but with everything going on right now in her life, she allowed the arms of slumber to claim her. Her last thought was of Gideon and what she should wear that night.

****

"Gideon are you listening?" Zacke's low rumble of a growl pulled him away from thoughts of Kat. Since their conversation had resumed about twenty minutes before, he had barely heard a thing Zacke said. Not good, and definitely something he needed to correct. He needed to get his head into the game.

"Yes, no, tell me again." Gideon met Zacke's exasperated expression with one of chagrin. "I'm sorry, I'm listening now. Promise."

"You'd better be. Now tell me again about the morning you found Kat."

Gideon knew why he was asking; they'd gone back to the alley but found nothing that shouldn't have been there. He wasn't sure what they were hoping to find, but a weapon would have been nice. A trail leading to their killer would have been better. But not a thing.

"Okay. Well I was just patrolling and I heard something like a kitten. I followed the sound and found Katheryne. There was no one else around that I could see."

"You're positive?" Zacke's question was asked in a tired tone. They both were exhausted from the night's events.

"Yeah, I'm sure." Gideon stood up and walked to the sink where he rinsed his coffee cup before pulling open the dishwasher and sticking it on one of the racks.

"Why don't we call it a night? If we need to go back to the station for paperwork, I can take care of it since you're home already. And if we need to talk more, we can do it after I bring Kat home."

"That works, thanks, and here take this." Zacke pulled out his wallet and handed Gideon a couple of George Washington's.

"Man that's too much." He kept his hand from reaching out and grabbing the bills.

"Keep it, you might want to take her out again before you get paid." Zacke followed Gideon to the back door.

"Just make sure you don't let things get out of hand, okay? I'm not trying to tell you what to do, but if you're indeed serious about Kat possibly being the one, you have time to get to know one another without jumping the gun. You and she both deserve that."

Gideon felt the rush of embarrassment heat his face, but he knew Zacke truly cared about what happened to Kat. And in his book that made him an even better partner and friend.

"I'll behave, I promise."

Gideon left with Zacke's laughter ringing in his ears. The early morning sun cast a pale glow over the driveway and coated the streets as he drove to the station. It looked like it would be a beautiful day, and if he had his way, it would be an even better night.

****

Gideon ushered Kat out to Zacke's car. His pickup truck had started smoking the minute he'd pulled into the Kensington's driveway. At the rate he was going, he would owe his partner for the next hundred years.

"Watch your head." Gideon smiled down at Kat and then felt a bit of lust so hard and heavy he almost groaned. The sleek little dress, someone, probably Miranda, had helped Kat shop for was a slide of sensual silk as she crossed her legs inside the car.

Remember, do not pounce on your date before dinner. Do not pounce on your date before you bring her home, and especially not with her vampire guardians around. He'd not only promised Zacke to give Kat space, he'd made a vow to himself. He just didn't realize how hard, pardon the pun, it would be at the time.

"Gideon, is there anything wrong?" Kat's voice, husky as all get out, but filled with slight apprehension, pulled him back from his thoughts of making love in Zacke's convertible. Probably not the smartest thing to do. The last time he'd tried that, way back in his teens, he'd ended up with a gearshift almost neutering him. And his partner would certainly not like it if he used his prize vehicle as a bed.

"Everything's fine, Kat." He patted her hand lightly and then closed the passenger door. A quick jog around the car and he climbed in the driver's seat.

"I thought we'd go somewhere quiet so we can talk over dinner. Is that okay with you?" His gaze slid over her fine-bone face, her silver fall of hair, and her full lips—now painted a show-stopping red instead of the natural pink he was used to seeing.

"Yes, that would be nice." As soon as that sentence was out of her lovely mouth, Kat closed her lips and looked down at her hands.

Surely she couldn't be shy? Well, he knew one way to warm her up. He'd called in a favor to a friend and after dinner he was going to try the carriage ride that had been such a disaster a few years back for Gideon and his date. With the cold weather, he wouldn't have to worry about a thunderstorm ruining the evening.

He would keep her warm, and at the same time try to carry on a casual conversation. All in an effort not to jump her bones.

****

Marcel watched as Katheryne was ushered out of a house in a better section of town than her escort lived. He had followed the policeman in hopes of finding his destined mate. His vampire sight had picked up on the lustful looks the man gave Katheryne. He wanted to sever the man's jugular and drink every drop of blood from his dead body, but that would only make them aware he was a vampire. Something he didn't want. He'd been so careful to keep his secret after coming to the states to search for Katheryne. His travels had been filled with the whores that filled the major cities he'd targeted. He'd enjoy each and every one of them before he sent them to their deaths. Now with his love so close, the blood lust had escalated. He could not bear the thought she was involved with another.

Chapter Twelve

Katheryne felt as if her incisors were glued to the roof of her mouth. She had sat like a lump of coal in the car instead of acting charming or witty. Two items most men from her century loved in a woman. Now as Gideon pulled her chair out and then seated her, she wondered what on earth she could say to save the evening.

"So what are you in the mood to eat? This place does some great steaks. You can also order about any meat you want." Gideon looked over the menu he held in his hands.

What to do? She really didn't want to eat, but Zacke told her Gideon would wonder why if she didn't. He'd suggested she stick to a medium rare steak, and a baked potato like Miranda had served.

"Could I have a steak medium rare with a baked potato?" Her words were as hesitant as her desire to consume the food. She was so nervous she wasn't sure her digestive system could tolerate anything.

Gideon grinned and her insides melted. She would probably eat glass if it made him happy.

"You can have anything you want. And you will love the cheesecake with raspberries. It's kinda like the house specialty."

"Are you ready to order, sir?"

Kat jumped. A younger man than the one who had seated them stood at Gideon's side. She needed to be more alert. This modern world could prove to be more dangerous than where she'd come from.

"Yes, we'll have..." Kat listened as Gideon ordered the same thing she'd requested but with a salad. He also ordered a bottle of wine. She could feel the tenseness inside her bones relaxing a bit. Zacke said wine would not hurt her at all. Just not to drink too much. A vampire could get alcohol poisoning.

"Now, that we are alone, tell me about where you come from, Kat." So busy entertaining thoughts of a drunken, poisoned vampire turning their evening into a nightmare, she again missed the waiter's movements.

"Uh, it was a small village outside Edinburgh. Nothing special." Katheryne didn't lie; she just didn't want to tell Gideon that at one time her father owned the village and that she was classified as a lady. Yes, it was so long ago, but she didn't want him to think she was a braggart or Heaven forbid look it up on the Internet.

This time Kat saw the waiter before he got close to them. Good, she'd actually heard his footsteps and the clink of the glasses against the wine bottle as he'd carried the tray on one hand raised above his head. She remained quiet as the wine was poured, Gideon tasted it, declared it to be good, and then the waiter left.

"So do you have any brothers or sisters?" Gideon's question expressed a mild curiosity, but she wished he'd leave her past alone.

"No, I lost my parents when I was young. My uncle moved into our home after they were buried."

The look of sadness in his gaze made her want to cry. Such a sweet wonderful man, and here she was doing her best to tell him nothing that would lead to her being a vampire.

"I'm sorry, Kat." He reached his hand out and she slid hers inside the large comforting clasp.

"It's okay. It was a long time ago." Katheryne used her free hand to pick up her wine and then took a tentative sip and swallowed. When the liquid did not cause her insides to twist, she took another before setting it on the table.

"I can't believe it's been that long. You look so young." His brown eyes smoldered with an emotion she wanted to explore, but it probably wouldn't be wise.

"Thank you." Kat heard the waiter's approach. "Oh look, the waiter is bringing our meal."

Gideon, who sat facing the direction of the kitchen, looked around and then looked confused. "I don't see him."

"Oh, well then, I must have been mistaken." She bit back a groan. Of all the crazy things to do, if she wasn't careful, she'd be hanging a sign around her neck that read, "Oh look, I'm a vampire."

As on cue, the waiter stepped up to their table, served their food with a flourish and left them alone.

Gideon picked up his fork, looked at Katheryne, but did not make an attempt to cut into his steak. Vamp's teeth, he was waiting for her to begin. She had to admit the sizzling scent of hickory-charbroiled meat did make her want to take a bite. She gave her date a slight smile, and picked up her cutlery. The first bite of steak delighted her taste buds. She bit back a moan. It seemed her appetite had returned.

"Good huh?" Gideon grinned before he popped a much larger piece of steak than the sliver she'd cut into his mouth.

She smiled back. "Yes, really good." For a few moments, silence reigned as they pretty much cleaned their plates. Katheryne drank the wine he continued to pour and marveled at how good everything tasted. Dessert, when it came, was in the form of a scrumptious chocolate raspberry cheesecake that positively melted on her tongue. Gideon must have liked it also, for there wasn't a crumb left on his plate either.

After paying the waiter, he escorted her out of the restaurant. His brown eyes danced with excitement, and the grin he sent her way was mischievous.

"Come on. The evening's not over yet."

He tugged her forward and then down a landing, until they came to a place where you could rent a horse and carriage.

"We're going for a carriage ride?" Katheryne could feel the anticipation of riding once more as she did in days of old. The night air crisp on her face, the moon hanging low, and the comfort of knowing she was safe.

"Yes, if you want to, and I hope you do." Gideon helped her onto the plush seat and then moved in close beside her.

"Of course I do. This is a wonderful way to end the evening. I love it. Thank you, Gideon."

As she watched, her errant knight's ears tinged pink and then his face followed suit. She wanted to kiss him so badly but denied herself the pleasure. Katheryne still wasn't sure she could manage to keep from tasting the rich nectar of his blood. It was as if she were addicted to Gideon. And the evening carried a magical promise. Katheryne felt she could reach up and touch the silver orb in the sky above them or fly to it.

Gideon placed an arm around her shoulders and pulled her close. "I don't want you to catch a chill. But just so you know, I will behave like the gentleman my mama raised." The twinkle in his eyes made her want to curl up closer. A soft, warmth teased her insides. He made her feel cherished.

"Is your mother still living?" She raised her voice to be heard over the noise of nearby passersby and the horse's hoofs clicking against the cobblestones.

"No, my mom and dad died right after I got out

of the Police Academy. I still miss them but it's like I always have them here." Gideon touched his heart. "I pretty much hear my mama's words when I start 'to act out' as she called it."

"That's wonderful."

"What about you, Kat, tell me about your childhood." His tone bordered on curious.

"My parents died in an accident. My uncle moved in, as I told you earlier, and he was supposed to take care of me. He didn't. I ended up on my own at a young age."

Gideon's expression looked confused. "But there should have been agencies in place to help. What happened?"

Katheryne's head hurt. If she only had the guts to tell him the truth, then she wouldn't have to muddle through trying to figure out what he meant.

"Look, it's a beautiful night. Can't we just enjoy it?" She knew she sounded terse, but she just didn't have the answers he would want to hear, and Katheryne would not lie to him. Even when he did discover all she kept from him, he would probably never speak to her again. She wanted this one night of romance.

"Sure, whatever you want, Kat." She heard the hidden hurt in his words and it tortured her heart, but it would be another burden she'd have to bear until she could gather the courage to speak the truth.

The old part of Savannah drifted by as they made their way through the different squares. Gideon's arm remained around her, and she reveled in the comfort it gave her. As they moved into a dimly lit area, his lips found the vein in her throat, and she stifled a moan as she angled her head to allow him better access.

Gideon knew he shouldn't but he couldn't help himself. He'd wanted to taste Kat ever since he'd picked her up for dinner. The softness of her skin appealed to him with its scent of lavender soap and woman, and he wanted to gobble her up. His lips nuzzled the lobe of her ear.

"Gideon..." Kat's husky tone only made his lust hotter.

Yes. She wanted him too! He wanted to high-five someone. This beautiful, fragile, lady wanted him. A redneck.

He caught her lips with his and then plummeted beyond for a taste of the dark desire he craved. His tongue stroked hers, gentle at first, and then harder as Gideon's desire grew. Kat allowed his touch and seemed to welcome it as she had a few nights before. He pressed her back against the carriage seat and prepared to mount another foray against her neck.

"Whoa! What do you think you're doing?" The carriage driver pulled back on the reins so hard, Gideon's weight went back and then forward again. He had to lurch sideways to keep from hitting Katheryne in the face.

She gave him a startled glance, and he patted her hand. "Hang on, love. Let me see what's going on."

"Driver..." Gideon's voice and subsequent question trailed off. Standing in front of the carriage was a woman whose clothes were soaked in blood. The shouts of passersby stopped, and he could hear her sobbing.

"She's dead, Gini's dead."

Gideon gave Kat an apologetic look and jumped out of the carriage. "Ma'am? Who's dead, and are you okay?" He pulled out his cell and tapped 911. "Detective Hawks here, I need an ambulance, possibly the ME, and tag my partner, Detective Kensington please. Also some uniforms for crowd control." Gideon reeled off the address and hung up, told the carriage driver to stay put, and approached the distraught woman.

"Ma'am, what's your name?" He kept his tone low, hoping she would respond in a calmer manner. Hysterics always made him nervous.

"It's April." The blonde blinked her eyes several times and tears washed her porcelain-colored cheeks.

"Can you tell me what happened, April?"

"Me and Gini were just getting ready to hit the streets for our..." She gave him an unsure look.

"It's okay, I'm not going to arrest you or anything, but I do need to know what happened."

"Gini was behind me, we had just come out of one of the back entrances of a bar, when she said she thought she heard a kitten."

April took several deep breaths and pinned her gaze back on Gideon. "I told her to leave the poor thing alone, it might be diseased, you know? But she wouldn't listen. She said she'd be along in a minute or two. I waited and waited and when she didn't come back, I went looking for her." Her face crumpled into more tears, the black eyeliner and mascara she wore ran in streaks down her cheeks.

"She was dead, lying in a pool of blood. I tried to find a pulse, but couldn't. I mean I hoped she was still alive. Then I heard a noise, and I got the hell out of there. I didn't want to be another corpse littering these streets. I've got kids, you know?"

Gideon patted her hand, as he heard sirens in the distance and then a couple of patrol cars pulled up.

"Detective Hawks?"

"Yeah, that would be me." He glanced at the man's badge. "Officer Marlow. I'd appreciate if you would go ahead and cordon off this area. When the ME gets here as well as my partner, tell them the body is farther back in the alley.

Gideon moved toward the alley, sidestepping

police personnel, and pulled his gun out. He held the Colt 45, his personal choice of weapon, cupped in his right hand as he moved deeper into the darken interior. Lord, he hated alleys. All kinds of vermin, four and two-legged kind. He wished he had his flashlight. He just hoped if there was a body, for he tended to believe the woman, that the killer was still there. No man had a right to kill a woman even if she wasn't pure as gold.

His boots played nice, keeping his steps from shattering the deep silence of the extremely long alleyway. He skirted around several turned over crates, a pile of refuse, he didn't want to think about what was in it, and then he heard a noise. It sounded like a shoe striking a loose bit of pavement. Gideon stayed his need to rush forward, exercising caution. He wanted to catch the guy, if indeed it was their suspect. He moved forward again, around a dumpster, and saw the body. The woman lay on her back, her skirts up around her waist. Her chest was drenched in blood as were her thighs. He knew she was dead but he felt for a pulse anyway. As he drew his hand back, bam, something or someone struck him. Gideon cursed when he landed in a puddle of liquid.

He bemoaned the dry cleaning bill he'd have to pay for his one good suit, and then eased his head around the side of the trash receptacle to find his assailant.

Nothing.

Another spasm of sound caused him to spin around. Zacke was hoofing it down the alley. "You okay?"

"Yeah, but not happy. Looks like he got away after jumping me." Gideon holstered his gun, eased to his feet, and then jogged to meet his partner.

"Looks like he nicked you with his knife." Zacke motioned toward Gideon's neck where a slow slightly burning pain was now making itself known.

"Ah, hell. How bad?" Gideon put his hand up to his neck and it came away covered in blood.

"Come on, let the paramedics clean it up and bandage it." Zacke walked by Gideon's side as they exited the alley.

"I need to check on Kat. I kinda left her in a hurry."

"All right, I'll walk with you." Zacke suited action to his words as they both made their way toward the impatient carriage driver.

"Look, I've got to get back. I've got other fares waiting."

"Yeah, well make sure you stay away from this section of town, it's now a crime scene." Gideon knew he sounded angry, but dammit a woman had died.

"Sure, just let me get back to work." The driver didn't hold out his hand for a tip, probably knew he wouldn't get one. The man needed to be more compassionate.

Gideon reached up and gently lifted Katheryne down from the carriage. It was then the scent of blood reached her nostrils. She inhaled the delicious scent, basking in the rich and tantalizing offering. Her eyes widened. She knew whose blood it was—Gideon's.

"You're hurt!" Her voice came out in a squeak and startled Gideon who almost dropped her. Zacke looked a bit disturbed as well.

"I'm fine. It was just a nick." Gideon set her on her feet and then pulled her closer as the carriage driver took off at a fast clip.

"I ought to give him a ticket for just being rude." He exchanged glances with Zacke, before turning back to her. Katheryne wasted no time in ferreting out the blood source.

"Gideon, you need to see a physician, so they can take care of this." Her words must have sounded a bit stressful.

"Honey, it's okay. I've been hurt a lot worse than this in the past. Now, let's get you home."

The scent of his blood continued to grow, teasing her senses. Lord above, she wanted to drink from the wound in his neck so badly. But she couldn't—not here and not ever unless she grew a backbone and told him the truth, what she was and then it would be a moot point. He'd hate her. She just knew he would.

"I'll take her back to the house. You were first officer to respond, so I'm making you primary on this one. We'll go over the notes to see if there's any correlation between this woman's murder and the other two." Zacke's tone was calm and the look he gave her reassuring.

"You know there is." Gideon looked mad enough to spit.

"I know. I still need you to stay here, but get that wound checked first." Zacke smiled at Katheryne and then Gideon leaned down and lightly brushed her lips with his.

It was enough to send shock waves of desire throughout her body. The sensuality of the kiss, the scent of blood, and the closeness of his muscle-packed body screamed soulmate.

"Come on, Kat." Zacke threw a hand Gideon's way and led her to his car. She glanced back and watched as Gideon allowed a man in uniform to look at his neck. She should stay but it would be best if she didn't. He had a job to do, and he certainly wouldn't appreciate it if she threw herself at his neck.

Zacke opened the car door and Katheryne climbed in, while he opened the car's trunk. A second later, he slid into the driver's seat and handed her a bottle.

"What is it?"

"Blood. I usually keep a bottle or two in the trunk for Miles or Hawk if they're with me. Less messy than bags. Drink it, now. I saw the way you looked at Gideon's neck—"

Katheryne wanted to crawl under the seat. "Oh no, do you think…"

"No, I don't think Gideon realized anything. You were good at hiding your feelings, but as a former vampire, I know the signs. It's hard to control your emotions when it comes to your soulmate."

Kat slugged down the blood, her gaze on Zacke over the lip of the bottle. Once she finished she took the handkerchief he offered and wiped her lips.

"Thank you, so what do I do? How do I control it?" She knew she sounded like a lost child, but that was how she felt. How on earth could she control her urge and what happened if she didn't.

Katheryne wrapped her arms around her body and hunched forward as much as the seatbelt would allow. She rocked back and forth. She'd seen too many men, good and bad, fall by Gabriella's hand and the vampiress' thirst for blood. Men who begged Gabriella to kill them, and then shuddered as she laughed at their whimpers.

"Katheryne? You okay?" Zacke's tone was concerned as he glanced her way. She caught his gaze but couldn't hold it. This man had been honorable as a mortal and as a vampire. How could she tell him she wasn't sure she would be able to stop herself from drinking Gideon's life-blood? Even as soulmates, he could still be in danger if she wasn't in control.

"No. I think I should never have come to this century. I should have stayed underground."

She blinked back tears that she knew would be blood red if they fell. Lord knew, she didn't want to cry in front of this man, this warrior who'd beaten Gabriella at her own game.

A warm gentle hand caught the hand plucking at the skirt of her dress. "It'll be okay, little one. You, I, and Miranda will talk this through. Just remember, Gideon cares for you."

"But what if that's not enough?" Katheryne continued to look at the tanned hand next to hers. This man believed in her, he and Miranda had taken a chance on her, so should she just run away, or should she stay put?

****

Tonight had been a close call. The detective had almost caught him. He would have to be more careful in the future. He didn't want to kill the mortal yet, although the blood he'd scented after nicking the man had tempted him. He preferred to drink from a woman. More satisfying. As for killing the detective, it would be much more poignant if he did so while Katheryne watched. Then he would offer her comfort and take her away.

Chapter Thirteen

"Here we go, home again." Zacke pulled the car into the garage, exited the vehicle, opened her door, and then walked her to the adjacent kitchen door.

"What if Miranda's asleep?" She couldn't decide if she wanted the kind-hearted doctor to be deep in slumber or not."

"She won't be. When I get called out on her night off, she won't go to bed until I get in." He sounded like it was perfectly normal for his wife to do that.

"Why on her night's off?" Curiosity tinged her question.

Zacke shrugged his broad shoulders. His dark blue gaze darkened. "I'm not sure but I think it dates back to when I was shot while on duty. That happened on Miranda's night off. The fact I'm human now makes her even more antsy.

Katheryne could understand Miranda's feelings. Her first thought when she saw Gideon's blood was of horror that he'd been wounded. And going back to when he was beaten up drove home the fact that he could die. No wonder Miranda didn't sleep until Zacke was home.

"Zacke?" Miranda's soft query meant the twins were already sound asleep in their beds.

"Yeah, it's me. I've got Katheryne with me." Zacke moved toward the den where Miranda's voice had come from.

"Hey you. I'm glad you're home." Miranda stood on tiptoes and pulled Zacke's head down. She placed a kiss on his lips before she greeted Katheryne.

"Sorry, but I always do that when he comes home and I'm here." Miranda's eyes glistened.

"It's all right. I do understand." Katheryne stood there feeling like a hindrance. Maybe she should just go to her room.

"Of course you do. I heard Gideon got nicked by a knife." Her host's tone was compassionate and concerned.

"How did you know?"

"Scanner." Zacke and Miranda both replied at the same time and laughed.

"Sorry, Kat, it's just easier to keep my peace of mind if I know who's involved in what when Zacke's working or in this case when he's not." Miranda caught Katheryne's arm. "Come on, let's have something to drink. I have a feeling you could use a friend tonight."

****

Gideon surveyed the crime scene. Almost all the other personnel had gone home. He wanted to do one more walk through and then he'd talk to the clutch of women standing near the front of the alleyway. They had started gathering before the ME had brought Gini out in a body bag. The woman would haunt him because of the depth of resignation in her death gaze.

The alley was almost reverent in its silence. As if the walls, the concrete, even the garbage knew someone had passed earth's boundaries. As he scanned the area, he found nothing to indicate who the killer was and who had jumped him. Hell, he should have been more on his toes. Not taken unaware like a rookie. He wanted to slam his fist into the brick wall but it would do no good. He needed to come up with something that would help find this guy.

He exited the alley, stopped and spoke to the weeping women, and told them he would do everything he could to find the killer. The look on their faces made him want to curse. Some had hope gleaming on their tearstained countenances, the others disbelief.

After looking around, he realized he didn't have a ride home. He could call Zacke but decided to walk the ten blocks to the station. The night was clear, only a bit colder than when he and Kat had started their evening out, and it would give him time to think.

The Savannah PD ball was creeping up fast. He needed to rent a tux, or perhaps he'd buy one. Maybe he'd need it for a wedding—hopefully his, if Katheryne said yes. And that presented another problem, was he rushing things? Yeah, maybe a bit. A part of him knew his beautiful, sensual Kat might decide to move on. She could always leave Savannah or if she didn't, she might decide she didn't want a detective for anything other than friendship.

The wind picked up as he walked, and the light breeze chilled the sudden anger and fear in his blood at the thought of Kat finding someone else. Allowing another man to kiss and touch her as Gideon had and continued to want to. That could not, would not happen if he had anything to say about it. He might not be worth a lot, but dammit, he would die trying to make her happy.

A few blocks from the station, he finally got his anger under control. His fear was another matter. He needed to talk to Katheryne. Yes, his friends thought he should wait, but life was too chancy and he didn't want to lose her, nor did he want to die before he made her his. And yes, he did want Kat and he wanted her forever.

The back of the station house came into view, and his steps were suddenly lighter. He would propose to Katheryne at the Policeman's Ball. Now, he had to ask her to the damned thing.

To Gideon's surprise, his pickup was parked in a spot near the back door. He checked and found the keys in the ignition. Zacke must have had the truck dropped off. Instead he found Zacke in his office. His partner looked a bit down, probably because he was here and not at home with the lovely and patient Miranda. Hopefully his luck would change and Kat would soon be waiting at home for him. And for that he would need a real home. He'd go check out realtors tomorrow afternoon.

"Hi, you look surprisingly happy for someone who just finished a murder scene." Zacke looked more than a bit confused.

"What are you doing here? I thought you were staying home with Miranda."

"I wanted to look over the other murder files."

Gideon shook his head. His partner had always been dogmatic when it came to sniffing out a case.

"Okay, fine by me, maybe I can help. And yes, I am happy. I've decided life is just too damn short not to live it. So, I'm going to ask Kat to the ball and then propose to her." Gideon's wait for congratulations turned into a long pause. What was wrong with Zacke? He looked like he'd seen a ghost.

Gideon remained standing. "What's the problem? I thought you'd be happy for me."

When he got no response, he began to see a bit of red. "You do think I'm not good enough for Kat, don't you?"

Zacke's mouth opened, "No, that's not it at all, I..."

"You what? I don't get it, Zacke. I thought you of all people would be happy I've finally and sincerely fallen in love." His anger turned into a wall of hurt.

"Gideon..." Zacke stood and started to move around his desk. "I'm just concerned you're moving too fast. Again, I stress you need to take the time to get to know Katheryne. Allow her to know you. To do anything else is unreasonable."

"You know what, good buddy, save it. I guess all these years I thought we were friends, I was just plain wrong." Gideon moved back toward the door. "It's still my night off. I'll do the paperwork when I get in tomorrow."

"Where are you going?" Zacke sounded worried.

"That's none of your business, detective." Gideon slammed through the station like a bear on a killing frenzy. So upset, he almost ran down an older gentleman who quickly stepped back out of his way. He put the brakes on his anger and stopped.

"I'm sorry. I was in a hurry. What can I do to help you?" He really didn't want a further delay getting out of Zacke's view, but all the other officers were either on the phone or booking suspects.

"I want to report an obnoxious smell." The man looked genuinely upset, but all kinds of flakes came out after dark.

"And where was this smell?" Gideon whipped out the small notebook he kept in his back hip pocket.

"It was at the intersection of Crescent and Boulder. I was walking my dog, and Ms. Ginger got away." The man unzipped his coat and a previously quiet fur ball began to yip. "It's okay baby, we're going home in a minute." He patted the little orange ball of fluff and pushed her gently back inside his coat.

"Now where was I? Oh yes, Ginger got away and I chased her for several blocks. When I caught up with her it was near an overgrown lot."

The man looked at Gideon to see if he was following.

"So what happened next?"

"Oh by the way, my name's Carter, Percy Carter." The man stuck his hand out which meant Gideon had to stick his pencil in his mouth, and switch the pad to his other hand in order to reach out and acknowledge the other's greeting. A second later, he wanted to spit out the taste of lead on his tongue but instead replied. "Thank you, Mr. Carter, now if we could get back to the smell."

For a moment, the man's brown eyes lost their twinkle. "Sure, I'm sorry. Well Ginger heard something like a cat meowing and took off through the tall grass. I followed her, but before I could reach her she came bounding back, looking like she was scared to death. I picked her up, got a whiff of something that smelled cankered, and came on over here."

Gideon looked the man up and down, he didn't look crazy, but you could never tell. "Okay, why did you think it was a matter for the police?"

For the first time since their conversation, the man's eyes went flat, his face stony, and he pulled himself up into a straight stance. "I might seem like a crazy fool to you, but I'm former Army. I've worked burial detail through several wars, and this smelled like decaying flesh."

"Can you take me to the lot?" Gideon stuck the pad in his pocket and tossed the pencil on the closest desk.

"Sure can." Mr. Carter grimaced. "I hope I'm wrong."

"So do I, sir, so do I. I'll be right back." Gideon didn't want to talk to Zacke but this was business and from the sounds of it a dead body.

"Zacke, we have a possible DB reported by a citizen. Do you want to ride along on this one?" He waited for Zacke to look up from the paperwork on his desk. When his partner did, Gideon was stunned to see regret etched deeply into his blue gaze.

"Gideon..."

"Forget about it. Let's concentrate on the possible corpse. Do you want to ride shotgun?" He wasn't sure if he wanted Zacke to say no or not.

"Why don't you check it out first, and let me know. I want to get home before Miranda has to go to work." His tone was apologetic. Did that mean he was sorry for butting in earlier also? Gideon didn't know and at the moment, he didn't give a flying donkey's ass.

"All right. Will call if it's a DB."

Gideon turned around and exited the office before Zacke could acknowledge his words. Mr. Carter followed him as he strode through the complex of desks and then out the back. Once the concerned citizen and his dog were seated in Gideon's truck, Gideon followed suite.

"So you say you didn't smell it until you actually walked into the lot?"

"Yes, and at first I thought I was imagining it, but then the wind picked up and I got a good whiff. Nothing like a dead body smell to make your stomach churn." Mr. Carter looked Gideon in the eyes.

"I know I don't look like a Vet, but believe me, after doing what I did for three tours I needed a change. After retiring, I sold my house up north, and moved here. Been dabbling in this and that to take my mind off of my former career. Lost my wife because she found someone else while I was overseas."

Gideon felt for the man. Anyone serving the public in a military, police or firemen fashion always ran the risk of having their relationships blow up in their faces. It was a tough life, but rewarding most times.

"Yeah, I can understand that." Gideon pulled out into the street and silence prevailed as he headed for Crescent & Boulder. A few moments later, he cut the engine, and both he and Mr. Carter, minus Ginger who whined as her owner left her in the truck, made their way to the beginning of the lot.

The smell hit Gideon almost immediately after entering the tall grass. Something had died, and he had a horrible feeling another woman had lost her life. God he hoped not. The brown patches rustled as he stepped gingerly toward the center of the lot. He sure as hell didn't want to step on the body. Dr. D hated it when evidence was contaminated.

His foot struck something soft, and he shone the flashlight gripped in his left hand over the area. His right hand was on the handle of his gun just as a precaution. The orb of light found a pale slender arm, attached to a blood-spattered torso. Gideon raised the light and wanted to curse as it highlighted the young and definitely dead features of a young woman. Dammit, they had to find this madman before he killed again.

"Damn. I hate I was right." Mr. Carter's eyes stared at the body.

"Yeah, me too. I have to call this in, so if you want to go back to the truck and wait, then that's all right by me. I appreciate your help tonight."

Mr. Carter straightened his stance and stepped back. "Glad I could help. I'm truly sorry." The man sounded sincere and his gut told him the man was only being a good law-abiding citizen but still...

"Mr. Carter, I hate to tell you—"

"No need. I don't plan on leaving town, and I'm available to answer any questions. I know with me finding the body, you have to look at me as a suspect also. I'm in the book, give me a call."

"Thanks again." Protocol would be to take him back to the station, but that would just cut into his time of trying to get this third murder tagged for the ME. Besides, he truly didn't think Mr. Carter had been involved at all.

He flipped his phone out and dialed the station.

Chapter Fourteen

Katheryne finally dragged herself to bed just as dawn broke the eastern sky. She'd hoped to hear from Gideon, but figured that wouldn't happen after Zacke returned a second time and said there might have been another murder. The evening, although horrendously interrupted, had been romantic in her mind. She hoped he felt the same way.

She closed her eyes, and just as she started to drift off to sleep, she picked up the sound of Gideon's truck about to pull into the driveway. The children had awakened when their dad came home and kept their parents up until about an hour before. Katheryne knew Gideon's arrival could wake all of them once again.

She pulled on her robe and teleported to the kitchen. Gideon usually used the back door as his entry point. She opened the door just as he raised his fist to knock.

"Uh, hi, darling. I didn't expect to see you, but glad you answered the door." Gideon gave her a quick peck on the cheek, which she cherished even as she wished for more, and then he stepped into the kitchen.

"I was hoping Zacke would be up. Guess he's not since you answered the door." Gideon raked a hand through his disheveled hair. His brown eyes looked tired, his smile a far cry from the grin he habitually wore.

"Sorry, both he and Miranda are still sleeping. The twins—"

"Kept them up, didn't they? I understand." He

117

looked around uncertainly. "I guess I should go. Would you tell Zacke to call me when he gets up? I'm going to hit the sheets, and then run some errands before work tonight."

Katheryne couldn't help herself. She raised her hand and caressed a slight smudge of dirt off his face.

"You look like your night got worse after I left." She noticed a small bandage on his neck. "How's your cut?"

He caught her hand and brought it to his lips. The kiss he placed against her fingers made her feel warm and fuzzy as Miranda would have said.

"Yeah, you could say that. The cut's fine. But there was another murder, another woman who should be alive. God, I hate not finding this maniac." Gideon slammed the hand that wasn't holding hers against the kitchen counter.

"Stop! You can't prevent every crime. You know that. You're a good man, Gideon. You can only do your best."

Gideon allowed her to place kisses on his fist before he pulled her into his embrace. She loved being in his arms. He made her feel so safe, so loved, so worthy. Which is why she had to tell him the truth. Now.

"Kat, you're the best thing that ever happened to me. I want you to know that before you I was empty. Just going through the motions of life. Nothing to look forward to except work." His words were hoarse but she welcomed every raspy note.

"I feel the same way about you, Gideon." Katheryne prayed she was doing the right thing. "But there's something I need—"

"Hey, I thought I heard voices." Zacke walked into the kitchen and headed for the coffee maker. Silence reigned while he programmed the appliance.

"Hi Zacke." Gideon looked relieved though a bit

miffed.

"Morning Zacke." Katheryne's greeting wasn't much warmer. She wasn't sure when she'd find the courage again to tell Gideon her secret.

"So, what happened last night?" Zacke's tone was inquisitive as he took down a couple of cups, and grabbed a box of donuts from the cabinet.

"You know Miranda's not going to like you eating those." Gideon arched a brow at Zacke.

"Well, that's why you're going to help me eat them." Zacke chuckled and then took the carafe and poured two cups before adding sugar to his coffee. He sat down at the table and motioned for Gideon and Kat to do the same. Katheryne didn't feel the least bit slighted her host didn't offer her any coffee. He knew she hated the taste. And besides it looked like it would be a long conversation, and as much as she'd like to stick around until it ended, Katheryne felt the pull of sleep tugging at her.

"I guess I'm going to go back to bed." She knew Zacke would know she had not yet been and had no choice in the matter. Gideon hopefully wouldn't think anything about her hasty exit.

"Uh, before you go, I wanted to talk to you about the Policeman's ball." Gideon shot her an apologetic look. "I was gonna do it earlier but things happened."

"Are you asking me to go with you?" Katheryne just knew she'd go to hell for being so forward. She was taught women did not do that type of thing, but this was a totally different century and with her newfound friends, she wanted to be daring.

Gideon's ears tinged a bit red, but his voice was sure when he replied. "Yes, I want you to go as my date."

"Why, I'd love to go." Katheryne applied a bit of the southern drawl she'd heard from Miranda to her answer.

Both Gideon and Zacke laughed.

"Don't worry darling, I love your old-world accent." Gideon kissed her on the lips and then lightly swatted her robe-clad bottom. "Now go get some rest. Oh yeah, the ball's in three days."

"Thanks, Miranda told me." Katheryne laughed, gave Zacke a wave, and then blew Gideon a kiss before backing out the kitchen door.

****

"So are we okay?" Zacke held up his coffee cup like a truce banner.

For the life of Gideon he didn't want to stay mad at his best friend and partner. Besides, Katheryne had said yes to the ball, and he felt in a benevolent mood despite the night he'd had.

"Yeah, we're okay, now let me tell you what happened."

****

Gideon made it to the realtor's office late that afternoon. He'd gone home after his chat with Zacke and fallen into bed fully dressed. Now, he dickered with the agent about bringing down the price on a two-story, four-bedroom, two-bathroom brick home. The place was in town, not too far from the station. Almost in the same neighborhood as Miles and Hope, and it had a fenced in backyard.

He could see little Katherynes playing on a swing-set or having tea parties out under the large weeping willow dominating the back.

"Mr. Hawks, $100,000 is the lowest I can go even in today's economy. This house was just built a few months ago. The owners have to sell; the husband's been transferred up North for his job. The Garrett's have already left and said they're willing to leave the furniture for the new owner. I understand all of it's new as well."

Gideon knew it was a great buy. He just hated to wipe out all his savings at once. He could finance the house, but would prefer to pay for it now. Although he'd given the idea more than a passing thought that Katheryne might turn down his marriage proposal, it was still a good deal.

"All right, I'll take it." Gideon held his hand out to shake Mr. White's hand, before taking a last look around his soon to be property.

"Great, just great. You want to come down to the office and we'll start the finance papers." The man was positively glowing.

"No, actually I prefer you follow me to my bank. I'll have them draw up a cashier's check for the full amount." Gideon started for the truck, leaving an open-mouthed agent behind.

An hour later, after assuring the bank he wasn't crazy he dropped by the realtor's to sign the paperwork. The family had told Mr. White to handle everything and given him power of attorney to sign the closure papers. All that remained now was for the deed to be recorded in Gideon's name and Mr. White would take care of that. Gideon left with a receipt in one hand and the keys to his new home in the other. With the family already out of state, he could move in whenever he wanted and he wanted to do that now. And he wanted to invite Katheryne, his buddies, and their wives to a spur of the moment house warming. First, he needed to grab what few belongings he had in his little hole in the wall, and some sheets. Tonight he was sleeping in the king-size bed the family left. In fact, the place already had more furniture than his little place did.

Gideon's walk was light as he grabbed what he needed, picked up some wine and beer, and called Zacke so he could pass the word to the others. He planned to pick up Katheryne a bit earlier than the eight o'clock meeting time.

****

Katheryne was out on the porch when Gideon

pulled up in his truck. Zacke had slid a note under her door telling her about something Gideon had planned.

"Hi beautiful, you ready to go?"

Katheryne didn't think she'd ever get used to being called beautiful, especially by Gideon. Yet, she'd pull every fang in her head to be able to hear him say it everyday for the rest of her life. A life that when she told him the truth would not be worth living. Should she try again now?

"Hi yourself. You look a lot happier than when I saw you last." Katheryne moved into his embrace and allowed herself the pleasure being in his arms always brought.

His lips caressed her hairline, and she wanted to crawl inside his body.

"You make me happy, Kat. Now come on, I want to beat Zacke and the rest over to—"

"Over where?"

"It's a surprise." He grinned at her, and Katheryne decided she didn't care where they went as long as she was with Gideon.

The ride was shorter than she expected, and when they pulled into a driveway with chrysanthemums blooming, shrubs, and trees surrounding the brick home, she was more than a bit confused.

"Gideon, I thought we were going to your place." Gideon, however, was no longer in the truck. Instead, he was almost around to her side.

"We *are* at my place. This is my new home." Gideon's smile was contagious.

"When did this happen?"

"Today, you're the first one to see it outside of me and the real estate agent. The family who owned it never even got to move in before they had to move up north."

"I'm flattered." And she was, but the look of

expectation in his brown eyes made her think he wanted her to say more about the house. Before Katheryne could respond, Zacke pulled up with Miranda and the twins in tow, followed by Hope, Miles, and their little one as well as Hawk.

"Hey, what are we doing here? I thought we were meeting at your place, but then we found the note." Zacke's eyes were full of curiosity, and Katheryne wasn't sure what he would say when Gideon told him.

"Well, I wanted ya'll to see this house." His words still didn't do a thing to clear up the confusion, but instead seemed to cause more.

"Why are we seeing this house?" Zacke asked patiently but he could see the questions in four more sets of eyes.

"Because it's my new home." Gideon's eyes gleamed with excitement. The tiny lines around his beautiful features were not as prominent as they had been that morning. So if he was happy she was happy, and hopefully, no one would take that away from him.

"You're buying a house?" Hawk sounded baffled.

"Yeah, well, I actually—"

"Come on, Gideon, you never have any money." Miles' disbelief was mirrored on Zacke's face as well as the women's.

"Hey, I just loaned you some money until payday. No way can you afford to buy a house this size." Zacke didn't pull any punches with his words, and Katheryne cringed waiting on Gideon's response.

"Good point, but the reason I usually run out of money between paydays is I put everything, and I have been for over ten years, in the bank after I pay my bills." Gideon grinned at the astonished faces staring at him; Katheryne's being one of them.

"And I'm not only going to buy this house, I

already have!" The man actually did some type of dance step.

"Look ya'll, I don't come from old money like you do. I invested mine in stocks and bonds, and I paid for the house today. There's no loan, just the title which is being transferred over to my name."

"Wow, I am a bit blown away." Zacke clapped Gideon on the back, and then grinned. "Does that mean I can get my loan back?"

"Sure when I get paid again, partner." Gideon laughed. "The house about wiped out my savings, so I have to do some financial finagling and buy up some more stock."

Hawk moved in close to Gideon. "You think you can help me pick up some prime stock. I've been wanting to build a house of my own."

"Sure, I've learned quite a bit in the last several years." Gideon shook hands with Hawk, accepted thanks from Miles, and then moved back to Katheryne's side.

"Now, are ya'll ready to party? I brought food and liqueur."

****

Katheryne sat on a window seat in the kitchen area. Gideon and the men had moved out to the side patio off the breakfast nook.

"So I hear Gideon asked you to the policeman's ball." Miranda grinned over a slice of pizza. It smelled good, but she'd rather have what the male vamps were having outside. It seemed Gideon had made sure all of his guests had a drink of choice. Kat pulled her mind away from the taste of blood to Miranda's statement.

"Yes, he asked me this morning before he left your house. I'm not exactly sure what it is."

"You'll love it." Hope laughed. "Even though Miles isn't a police officer, we buy tickets and it's always a blast."

"It's dressy isn't it?" Katheryne hated that she sounded uncertain, but this seemed like a big affair. She didn't have anything that would be suitable.

"Oh yes, dressy and a big deal. All the big shot ranking officers are there, as well as the mayor, the police commissioner, you name it. And their girl friends and wives." Miranda's words did not help disperse the unsettled feeling in the pit of Katheryne's stomach. She did not want to embarrass Gideon.

"Hey babe." Miles popped his head and then his body into the kitchen. I thought you might like what I'm having, since you didn't get a chance to eat before we left."

He handed Hope a bag of blood, and then pulled another one from under his shirt. "Here you go, Kat. I know you as well as Hope can manage some food, but until you can tell Gideon, I thought you might need some help." Miles grinned. "And don't worry, we'll keep Gideon busy until you're finished."

"Thank you." Katheryne smiled, grabbed the offering, and turned her back to the doorway. She suppressed a moan of delight as her incisors came down and ruptured the plastic. Once the blood was consumed, she turned back.

"Feel better?" Hope took the empty bag and tossed it as well as her own into a garbage bag.

"Yes, thank you. It's a bit disconcerting having you all know what I am, but still having to hide it from Gideon." Katheryne's gaze locked on Gideon as he laughed at something one of the other men had said.

Lord, she loved him. His laugh, his commitment to help others, the way he held her when she just needed comfort, and the way he loved her all the way to her toes.

"Kat? Kat? Are you listening?" Miranda's question pulled her from a daydream of making love to Gideon.

"I'm sorry. What did you say?" Katheryne forced her gaze to Miranda's.

"What on earth were you thinking about? You were miles away." Hope's tone was curious as well as humorous.

"Actually only a few feet." Kat's sigh came out almost on a moan. "I have to tell him what I am. I've tried twice and something always happens before I get the words out."

"Trust in yourself and Gideon, Kat. The man really loves you." Miranda's words sounded wonderful, but Katheryne had seen the looks of horror on men's faces when Gabriella revealed her true self. What if...no she couldn't think that way. If Gideon turned from her then there would be no tomorrow for Katheryne. She had to tell him before the ball, before he could bring her closer into his life, before he tore her heart completely in two.

Yes, she needed to tell him tonight.

****

Marcel watched the gathering of mortals and vampires. It was odd seeing them interact, but he needed to know more about Detective Hawks. A name he'd gotten from the man's next-door neighbor. He'd also found a willing clerk at the local library who found him all sorts of trivia on Katheryne's beau. After that, he'd trailed Gideon on his myriad of errands and watched him move into this more impressive house. Still it was not good enough for his Katheryne. She deserved the best and she would have it when Marcel had her.

Chapter Fifteen

Katheryne wanted to pull out her fangs. Her plan to tell Gideon she was a vampire had been yanked out from under her once again. Not long after the pizza, beer, and in some cases blood had been demolished, Gideon got a call on his cell phone. A quick kiss on the lips, a promise from Zacke that he'd lock up, and the man took off.

The bad thing...she couldn't be upset with him for leaving. One of the women, a friend to one of the women killed, had called—frightened to death. He was a good man and a good detective, so she either loved them both or not all.

Now, three days later, she waited on her date to the ball to arrive. Miranda had hinted while they had gone dress shopping that Gideon, by way of Zacke, had pretty much said he wanted to ask her to marry him. She couldn't allow him to do it, not yet, not until he knew what type of creature he would be marrying.

Then again, he might decide he didn't want her any more.

Stop it! *I can't think that way. I won't.* Gideon would still love her, he had to, Katheryne didn't know what she would do if he changed his mind. The few times she'd seen him in the last three days, he'd smiled that heart warming smile of his, kissed her until her toes curled up, and his eyes had promised forever.

She smoothed down the red satin of her evening gown. Miranda and Hope both thought she needed a bit of color for this important occasion, but

127

Katheryne wondered if she'd made a mistake. Blending in would be good since she'd be meeting some of his co-workers and boss, but now she was afraid she'd stick out like a clown.

"Stop fidgeting, Kat. The dress is fine, you look lovely, and Gideon will love it and you." Miranda's calm voice of reason helped settle some of her nerves, but the part still galloping like a runaway horse wanted to throw up the blood she'd consumed prior to getting dressed.

"Yes, and now I won't feel so flamboyant myself." Hope curtseyed in her peach off the shoulder dress.

"You look wonderful, and besides I thought this wasn't your first ball." Katheryne sounded petulant and hated herself, but she just knew one look at her and Gideon would have a cow as Miranda would say.

"Well, no, but it's my first time to wear this much color at the policemen's ball. I usually go in black, but Miles put his foot down. Said I wasn't to go all somber like and hide in a corner like I did last year." Hope laughed.

"Did you really?" Katheryne was astonished that the so self-assured physician/vampire married to one of the most handsome men in Savannah could ever be shy.

"Oh yes she did. It took me and Zacke and Miles to drag her out to the dance floor." Miranda giggled. "But once there Hope actually put the rest of us to shame."

"Yeah well don't count on that happening again. Everyone thought I was drunk just because I loosened up a bit."

"Well, if you want to hide in the corner, then I'll hide with you." Katheryne could only pray Hope would do just that.

"You ladies ready?" Zacke's baritone came from behind the group of women, but instead of jumping at his silent approach, Miranda melted back against him. Katheryne envied the comfortable and loving relationship the couple enjoyed.

"Yes, just waiting on the limo to arrive with Gideon. And I'm ready and more than willing to gorge out on some of the fantastic food. What about you two?" Miranda looked at Hope and Katheryne.

"I'm willing to nibble a bit." She inserted at almost the same time, Hope blurted out, "Oh yes!"

"Hope, you look gorgeous." Miles' gaze slid over his wife's body and brought a shiver of awareness to even Katheryne. The man positively ate Hope up with his eyes.

"Well, I see Gideon is late as usual." Hawk's droll tone and amber eyes lit with humor. "And if he doesn't make an appearance soon, I think I'm going to steal his date."

Before Katheryne could say a word, the vamps in the room heard the sound of a vehicle's motor. A moment later, Zacke and Miranda smiled.

"Looks like Gideon's here. Guess I'll be going stag after all." Hawk's laughter, joined by all of them, preceded Gideon's knock on the door.

At a nod from Zacke, Katheryne did the honors. Gideon stood motionless, highlighted in the moonlight, in what she could only call regal splendor. His blond hair lay over the collar of his black tuxedo coat. His chest looked muscular in the silk shirt and vest. The cummerbund banding his waist made her want to tangle her hands in it and then strip it away. The satin pants drew her attention to the masculinity hanging low but full against the material. Lord she loved and lusted for this man.

"You take my breath away, woman!" Gideon's hoarse greeting pulled her gaze back to his face.

"I'm glad. You make me breathless also."

"Shall we go, my lady?" Gideon crooked his arm

toward Katheryne and she laid her palm on his sleeve. If she died tonight, she would always remember this moment. Her first ball, her first love, and the reality this man loved her back.

"Yes, I can't wait to dance with you."

The guffaws coming from the men turned her escort's ears a lovely shade of pink.

"Good luck with that, Kat. The man can't dance." Miles' baritone caused another chorus of guffaws.

"That's enough. I can slow dance and that's all that matters. Now let's get a move on. I'm ready for some fun and other stuff." Gideon waggled his eyebrows at Katheryne, and the giggles escaping from her throat caused the women to burst into laughter.

"I agree, let's get this show on the road." Miranda grabbed Zacke's arm, and Hope herded Miles as well as Hawk out the door to the limo Zacke had rented.

"You ready?" Gideon's question caressed her ear right below the lobe. Shivers danced up her spine, even as the blood heated inside her body.

"Yes, more than ready." She just hoped he was for what she had to tell him.

****

Katheryne wiggled her abused toes as she sat at one of the tables. Gideon had gone to get her a plate of food she would have to try to eat. Miles and Hawk gave her sympathetic looks, as did Hope who for some reason when she was turned could still tolerate almost all-mortal food. She only hoped she wouldn't disgrace herself and be sick on her gown. She was already nervous enough.

"Here you go." Gideon handed her a plate, and then sat next to her with one filled to the brim for himself. Thank God, he'd chosen small samples of different foods for her. Maybe she could just nibble this and that.

Katheryne brought a crisp cracker to her mouth and while the others were eating, she chewed slowly and glanced around the room.

There seemed to be a lot of people eating and milling around, although Miranda said attendance was down somewhat from the previous year. The music was a lot different than she recalled from when she was forced to serve while Gabriella entertained, but it had a nice sound.

"You don't eat enough to keep a bird alive, Kat. Try some of this." She turned her head and opened her mouth to say no when a nice plump strawberry popped onto her tongue. Out of habit, she bit down and the luscious, ripe flavor teased her taste buds. Katheryne closed her eyes to savor the fruit and opened them only after she felt the touch of Gideon's lips against hers.

All too soon, he pulled away. She smiled back at him and then dropped her gaze upon noticing she and Gideon were the center of attention at their table as well as a few others.

****

Gideon didn't know how much more he could take. From the moment Kat opened the door, he'd wanted to take her in his arms and make love to her. Not just dance, all that did was give her crushed toes and make him horny as hell. Not what he wanted, scratch that, he did want that, but he wanted the evening to be romantic for Kat.

He wanted the mood just right for his proposal.

How much longer did they have to stay at this damn ball?

Oh yeah, until the awards and commendations were handed out. And by the way the commissioner and the mayor were throwing back the drinks it could be awhile. Mere Hamilton, aka, Mrs. Mayor would be giving her husband a talking to before she allowed him behind the podium for anything.

Gideon glanced at his watch again and looked around. The wait staff was replenishing the buffet, which meant they had roughly half hour or more before they brought out the desserts. Then that would take up, if he remembered correctly from last year, another thirty minutes or so.

Yep, plenty of time to propose to Kat.

"Excuse us." Gideon gently tugged Kat to her feet, ignored the "Hey, where are you going?" coming from several of their tablemates, and ushered his date through the throngs of people in the ballroom.

"Gideon?" He heard the question in her voice, but chose to ignore it for the moment. The ring he planned to place on her finger, if she said yes, burned a hole in his pocket. His nerve endings were bouncing around like he'd stepped on a live wire. His heart raced, and his pulse pounded as he guided her to the elevator, then changed his mind—the escalator would be quicker.

He tucked her gown up a bit, so it wouldn't catch in the glide and once they were in the lobby, he tugged her toward the hallway leading to the gardens.

The moon's glow cast the late blooming roses, azaleas, and camellias into a seductive blend of scents and color. Good, he needed all the help he could get. Gideon glanced down at Kat, whose eyes were wide open, her lavender gaze filled with curiosity. Gideon tugged her forward to a bench and then gently guided her down.

Okay, he had one chance at this. He'd never proposed to anyone in his life unless it was indecent. This was so different, and he wanted it to be perfect.

The light breeze whirled tendrils of Kat's hair around her shoulders. The silver halo from above turned her skin into an alabaster glow. If he had tried, he would never have been able to create such a beautiful scenario. Now only one thing would make it complete.

Gideon dropped to one knee and took Kat's hand in his. "Kat, I know you know how I feel. You couldn't help but notice that I'm crazy in love with you." He caressed the top of her hand with his thumb. "What you don't know is that I don't think I can live without you in my life forever. You're everything I've always wanted in a lover, wife, friend. You make me feel worthy. For so long I've muddled around trying to find someone."

He kissed her hand before releasing it. "I guess what I'm trying to say is, I love you more than I love my own life. Would you please marry me?" Gideon drew out the jeweler's box and opened the lid.

Katheryne sat in stunned wonder. She knew he planned to propose but having him do so was something else entirely. God how she wanted to say yes. Yet, she needed to tell him what she was before turning his life upside down.

"Gideon, I..."

The glow in his brown eyes, so full of hope a second before, became dull.

"Kat, I know you could do much better than me, but no one else could ever love you as much as I do. I pledge to always keep you safe and love you until the day I die."

Oh Lord, she'd hurt him, made him doubt himself. Her shining knight in police armor who rescued damsels in distress and protected the innocent.

"Yes." The moment her mouth uttered that word she wanted to call it back, yet for the first time in decades she felt a peace that enveloped her completely. This was right. Now if only he would understand what she had to tell him.

"Yes? You said yes?" Gideon's mouth, which had turned down lit up with a smile that put the moon to shame. His gaze twinkled with a combination of love, happiness, and disbelief if she read him right.

"Yes, but I need to tell you something—"

"You've already told me what I want to hear, my love." Gideon got up off the ground, and sat next to Katheryne on the bench. The ring he slid on her finger shimmered with a rainbow of colors as the moonlight hit it. It was lovely, but she still needed to confess before she could wear the ring with any type of assurance.

"No...I really have to tell you about me. What I—"

"Gideon? You out here?" Hawk's voice cut through her words.

Why couldn't he have waited just a minute longer? Who was she kidding? It would take her at least five minutes to work up the courage to spit out the word vampire.

"Yeah, back here." Gideon turned toward the tall handsome vampire just now walking into view. Hawk's mane of hair was golden and his amber eyes meshed with the bronze tone of his skin. Too bad she'd been turned while still a pasty white skin tone.

"Hey, Zacke sent me, the award ceremony is fixing to start."

"Well, I have my own ceremony going on. Be the first to congratulate me, I'm getting married." Gideon positively crowed his announcement.

Hawk shook Gideon's hand, then clapped him on the back. Katheryne could hear the thoughts in his mind.

"Did you tell him?"

"No, I didn't tell him."

"Why not?"

"Because you interrupted me before I could. I have to tell him."

"Now let me congratulate your bride to be." Hawk pulled her into an embrace and whispered.

"Sorry about the timing. Maybe you can tell him later?"

"I hope so. I can't marry him without him knowing." She whispered back.

"Okay you guys break it up, I want to get back inside and tell the rest of the crew." Gideon pulled Katheryne to him and then encircled her waist.

"Come on darling. We've got a lot to celebrate." She smiled up into his gaze and prayed he'd still be calling her darling before the night was over.

****

His plan to snatch Katheryne at this so-called ball had been a good one but had quickly come unraveled. He was so close when the male vampire interrupted the tender scene between his beloved Katheryne and the detective. Next time there would be no interruption, he would kill the man usurping his place, and take Katheryne away.

Chapter Sixteen

Gideon raised his glass for the fourth or fifth time, he'd lost count, as his friends toasted their good wishes. His hand still held onto Kat's. He didn't want to let her go. If he was dreaming, then he'd like to keep dreaming a bit longer.

Yes, she'd said yes, but her eyes didn't smolder with the happiness he felt deep within his heart. Something was bothering Kat, and he just prayed she hadn't changed her mind about marrying him. Of course he'd sorta, even though he'd hinted at it before, thrown it at Kat pretty fast.

He downed the champagne and set his glass down. Maybe he just needed to talk to her somewhere quiet. His house maybe.

"You about ready to go?" He took Kat's almost full glass from her and placed it next to his.

"Yes. I think I am." She smiled at him but it still didn't light up her face like he loved.

"Okay then, we're out of here." He caught Kat's hand and then spoke to his only family. "I'll catch you guys later. I'll send the limo back to pick ya'll up. Thank you for your well wishes."

"Night, you two!" Those words followed him from various sets of lips as he and Kat made their way out of the ballroom and the hotel. Once seated in the limousine he turned to her.

"Look, I may have rushed things tonight." His words sounded flat just like the night seemed to have become.

"No—Gideon I'm thrilled, I mean I love—It's just I think we need to talk about things." Kat's eyes glistened but her words were gentle.

Great, she *had* changed her mind.

"Okay, let's go back to my place and we'll hash everything out. Is that all right with you?" He prayed she'd say yes, that somehow he could convince her things weren't moving too quickly. That they were right where they should be.

"Yes, that's fine with me."

The ride to his new home, and hopefully Kat's in the near future continued in silence. Gideon tried to plug the hole in his heart that was getting bigger all the time. Why wouldn't she smile at him? Why did she look like her heart was the one breaking?

Once there they entered through the front door. Gideon moved through the house to the kitchen. Moonlight shone through the large bay window ingrained in the kitchen facing the back of the property.

"Here have a seat. I want a beer. Drinking Champagne is like drinking water. You want anything?" Gideon tried to smile but felt like his face would crack.

"Uh, yes, if there's any wine left, I'd like to have a glass." Kat's sultry voice was the opposite of the dread he spotted in her gaze. Did she want to change her mind?

He pulled the wine from the refrigerator and poured her a glass. Kat took several sips and when it looked as if she was going to take another he couldn't stop himself.

"Okay, Kat, out with it. Why are you so upset? Do you regret saying you would marry me? Is that it? Do you want to back out?" His words sounded as desperate as he felt.

"No, not at all. I just need to clarify some things about myself." The look she gave him was hopeful but definite in the implication that she meant what she said.

"I can accept that. We probably don't know everything about one another. Lord, I snore." He tried to smile.

She did manage a slight smile. "I already know that much." Then her smile faded, "Gideon it's something that could change how you feel about me." Kat's hand clenched around the stem of her glass.

"Nothing you could ever tell me would change the fact I love you. Nothing, Kat." Gideon moved from the counter to stand with his back to the window. His stance was relaxed but his muscles jumped within his skin. Kat sounded so serious.

"What is it, baby? You can tell me anything."

Katheryne opened her mouth to release the words that would grant her heart's desire or seal her hopes of love forever. But before she could the bay window shattered, and the front of Gideon's shirt blossomed red. She could smell the metallic scent of blood. Someone had shot him.

Oh God above. She jumped up and caught him in her arms before he could pitch forward.

"Kat, I..." His voice trailed off as his eyes closed. She lowered him gently to the floor. Another pinging sound echoed around the kitchen. Whoever had shot Gideon was still shooting. Was she the quarry now? It didn't matter, if they hit her she'd survive, but she had to help Gideon or he might not.

Blood poured from his chest in copious amounts. She needed to stop the blood. Ah the blood, the scent called to her like nothing else could. She dragged her mind from the temptation before her, and her gaze lit on the cummerbund around his waist, it could help stop the blood. She yanked it off and pressed it against the wound. Crimson bled into the material turning it into a sodden mass.

It wasn't working. She needed to call someone... Miranda, she could save Gideon. The phone! Where was his phone? Her search for the phone reminded her of another time he'd been injured. She prayed tonight's outcome would be as good.

She dropped the phone twice, her hands slippery with his blood, but finally managed to get it open. She looked for, found Zack's number, and punched it. Her fingertip left a bloodstain on the faceplate.

"Hello." Zacke's greeting registered above several background sounds. They must still be at the hotel.

"Zacke, it's Kat. We're at Gideon's house. Someone shot him. He's bleeding badly."

"Kat?" His tone turned into an authoritive rumble.

"Yes, it's me. Gideon's hurt." She looked down at his washed out features, the blood staining the floor, and the wash of crimson covering the front of his body. "I think he's dying. You have to do something."

"Did you call for an ambulance?"

"No, I don't know how, and besides he'll die before they get here. You have to come now. We have to save him. Please." Kat swallowed against the bubble of tears in the back of her throat. She knew death up close and personal. She'd seen men die before. Gideon would not last if something wasn't done soon.

"Kat, call 9-1-1. We're on our way."

She didn't bother to reply but tossed the phone down. Even if they drove like mad, Gideon would be dead before they reached him. She didn't have to have a doctor's degree to know this—she could feel the life leeching from her heart. His eyes remained closed, and his chest rose slower than before.

No, she had to do something and the only thing to do was turn him. Yet, if she did he would hate her, and wasn't there a code about turning mortals? "Damn," the curse rolled off her tongue as she tried to think. The one thing she was sure of was she would not lose Gideon to death. She might have to give him up after he realized what she'd done, if he survived, but at least he'd be alive to make the choice.

All right, she could do this. Once his blood was drained completely, she would need to give him hers. Should she drink the blood spilling from him? No, she couldn't bear the thought of helping him die. She would wait until the wound stole his life and then she would give him what he needed to live. And it needed to be done at the same time he took his last breath. At least that's what she thought. Maybe she should wait for Zacke and the rest; they had turned Hope and would be better at this than Katheryne, but she feared he would not last that long.

It could have been a second but it seemed like an eternity before Gideon took his last breath. Her heart almost stopped beating the same moment his did, but she had a job to do. Katheryne allowed her fangs to descend and ripped open her wrist. She held it over Gideon's mouth, but when he didn't respond, she pressed it against his lips.

Nothing. Oh God, what to do now?

She felt rather than saw the group that teleported into the room. The gasps of horror quickly extinguished when she turned and growled. "It's not working, do something!"

"Why didn't you call 9-1-1?" Zacke's question was a stunned inquiry.

"Because it would have been too late. And if they arrived, then we would not be able to try to save him by turning him. Now help me... please." Katheryne's voice shook, as did her entire body.

"She's right, Zacke. It looks as if the bullet nicked an artery in his heart." Hope's statement was calm, but her hands shook as she tore open Gideon's shirt.

"How long has he be..." Hawk's question bled into Katheryne's brain. *Dead? Oh God he's dead.*

"Katheryne? How long?" Miranda's gentle tone was the total opposite to the wild and desolate look in her blue-eyed gaze.

"No more than a minute. I tried to stop the bleeding, and when I couldn't I waited. As soon as his heart stopped, I tried to give him my blood. He wouldn't drink." Her words came out on a wail. "Why isn't it working? He can't die."

"Come on little one, let's give Hope and Miranda some room."

Both women, regardless of their evening apparel were already examining Gideon as Miles helped Katheryne to her feet. She allowed him to turn her face into his shirtfront and her sobs soaked the material. God, she'd been so stupid. She should have told him what she was, she should have done it sooner, and then maybe he'd be alive.

"Katheryne, did you see the shooter?" Zacke seemed to have retained his usual calm manner, but she knew from the slight trembling in his hands when she raised her head to look at him, he was far from calm.

"No. Gideon had just moved in front of the window. We were talking and then the glass shattered." Kat's gaze returned to the ashen-faced man at her feet. She pulled away from Miles and dropped to her knees.

"Is he going to...?" She couldn't bear to finish the question.

"Technically, he's already dead, Kat, but he does have an arterial pulse in his abdomen. I'm hoping once that stops, we can give him the blood and he'll take it. I'm not sure." Hope sounded as defeated as Katheryne felt.

"How long?" She took Gideon's hand in hers and just held it in her lap.

"Not long, Kat." Miranda reached up and wiped a tear away. "I don't know what else to do after that."

"What about any of you? Is there anything that can be done to help Gideon?" Katheryne knew she was pleading but didn't care.

"No, we turned Hope but that's all the experience I've had. I think we probably need to set up some blood for him so we'll have it on hand." Hawk inserted but then looked at Zacke.

"I think that's it. We just have to get him to take the blood when it's offered." Zacke rolled up his sleeve. "I want to donate some."

"Yes, the rest of us will too. Maybe with all of us contributing it might make a difference." Hope's smile at Kat was dismal, but still appreciated.

"Okay, it's almost time. His pulse is almost gone." Miranda looked at Kat. "Do you want to try again first?"

"Yes, please, I need to do this." Katheryne laid Gideon's hand gently on the floor and waited for Miranda's nod.

Again, she slit her wrist and held it to his lips. His face remained motionless, his lips a hard unyielding line, a bluish tint to his eyelids.

Dammit, he couldn't die. She loved him. Before she could think twice, she pinched his nostrils together and pried open his lips. The blood, although it had slowed, still flowed enough to drip into his mouth.

The silence was audible as they all waited to see what Gideon would do. She wanted to laugh when his nose wrinkled up before his tongue searched out the life-giving liquid he so needed. Then his mouth attached itself to Katheryne's wrist. The more he suckled, the more hopeful she became.

So intent with watching Gideon's life force return, she didn't realize she was slumping forward until several pairs of hands caught her.

"Enough, Kat. Let us help tend Gideon." This

time Hawk lifted her to her feet and then sat her in a chair. He dropped to the floor beside Zacke who took the scalpel Miranda offered from her bag and opened a cut in his wrist. Gideon took his partner's offering as he had Katheryne's. And so it went, Hawk, Miles, Hope, and Miranda all gave of their blood to ensure Gideon would survive.

Katheryne didn't know how long she sat there watching but sometime later, Hope handed her a bag of blood. "Sorry, I should have given this to you before. I just..."

"Don't worry about it. We were all too upset and worried to think of anything but Gideon." Katheryne patted her hand and then slapped the bag to her mouth. She sucked it down so quickly the rush went to her head, and she had to lean forward again.

"Take it easy, you need to be your best when Gideon awakens." Zacke's words did what the blood couldn't. It mobilized her heart and soul into believing Gideon would recover.

"Thanks for everything. Gideon has such wonderful friends."

"We're your friends also, Kat." Zacke smiled for the first time since arriving. He pulled up a chair and then sat next to her.

"I know you didn't get a chance to tell him about being a vampire before you left the hotel. Were you able to before...?"

"No. I opened my mouth to tell him and then he was shot." Kat looked to where Gideon still lay on the floor. Miles had stuffed his tuxedo coat under Gideon's head, and he was still suckling just a bit from Miranda. A Miranda who looked like she wasn't sure about what she was doing but would do it anyway to save a friend.

"Well, when he awakens, we'll be with you. We'll all explain what happened if you like." Zacke stifled a yawn. Sometimes she forgot he wasn't a vampire.

He still maintained so many of the strong traits Miles and Hawk carried.

"You need some rest, both you and Miranda. And what about the twins?" In all the chaos, Katheryne had forgotten the captivating pair.

"They are fine. The babysitter is staying until we get back. She's used to us keeping odd hours. And since it will be several hours before Gideon awakens, I'm going to talk Miranda into lying down."

"Where?"

"I think Hawk and Miles are going to get us some sleeping bags in a bit. It'll be fine. What we have to do now is wait on the change to take over." For a moment, the detective's calm slipped as he ran a hand through his hair.

"What do you mean change? I thought this was it?"

"Kat, do you remember when Gabriella changed you?" His look was curious.

Katheryne gripped her trembling hands together. Any mention of her sire made her want to wail in terror. "I don't remember much. I felt the pain when she tore into my throat, but after that it got really hazy and then dark. My next memory was waking up hungry."

"Sounds like you were unconscious for the undesirable aspects of the change. Hope slept but she thrashed around and had nightmares before she awakened." He sounded regretful.

"Yes, but if ya'll hadn't change me, I would have died and my baby with me. You are sometimes worse than Miles. Quit beating yourself up over it. If you love someone you will do all you can to make sure they survive." Hope's calm words mixed with a bit of fire. It seemed she'd had this conversation before with Zacke and certainly with her husband.

"So now we just wait?"

"Yes, and be patient when he awakens. My

partner is a good man, but this is not going to be something he can swallow down without it taking some time." Zacke patted her hand again.

"What you're saying is that Gideon is not only going to be upset with what he's become but with us or rather me more specifically."

"Yes. I'm sorry." Again the pat.

"Well then, I guess I'll just have to hold on until he gets over it. And then maybe he'll see that there was nothing else to be done." Or, at least Katheryne prayed it would be so.

Since Gideon apparently and finally had enough sustenance, and since Miranda's wrist couldn't heal on it's own, Hope wrapped a piece of gauze around the wound. Now both Miranda and Zacke wore matching wristbands. Lord, she wished she could see the humor in this. The futility of trying to figure out why someone would kill Gideon weighed on Kat's mind.

"Okay, guess we need to move him to a bed." Miles reached under Gideon's arms to grasp his shoulders at the same time Hawk and Zacke grabbed for his legs. Hawk gave Zack an apologetic smile. "Why don't you stay with the women, and we'll get him up the stairs. I think he weighs more as a vampire than he did a human."

Zacke stepped back but not before Katheryne saw a look of sadness so deep cross his features it actually hurt her. Was he sad he'd lost his friend to vampirism or because he could no longer claim it as a brotherhood?

Once the men left with Gideon's inert body, the tension seemed to deflate from the air. Hope moved to the refrigerator, looked in and scowled. "No food. I know that most of us can only eat a bit, and some of us none, but Zacke you and Miranda are going to need to eat soon or you're going to fall on your face."

Katheryne looked out the window. Dawn was

just around the corner, and she knew the other vampires would have to sleep. She would too, but could manage to stay up past the morning sunrise.

"I can teleport out to a fast food place and be back before dawn. I'll grab ya'll up some breakfast, and swing by the house and get some more blood. I'm also thinking what if we set up a slow drip of blood going into Gideon's veins, it could keep him from waking up ravenous for blood." She turned to Miranda, "What do you think?"

"I think it might work. Lord, I'm tired, and I wished this had never happened. I know it's no one's fault but Gideon is such a mortal." Miranda giggled for a minute. "I mean he's always been such a guy guy and now to have to learn how to do certain things is going to annoy the heck out of him."

"You can say that again." Zacke's tired laughter filled the room. "We used to talk about him being a vampire just in jest. He said no thanks. He'd rather do his eating with a fork and spoon without a set of fangs. Now it looks like he's going to have to learn new tricks. And for Gideon that's not going to be easy."

"Well, we'll help him. All of us. I mean there was no choice. We couldn't just let him die, could we?" Katheryne practically begged her question.

"No, you're right. There was no choice. I can't imagine not having Gideon around. It's going to be strange working with him as a vampire. Guess I'll get a taste of what he put up with for years." Zacke pulled Miranda down to sit on his lap.

"Yeah, what will I do with all the beer we have in the fridge for him?" Miranda giggled.

"Knowing Gideon, he'll drink it or bust trying."

Katheryne listened to the sound of their laughter and for the first time since she'd watched Gideon's life bleed away on the floor she felt a smidgen of hope. Maybe he would take to his new life without any problems. Of course that didn't mean he'd want her in that life. The ring he slid on her finger an eternity ago felt heavy, dull, and lifeless against her skin. The what if's were killing her.

Chapter Seventeen

"Kat!"

Her name being shouted woke Katheryne from a sleep she hadn't realized she'd fallen into. She shook her head and jumped up from the table where she'd been resting her head.

"Kat!"

Gideon's awake. She looked out the window as she headed for the stairs. Day had come and gone again, but he should still be sleeping. She raced up the stairs and once she reached the landing, she followed his shouts to the bedroom.

"Kat!"

"Hush Gideon, the women are still asleep. I'll get Kat in a few minutes, but you need to calm down. There are some things you need to know." Zacke sounded exhausted. He should have called her to help.

"I'll calm down when you tell me where the hell Kat is. The last thing I remember is being shot. Is she okay?" Gideon sounded frantic.

"I'm fine, Gideon. You're the one that was hurt." Katheryne moved to stand beside the bed.

Gideon clutched her hand, and she barely stopped herself from flinching. As a mortal, he'd been strong, healthy, and handsome. As a vampire, even newly converted, he was all those things and more.

"Baby, are you sure you're okay?"

"Yes, but Zacke's right, Gideon, we need to talk about what happened after you were shot." Katheryne looked at the newly arrived Miles and

Hawk.

"Yeah, some things went down that weren't so good." Miles' words were an understatement.

"And remember the important thing is you're alive." Hawk's statement caused a frown to chase across Gideon's forehead. He turned and confusion filled his brown-eyed gaze.

"What's going on? Why am I here and not in the hospital?"

"Gideon, everything happened so fast. You were bleeding to death. I didn't know what to do." Katheryne tried to turn her gaze away from his but she couldn't.

"I can understand that, Kat, but that doesn't explain anything." His frown intensified, and Katheryne wished she could run away.

"Well, I called Zacke, who did tell me to call 9-1-1, but I knew there wasn't time. I uh..."

"You what?" His grip tightened again on her hand almost crushing the bones.

"I... well...I tried to tell you several times about something you needed to know, but we kept getting interrupted."

"I'm losing patience, Kat."

While she was trying to find the courage to tell him, Miranda and Hope slipped into the room. She tried to take their supportive smiles to heart but they did nothing to warm her frigid insides.

"Okay, I'm just going to say it. I know about vampires, I know about your friends." Katheryne's gaze encompassed the room before sliding back to meet his.

"How? I never told you, and what has that got to do with me being here and not in a hospital or dead?" The words dripped from his lips in a wealth of confusion. As she tried to find the words to say anything, a flicker of awareness invaded his gaze.

"Son Of A Bitch! You let them turn me into a

damn vampire, didn't you?"

Gideon's snarl scared the life or what life she had out of Katheryne. And the vicious looking fangs he sported didn't help her peace of mind.

There were collective snarls from the other male vampires, and Hope looked like she wanted to rip Gideon's throat out herself. Zacke and Miranda just stood and stared as if they were reliving a nightmare.

"What else could I do? Let you die?" Katheryne tried to reason with him.

"Yes, dammit." Gideon's gaze turned almost black.

"Well, I didn't, so live with it. I love you, and I wasn't going to watch you bleed to death. And would you really rather be dead than here with us?" Katheryne allowed her own incisors to come down and snarled back at him.

"Hell, you're one too!" Gideon's look of horror caused a pain so severe inside her chest, she knew her heart was slashed in half. So much for the dream he'd understand. Well, so be it.

"Yes, that's right. I'm the same as I was when you found me in the alley. Only now instead of wanting to die because I couldn't face living without friends or family." Her gaze encircled the husbands and wives standing stock-still as well as Hawk. "I found my family and friends. I thought I'd found love, but you know what, even Gabriella, yes, she was the witch that turned me didn't look at me with such horror and loathing in her eyes. I'm done."

Before anyone could think about stopping her, Katheryne teleported out of the house. She wasn't sure where to go. She wouldn't feel right just teleporting into the Kensington's home. Yet, she couldn't stay here. As she tried to decide, the moonlight just now coming across the horizon touched the stone of her engagement ring. She wanted to weep with fury, self-hate, and self-pity, but what good would it do? She'd lost. And now she had to find a way to deal with what happened.

Only a month before she would have thought nothing about walking out in the sunlight, but now, she realized she cared about the people who had taken her in, made her a part of their family. She wanted to watch the twins and Hope's little girl grow up, to be there when they graduated high school. Damn Gideon for being so stubborn.

She began to walk and found her steps leading to the back of the house. The moon's weak beams did nothing to dispense the murky darkness of the distant tree line. Katheryne focused and scanned the area. Nothing to show someone had attempted murder. The leaves still left on the massive oaks, the moss adorning some of the naked branches, and the tangled growth of overgrown bushes gave an unreal sense of mystery and just a bit of apprehension.

As Katheryne watched a shadow broke off from the others and a chill touched her spine. She knew she shouldn't be frightened, after all she was the undead, capable of fighting mortals and immortals alike, but she couldn't shake a sense of evil. Did it originate from Gideon's almost death, could the evil somehow be connected to him? She should probably try to find out, but her body felt frozen. Her feet would neither go forward nor backward. It seemed that whatever was out there had caught her in its grip.

"You are mine." The whispered words stunned her even as she realized they were not spoken aloud but directly in her mind.

"Come to me."

Katheryne's shock grew as first one foot and then the other began to move toward the trees. The chill on her spine turned to ice, and she forced her mind to block out the mesmerizing command. She shut her eyes, thought of Gideon, and then with limbs that resembled molasses she teleported to the driveway at the front of the house. She thought she heard a muffled curse but then her mind heard the rumblings going on inside the house and she began to walk briskly back and forth. Surely what or whoever had tried to call her to them would not come this close to a house full of vampires. She needed to think about what to do, what to say to Gideon if and when he spoke to her again.

****

Gideon grumbled under his breath as Miranda unhooked the IV from his arm. He ignored the frown Hope gave him, and totally blew off the comments made by his so-called brothers.

As soon as he was free, he yanked the sheet off his lower body and then hit the bathroom. He needed to see for himself if he truly was a vampire. He knew from Zacke's history, as a fanged creature, if he truly was one then his wound would be healed. He didn't hurt so it was probably true, but he just needed to know.

The mirror over the sink revealed what he feared. The hole he'd felt drilled straight into his heart was gone. He turned his back to the mirror and then glanced over his shoulder. The entry hole had also disappeared. Next was the tricky part. He opened his mouth and pushed on his gums. Damn, he did have fangs. He'd thought he felt them in the bedroom but couldn't be sure. Gideon looked at his unblemished chest again. He should be dead and would have been if not for... He didn't want to think about what had happened. He knew he had died, he'd seen Hope's turning. And as hard as it was for him to accept what had happened, it had to be harder on his friends and Kat.

Gideon glared at his image in the mirror, and then whirled when he heard a thudding sound.

Zacke stood in the doorway.

"Did you hear that?" Gideon wasn't sure if his probably ex-partner, certainly ex-friend would answer.

"No, what did it sound like?" Zacke's answer and question was uttered in a monotone.

"A thudding sound."

For a split instance, Zacke's lips curved upward. "You probably heard my heartbeat. When you are newly turned, all sounds seem twice as loud."

"Oh." Gideon didn't know what else to say. His anger and shock was still there but muted compared to before. The man standing before him was someone he trusted, had trusted with his life. And although he had no clue as to how to treat his present circumstances, he knew Zacke only participated in the turning because he cared. And it wasn't only Zacke but the others and especially Kat.

Oh God help him, what he'd said to Kat could not be taken back.

Gideon wasn't sure what to do next, but he did know he needed time to think about what had happened and then plan his next move. But first he owed a lot of people apologies, Kat being the first on his list.

"Look man, I, uh, I...I need to see Kat, then we'll talk if you want to talk to me. I know I messed things up in there, but..."

"Forget it. I remember what it felt like to wake up from the dead and be the undead." Zacke's smile disappeared.

"Thanks, I'm gonna go find Katheryne. I guess ya'll will be tutoring me in Vampire 101?"

"You can count on it, my friend." Zacke and Gideon bear hugged and then Gideon stepped back. "Hey how come I didn't wake up screaming for blood? I thought that was what a new vamp did?"

"It is, but with the blood being infused into your

body during the change by the IV, you didn't have the starvation syndrome most of us had upon being changed. Hope came up with the idea and together she and Miranda set it up." Zacke grinned.

"Another thing to thank them for. I'll be back after I talk to Kat." Gideon left the bathroom, and upon finding the bedroom empty raced down the stairs, and nodded at the cluster of vamps and Miranda in the kitchen before asking. "Do any of you know where Kat went?"

"Why do you care?" Miranda didn't have fangs but the snarl she sent his way was even more dangerous.

"Because I love her. Look, I owe you all an apology. I think everyone but you, Miranda, can understand what it means to die and then wake up as a vampire. It's a bit unnerving. I'm still not sure what is going on inside my body, so please cut me some slack." Gideon walked over to Miranda.

"You've been a sister to me. I love you, and I know why you fought to keep me alive. I thank you for that even though I had a piss-poor way of showing it." He kissed her on the cheek and rejoiced when, this woman he admired so much, hugged him. He needed to go after Kat but he couldn't leave the others without making it right.

Once Miranda released him, he stepped to Hope's side and gave her a hug. "Hope, you're also family to me. Thank you." He then turned to Miles and Hawk.

"Okay, fang face, don't even think about hugging me." Miles' snarky grin gladdened Gideon's heart.

"Don't worry, it never crossed my mind. But, I do want you and Hawk," his glance now included the other vampire, "to know I count you as brothers as well as I do Zacke. I'll need some tutoring in how to be a vampire and survive."

"Don't worry little bro, we'll teach you just as we

are teaching Kat." Hawk also grinned.

"Kat? But she's already a vampire." Gideon's puzzlement must have shown on his face.

"Talk to your fiancée, and make sure she stays that way, or I'll fight you for her, hear me?" Hawk's grin disappeared. He looked dead serious.

"No problem on that score. I'm going to grovel and tell her what kind of ass I've been. Now, do any of you know where she is?"

"The last time I looked she was just walking up and down your driveway." Hope looked at her watch. "I think I'm going to head home and check on Samantha."

Her words galvanized the others, as well as Zacke, who'd followed Gideon downstairs, into action. "Yeah, we need to get home to the twins." Miranda picked up her coat.

"I'm going to get someone to cover for both of us tonight." Zacke helped his wife fasten the buttons and then held his hand out to Gideon. "If you need anything let me know. And for pity's sake, stay clear of the windows. There's blood packets in the refrigerator, but you might be able to eat like Hope and Katheryne can as long as you don't over do it."

"Thanks bro." Gideon said goodbye to the others and promised to carry their goodbyes to Katheryne. "And if you decide to bring Kat back to our house, let me know. After what happened tonight, I'm not taking any chances on either of you getting in the way of some maniac's rage." Zacke sent him a look that brooked no argument.

"You think the prostitute killer is after me?"

"I don't know, but the fact you were attacked in the alley, and then shot here, after just moving in, makes me think someone's following you."

"Yeah, that makes sense." Gideon waited until Hawk teleported out with Zacke and Miranda holding on to each of his arms and then Miles and

Hope's departure before he tore through the house. After he got to the front door, he realized he barely felt his feet moving. A perk he could get used to.

He peeked through the front side glass of the door. Kat's form looked small, desolate, as she walked the rather long driveway back and forth from the street to the house. Although it was dark and the porch light wasn't on, he could see her features clearly. Her beautiful lavender eyes were misty in the dim moonlight. Her shoulders were hunched against the wind skittering leaves around the yard. He wanted to go to her, to hold her, but how on earth could he apologize and make her believe him?

After staring a few minutes longer, he shrugged his shoulders. Kat loved him, and he loved her. Of that one thing, he was certain. Even if she snarled, flashed her fangs, a concept he would have to get used to along with his own newly vamped nature, he knew she had been desperate to save him. On that thought, he opened the door and stepped barefooted out onto the porch.

The cold air he'd felt last night no longer chilled his skin. Another plus, and his view of his beloved was even clearer now. He watched as she continued to pace, then hesitate, before spinning around.

The look on her face tore at his heart. Undecided, unhappy and definitely undone when she saw him. God, how he hated himself.

"No, don't. It's not your fault." Her words although whispered were clear as a bell. Yet how did she know what he was thinking?

"I can hear your thoughts in my head." Kat smiled. "I didn't know I could until last night at the ball. I mean I'd never done that before, but I heard Hawk ask me a question, and I answered him back without speaking out loud. It's something I think we have to learn as we go."

"Amazing. And it's amazing you would even talk

to me after what I said." Gideon kept his gaze on Kat, but held his breath waiting for her to answer.

"Yes you are breathing. We do that when we're awake. And I think when we sleep but it's so faint a mortal might not see it. Now, are you ready to talk?" Katheryne stayed where she was as she waited for Gideon to answer. They did need to talk, and he prayed she could forgive him, and that they would be able to work everything through.

"I'm ready. You want to come inside?" Gideon knew she wasn't any colder than he was, but she looked like it, and he couldn't bear the thought of her suffering in any way. Not now and not ever, even if he had to cut out his own bumbling tongue to make sure it never happened again.

Katheryne chose not to answer him, but instead walked to the porch and then up the few steps. She held her hand out to him and when he took it, she wanted to shout with joy. Maybe things would be all right. She needed them to be.

"Kat, I..."

"Not yet, Gideon, just let me look at you. When you were shot, I thought I would never see you alive again, and when you had to be changed, I was scared to death. Knowing you are all right makes me feel like I own the moon and stars."

"I'm sorry—"

"No, you have no reason to be. Your actions were justified. I should have told you I was a vampire. Instead, I allowed myself to be sidetracked by the idea of being and feeling normal for the first time in so long." Katheryne slid her arms up to where the gunshot wound had been. Her fingers caressed the skin that last night was torn and bloody.

Gideon captured both of her hands in one of his. The other caressed her face. She wanted to purr her pleasure, to give herself to him and never come up for air, but they needed to talk.

"Kat, I think, no I know, at this moment, I've never been more certain that we were meant to meet. Life is crazy, you know?"

When she nodded, he continued. "We never know what's gonna happen, and if you told me ten years ago, there were really vampires in the world, I'd locked you in our psyche cell."

Gideon slid his hand down to her waist and pulled her a bit closer. "Now, not only am I of the fanged variety, but I've fallen in love and want to spend eternity with the most beautiful lady vampire to ever live."

Katheryne wanted to cry but didn't. "And I fell in love with the most fantastic, romantic, and sexiest mortal and vampire alive."

Gideon's chuckle was music to her ears.

"So are we good? I'm sorry for what I did, but I'll make it up to you." Gideon dropped a gentle kiss on her open mouth. She waited for him to follow it with a deeper one and when he didn't she opened her eyes.

"Is something wrong?"

"Nope not a thing that can't be fixed with a phone call or maybe two." Gideon grinned.

"What are you up to?" Katheryne loved he was smiling but wasn't sure she trusted his mischievous expression.

"I say we get married tonight." His now expectant look took her by surprise. He was serious. And that meant everything truly was all right.

"Gideon, I'd love to get married tonight, but how can we?"

"Well, I'm not sure, but I think Zacke might be able to help. I'll give him a call, tell him we're on the way over, and we'll go from there." Again, the hopeful look gleamed in his eyes.

When she remained silent, he spoke again. "Am I going too fast? I just want us to be together, and I'd prefer to make it legal. Call me old-fashioned but I want the mate to the ring you're wearing on your hand before I take you to bed. My mama always said if she's the right one, you can wait."

"I think I would have liked your mother." Katheryne touched her ring.

"And she would have loved you, darling. So do you want a big wedding with all the fixings? If you do we'll wait and do it up right." The tender look he gave her made Katheryne want to jump up and down for joy after she kissed him senseless.

"No, I don't need a big wedding. I'd much rather get married and have you all to myself." Katheryne touched his face. "I don't need anything but you, Gideon."

"Whoo hoo!" Gideon clutched her to him, lifted her off her feet, and spun her around until she was almost dizzy. He kissed her so hard after he set her down, she almost lost her balance. The kiss was hot, sensual, and so lustful, she didn't want him to ever stop, but he did.

"Come on, I'll call Zacke on the way to their house." Gideon started out the door tugging her with him.

"Gideon, don't you think you should put on some shoes and a shirt first?" She giggled when he looked down at his body and then back at her with a dumbfounded look on his face.

"Woman, you make me forget everything but you. Hold on a minute and I'll be right back." He hit the stairs at a run, and a second later she heard several thunks coming from overhead, and then he was back. A pair of jeans replaced his bloodstained pants, a cobalt sweater hugged his wide chest, and a pair of sneakers covered his feet.

"I'm ready. Let's go."

****

Gideon Hawks had cheated death. Not only

cheated but now he was a vampire. Marcel wanted to rail against the fates that had done this to him. His chances of taking Katheryne were slipping away. Her force of will when he'd called her to him had been stronger than he'd imagined. He should have just taken her forcibly. Now he no longer dealt with a mortal man, but one of his own kind, albeit a young one. Still, the detective had proven to be a strong adversary as well as a thorn in Marcel's side. He would have to think hard on how to get rid of Kat's love interest and if he had to the other vampires who always seemed to cloak around him and Katheryne—without getting himself caught in the crossfire.

Chapter Eighteen

"You're what?" Zacke's question was peppered with disbelief. "You just got turned into a vampire."

"You can't." Miranda sounded like she wanted to cry.

Now what? She agreed with Gideon there was no point in wasting time on a big wedding. Yet, she didn't want to upset Miranda. Maybe there was a way to compromise.

"Miranda, it's not like I have family that can be invited, I mean excluding you, Zacke and my new vampire family." Gideon turned toward Kat. "And you know Kat's family can't be here."

"Gideon's right. All the family we have are you two, Miles and Hope and Hawk. There's no point in planning some fancy affair. We just want to get married." Katheryne moved to Miranda's side.

"When I thought I'd lost Gideon in death and then after he learned he was a vampire, all I wanted was things to be back like they were. We just want to be together, and believe it or not, we can live without the fuss."

"But I wanted to plan—" Miranda broke off her words when Zacke shook his head.

"It's their decision, my love."

"But to just be married by a justice of the peace in a cold austere office..." Miranda looked at Katheryne. "When do you want to do this?"

"Tonight." Gideon's words barely left his lips before an explosion happened.

"No way, you have to let me plan something. Besides, we can't get a JP this late." Miranda was wailing at the same time she hit a button on her cell phone. Zacke looked incredulous before bursting into laughter.

While Katheryne stared at Gideon and he stared back, Hope teleported into the Kensington's living room, followed by a disgruntled Miles.

"What's going on, Miranda?" Hope ran a hand through her hair and then flicked her robe closed over an almost sheer nightgown as she walked to where Miranda sat.

"You aren't going to believe this, but Gideon has some lame idea he and Kat can get married tonight."

Hope shot a look at Katheryne before giving Gideon a once over. "No way. You couldn't bribe anyone to do a service this late, and besides I thought when you two got married it'd be in a church."

"Hell, is this why you called an emergency meeting? Lord Miranda, we were in the mid—" Miles looked like he was ready to grind nails.

"Don't say it, Miles." Hope gave him a look that had him moving closer to the other men.

"Sorry. I knew Miranda wouldn't be too happy, but this is..." Gideon couldn't find a word that wouldn't make the situation worse.

"Trouble? Tell me about it. I was this close to having my wife right where I wanted her, and her cell rings and she just disappears." Miles gave him a look he could only commiserate with.

"Again, sorry. We stopped by after we got everything straightened out, and told Zacke and Miranda we planned to get married tonight. Miranda didn't take it very well."

Miles chuckled despite the annoyed look still on his face. "Well little brother, even you ought to know not to cheat Miranda out of planning a wedding. The woman's a drill sergeant when it comes to tying people in knots." At Zacke's slight glower, he spoke again. "And I love her for being such a good hearted soul, but seriously, I was this close—"

"Miles!" Hope's screech cut through the women's chatter. Her husband clamped his mouth shut.

"Look, I know it's not conventional, but face it, the last thirty-something hours haven't been. Kat and I just want to get married. No fuss. Just married." His sigh ruffled the hair that had fallen into his eyes.

"Okay, let me see what I can do." Zacke pulled out his cell and moved into the kitchen. Gideon stayed put, as did Miles, well away from the women.

A brief moment later, Zacke returned, gave Gideon a thumbs up, and obviously a lot braver than Gideon stepped over to the women.

"Okay love, this is what's going to happen. A friend of mine will be here about nine to perform a wedding. That gives you and Hope one hour to do your magic." He placed his hand over Miranda's open mouth. "It's their time. Let them do it their way."

Miranda looked at Katheryne then over to Gideon before nodding her head. The moment he removed his hand, she started firing orders. "Find Gideon one of your suits, no way is he getting married looking like a hedge hog, and Hope, I think I remember you have a lovely cream dress, street length that would work for Katheryne. Can you get it?"

Hope jumped up and high-fived Miranda before teleporting out of the room. Gideon stood riveted as he watched the petite doctor drag his wife-to-be upstairs.

"Well..."

"Yeah, not much else to say is there?" Zacke grinned. "Miranda's like a mini-tornado, and it's best to stay out of her way."

"I agree. Guess I ought to get cleaned up a bit

too." Gideon waved toward what he had on his body.

"Come on. You too, Miles. If I have to go through another wedding then so do you!" His partner's grin was evil.

"Yeah, well let me go check on Sammie and then I'm calling Hawk. Let him share some of the fun!" Miles looked beleaguered as he teleported out of sight.

Five minutes later, Gideon was trying on dress pants and suit coats. They weren't a perfect fit, but he didn't care. The outfit just brought him closer to the reality of having Kat as his wife for all eternity. He barely noticed when Miles popped into the room with a sleeping toddler.

Eternity, wow, it certainly took on a whole new meaning as a vampire. He couldn't wait to have her on her backside.

"Gideon."

"Yeah Miles." Gideon held up a tie that might look good with the blue pinstripe suit he'd settled on.

"You're broadcasting your thoughts about Katheryne so loudly, Hope can probably hear them in the next room."

His head jerked up so fast he almost lost his balance. "You're kidding, right?"

"Nope." Miles looked at Zacke who grinned before looking back at Miles.

"Don't worry, grasshopper, I will teach you all you need to know." Miles droll wit caused Zacke to double up with laughter and the other vampire did the same. Gideon tried to hide his own smile but failed. The only thing that saved all three men from rolling on the floor was a rapid and ear-hurting banging on the wall.

"Stop wasting time. The justice of the peace will be here in a few minutes." Miranda's tone wasn't exactly low, and Gideon prayed she didn't wake up the twins or Sammie.

"Hey, how did you get a JP out this time of night?" Gideon asked as he stripped to his briefs and began to throw on the clothes.

Zacke sat on the edge of the bed. "A couple of years ago, when you were off one night, Craig Jackson left the courthouse way after dark. I happened by in time to keep someone from knocking him unconscious and stealing the diamond necklace he'd bought his wife for their anniversary. He told me then if I ever needed anything to let him know." Zacke looked at Gideon. "I just called in a favor for family."

"Thanks. Only you and Miranda could make this happen. Oh shit. What about the blood tests and the license?" In his zeal to get married and bedded he'd forgotten those small items.

"No worries, he's waving the blood work and bringing the license. You're good to go." Zacke stood to his feet and moved to the mirror where Gideon was trying to tie his tie.

"Let me do it, you're ruining the last one Miranda gave me. And believe me, she'll notice every wrinkle you leave in it." Zacke grimaced.

Miles chuckled. "Thank God Hope isn't that picky, I'd be in hot water all the time."

"You're in hot water anyway, Miles." Zacke pulled the tie through the loop he made and then finished tying it in a perfect knot.

"Okay, how do I look?" Gideon stood back and waited.

"You'll do for a new vamp." Miles grinned.

"Not bad, Gideon," Zacke responded.

"Gee thanks, you two. I'm nervous enough. Didn't think I would be, but shit, what if I mess up." He sat down on the bed, despite the threat of a raging Miranda.

"You can't. It's a short ceremony. Just say what Craig tells you to. It's not like you haven't witnessed ceremonies before." Zacke sat down beside Gideon.

"It's not the ceremony I'm worried about." Gideon knew he was opening up a whoop ass can of ridicule but he needed answers.

"Don't tell me you don't know what to do with a woman. Maybe I need to start your lessons early, grasshopper." Gideon wanted to knock the smirk off Miles' face, but instead he snarled.

"No, I don't need damn lessons, but I do need to know if my fangs will interfere if I kiss Kat. They didn't earlier, but could they? And do they just pop down, and how will being a vamp affect my uh, uh..."

"Performance?" Zacke wiped the smirk off his lips when Gideon glared at him.

"Well, I guess if you had to call it something, then yes, performance." He knew that Kat could blush as a vampire, but he hoped he wasn't turning all types of shades of red.

As soon as he had that thought another one popped into his mind. Was he still spewing all his thoughts for everyone to hear?

"No, you're holding the thoughts in pretty good. Seriously, fangs won't interfere when you kiss. They will however come down when you taste her blood."

Miles nonchalant statement caused Gideon's throat to close up. When he finally got his breath back, he wheezed out a few brief words. "I can't do that."

"Yeah you can and will when the blood lust is riding you hard, and you're hard in other spots as well." Miles looked at Zacke. "Just remember if you treat Kat like she's mortal, then you should be fine. Of course, she'll bite you too."

"She will?"

"Yeah, it's only natural for soulmates to suckle their partner's blood. Just go easy. And as for affecting your performance, let's put it this way, you won't have a problem."

At Gideon's inquiring look, Miles chuckled. "It's one of the best perks of being a vampire. It's great even if your wife's a mortal, but when there's two vamps, it rocks."

Before Gideon could reply the doorbell rang, and then Hawk who must have teleported in downstairs was standing at the threshold of the room. "Miranda said to get your butts downstairs unless you want her to come up here after you." Hawk's smile was genuine but not as ear splitting as the other two men.

"Okay, I'm ready." Gideon patted the suit's pocket. "Hold on, gotta get the wedding band."

He took the silver band out of its box and held it out to Zacke. "Would you do the honors? I didn't ask but I want my best friend and partner to be my best man."

"You bet. Now come on, Miranda's going to hurt all four of us if we don't get downstairs."

****

Marcel waited for the woman to exit the bar and then he followed her. He needed to exorcize his still hot rage at not killing the detective. He wasn't sure whom he should blame for turning his enemy into a vampire, but he had a feeling it was Katheryne as well as the detective's partner. Both needed to be punished, but he would have to come up with a plan to get Katheryne alone. In the meantime, he needed an outlet. He caught up with the blue-eyed blonde and asked. "How much for the night?"

Chapter Nineteen

Katheryne tried to slow her heartbeat. Everything was moving so fast. Miranda had been a dervish getting everything ready for the wedding. Of course, no matter how much she tried to tell her she didn't need something old, something borrowed, etc, the woman would not listen.

Finally she'd exchanged smiles with Hope and just gave up. Now she stood in a dress that wasn't her own. New and very scandalous unmentionables, (Hope said she'd popped into a mall and grabbed a few things) but one article of clothing looked too small to be a nightgown.

"So are you ready?" Miranda pushed a beautiful bouquet of Camilla's into Katheryne's hands, straightened the locket she loaned her, and then slapped her hand over her mouth. "Oh Lord I need to change too."

The next few minutes were a blur as Miranda pulled out a dress and flung it on, and fiddled with her hair—all the time firing questions at Katheryne.

"So I know, you're a vampire and all, but do you have any questions about what happens after the wedding..."

Katheryne knew her face was heating up, as was her blood at what would happen. No, she didn't have questions. She'd walked in on several of Gabriella's couplings.

"Honey, it's not exactly the same." Hope's words fell into Katheryne's mind.

"I know. She was never in love and that makes the difference." She spoke in kind back to Hope and

then smiled at her hostess.

"No, I'm okay. It will be perfect. And Miranda thanks for all you are doing. I don't know what would have happened if I hadn't met all of you."

"Well, I know you've made Gideon happy and for that I will always be grateful. He is one of the kindest men I've ever known, and now that he's a...he can protect Zacke." Miranda's eyes filled with tears.

Katheryne sat on the bed next to Miranda. "What is it, Miranda?"

"When Zacke was a vampire he was having problems, so I worried of course, and then when he became mortal it got harder to not be on pins and needles every time he was on the job. And now with this psycho who shot Gideon still on the loose, and it possibly having something to do with the case they're working on, I'm glad Gideon can protect Zacke."

"Miranda why didn't you say anything." Hope joined them on the bed. "You know Miles would have shadowed Zacke's every move, not to mention Hawk. Honey, this is something you shouldn't have kept to yourself."

"I know, but I just feel like such a wimp to complain." Miranda wiped an errant tear off her cheek and then gave a slight smile.

"It's just me being me. I'm fine. Now let's get Katheryne married."

Katheryne returned several tight hugs before being ushered down the stairs.

A man stood in the living room talking to Zacke, while her beloved, and Miles and Hawk stood off to the side.

Gideon looked up and Katheryne vowed she'd never forget the look in his eyes if she lived an eternity. The love shining back at her went straight to her heart. She'd cherish this man, soulmate, until the end of time. Lord how she loved him. Nothing or no one would ever take him away from her.

The ceremony itself was a blur for Katheryne after Gideon took her left hand. His strong and southern drawl when he'd said "I do," touched her soul.

As she listened to her vows and then her affirmation to take this man until death do them part, she prayed they would have centuries together.

The gaze in his brown eyes as he leaned down to kiss her turned her knees into useless appendages. The first taste of his lips as man and wife melted her heart and heated every pulse point in her body, especially the one between her legs. Once he released her lips, she glanced around hopeful that no one else had heard her thoughts.

Gideon leaned down once again for a quick peck on her cheek. "I love you, and woman as soon as we can gracefully leave, I'm going to explore every pulse beat you have."

Katheryne whispered back, "And I plan to do the same to you."

****

It seemed an eternity until they could leave. First they drank the champagne Miranda unearthed from somewhere, took tiny bites of a small red velvet cake Hope had bought at a twenty-four seven grocery store, and after that, Gideon was more than ready to vacate the premises. The looks his adopted brothers were giving him signified they sympathized with him. He just hated hurting Miranda's feelings. She'd gone to a lot of trouble, both her and Hope. Still much more of the social niceties and he wasn't going to be able to control his raging desire. His shaft was hard as a two by four, and he was fast losing control.

"Come with me." Gideon looked over his shoulder to see who'd tapped him. Miles stood there with Hawk and Zacke flanking him. He followed the men to the kitchen.

"What's wrong?"

"You're as pale as a one day corpse. You need more blood before you bed Katheryne." Miles took the bag of blood Zacke tossed him. "You don't want to pass out on your wedding night, and you certainly don't want to take too much blood when you bite her. Now sit down, and I'll show you how to just slap the bag to your teeth."

Gideon did feel a bit woozy. He wasn't sure if it was the lack of blood or the thought of drinking the blood causing the problem.

"It's really not that bad, Gideon, and once your body adjusts you'll be a pro." Zacke tried to encourage him, but Gideon felt like he wanted to gag. Yet, he had no choice, he might not have wanted his new way of life, but he had it now and a wife. He needed to suck it up and be a vamp.

"I'm fine. Just show me what to do." His words came out as a growl. He looked at his friends but none of them looked offended. It must be a natural thing then. Okay, good.

"Just put it to your mouth. Your fangs should slide down and then latch onto the bag. The rest is up to your vampire nature." Hawk offered.

Gideon did as he was told, and felt a shifting of teeth in his mouth. The next thing he knew his fangs were embedded in the plastic and he was guzzling blood like he would a beer. Once he consumed that bag and one more he accepted the cloth Zacke handed him and wiped his mouth. "Hey before I forget, did you get a line on the guy that killed me?" He knew that sounded crazy but sometimes truth was crazier than fiction.

"No, Miranda didn't find a bullet inside your wound, but we found one in the kitchen wall. A high caliber, but when I scoured the woods facing your bay window, I came up with zilch. Its like the shooter wasn't even there."

"Shit, I'd feel a whole lot better if we could nail his ass. I don't like being shot or killed, but dammit, Katheryne was in that kitchen with me. He could have hurt her." Gideon felt his fangs slide free with his anger. He'd have to learn how to keep them out of sight.

"Yes, but remember even if he'd shot her, it wouldn't have killed her. Vampires can be hurt, but we heal. You know the only way to make sure we don't is to take our heads and hearts."

"Wow, comforting thought. Also too bloodthirsty for my peace of mind. I'll just hope I don't run into any unfriendly fang peers."

Gideon joined in his friends' laughter. A moment later, Miranda led the way into the kitchen with Katheryne and Hope right behind. "Okay, I said your goodbyes to Craig. I also packed up the pizza, cake, and I'm going to throw in your beer, just in case, a bottle of wine for your bride, and whatever blood we have on hand. You can take it with you."

Gideon wasn't sure if Miranda expected him to reply or not, but now with Kat in the room his lust came flooding back tenfold. Katheryne came to him. "Hey you."

"Hey back," he responded as he pulled her down to hide the arousal threatening to punch a hole in his pants. Only the seductive feel of her backside made it worse. He needed another plan of action to keep from embarrassing himself and Kat, but one look around the room and he knew that once again his thoughts had gone galloping out of his mind for almost the entire room to hear. "Well hell." He stood to his feet taking his wife with him. Damn that had a right nice sound to it. "If ya'll will excuse us, I'm taking my wife home—now."

He started to pick up the cooler Miranda had

finished packing, but Miles stopped him. "Leave it. Since you're driving home, I'll teleport over with this stuff and be gone before you get to the house."

"Thanks, I appreciate it." He shook hands with Miles who spoke again. "I expect you both to be ready for vampire training two nights from now."

Hawk laughed as he and Gideon shook hands, before he turned to Zacke. "Thanks bud, for...ah, you know for everything." He accepted Zacke's slap on his back, and then kissed Miranda and Hope on the cheek. After grabbing Kat's hand, he caught the truck keys Zacke flung his way in the other and then headed for the door.

They were halfway to her new home when Katheryne finally spoke. "I guess I could have teleported us both home." Gideon took his gaze off the road for a split second and glanced at her but didn't say a word, although his eyes did take on a startled look. She sat there and fiddled with the bit of lace on Hope's dress she still wore. Maybe she should have changed, but Gideon still wore the suit he borrowed from Zacke. The entire ceremony and events before and after their wedding were almost like a dream. All she could really see was Gideon lying on the floor dying, then him awakening as a vampire. Did he truly forgive her? Was he over the deception of her not telling him she was also a vampire? And did he only want to get married this quickly just so he could make love to her?

"Hey, darlin' you okay?" Gideon's chocolate soft tone did what it always did—turned her insides to mush.

"I'm fine. Just tired, I guess. It's been a long twenty-four hours or so, but I don't have to tell you. Your entire life has experienced an upheaval." Kat hesitated to look at her new husband. What if he already regretted his decision to marry?

"Well, yeah, but what's done is done. I can't go

back, and I'd much rather go forward with you." The affirmation she saw shining back at her made Katheryne's heart quicken with speed and joy.

While they had been talking, Gideon's truck had eaten up the distance between the Kensington's and her new home.

He parked, turned off the engine and then raced around to her side of the truck.

"Come on babe. Now I plan to show you how I mean to go on and how much you mean to me."

She took the hand he held out, and welcomed how he pulled her close before walking them both to the door. "Now, Mrs. Hawks, lets get inside." Gideon lifted her in his arms and carried Katheryne over the threshold.

****

As Katheryne walked through the house at Gideon's side, she dreaded seeing the kitchen. When she'd awakened earlier someone had tried to get Gideon's blood off the floor, but there still remained a hazy reminder of what had transpired. But now, she was amazed to discover even more of the stain had been lifted out of the planking. She only wished the memory of that nightmare and the voice she'd heard within her head could be as easily erased.

"Miles left us a note when he delivered our care package. He says he did a bit more cleaning, he moves fast, and put all our items up. He also said Zacke forgot to mention it, but he would make my excuses at work for at least three nights. That way we can have our honeymoon and my first training session before I go back."

"That's good." Katheryne just stood there. All the desire she felt for him seemed to have dwindled away to nothing now that they were alone. All she could think of was the horrible acts of lust and perversion she'd witnessed while being a servant to Gabriella.

What did he expect from her? It was different now that he was a vampire. Even untrained, he would be stronger than Katheryne. What if she wanted to stop, would he? Oh Lord this marriage thing was going to shatter what peace she'd found after knowing he was no longer angry with her.

So occupied with her thoughts the touch of Gideon's hands on her shoulders startled her. She should be more aware, but did that work if it was your mate?

"Kat, I've been watching all sorts of expressions run across your face and inside those gorgeous eyes of yours." Gideon stroked a hand down her arm. "And I've got to tell you I don't know what's worse, the fear, the uncertainty, or the plain out I wanta run away look."

Katheryne turned and pressed her face against his chest. Fear left on the wings of love, as did the uncertainty. He was right; she had wanted to run but that desire was stamped out by the gentle way he held her.

He would never hurt her. She knew that as well as she knew her name. So now she needed to show him that she wasn't just a weak-kneed vampire who didn't know her own mind.

"I'm sorry. It's not you; it's memories of the past. How Gabriella behaved." Her breath quickened when she spoke the woman's name, and she loved how his hold tightened around her—shutting out the horror of deeds no mortal or immortal should witness.

"She was truly a monster, and the men she took to her bed rivaled her in their cruelty and perversion. For a moment, I could only think of that and not what we have or how you make me feel."

Gideon's heart hurt for Kat. To have been in the clutches of one as evil as Gabriella, and still maintain the innocence she did, was miraculous. No a blessing for he truly believed he and Kat were meant to be together forever.

"What else is bothering you?" He dreaded her answer—what if she'd changed her mind about loving him?

"Well, I did something that you don't know about." Her breath hitched, and he prayed she wouldn't cry.

"Knowing you it couldn't be that horrible, Kat. Now tell me."

"I bit you that night when we were...uh... at your pickup." She dropped her gaze back down to the floor.

Gideon thought back, and then the light bulb lit inside his brain. That's where the cut or what he thought was a cut came from.

"So you bit me, it's not a crime from what I've been told for a vampire to bite when caught up in desire."

"Yes, but I did it without your knowledge." Kat looked up at him.

"Oh baby, I knew you nipped me, but I didn't care. You were making me so hot; I thought I'd explode. Now, if I'd known the woman nibbling on my neck was a vampire, I might have stopped you." The grin he sent her way was to insure she would know he was kidding.

Kat's mouth fell open and then she did something he didn't expect, punched him in the arm. "Now I wish I'd bitten you harder."

The thought of Kat's lips anywhere on his body brought back a lust so strong his knees almost buckled. Did he dare trust his instinct to make love to her now? Should he wait until he had his desire under a tighter rein? To hell with that, he'd waited long enough.

Chapter Twenty

Gideon scooped Kat into his arms, cradling her body against his chest. He walked as quickly as he dared to the stairs. He didn't want to scare her by running like a mad man, but that's what he felt like. Mad with lust, mad to possess this woman who'd stolen his heart.

Her eyes widened as he traversed the steps two at a time, then she clutched him tightly as he scooted down the hallway. He was almost at the door when he remembered the mess his room was in when they'd left earlier. Dirty, bloody, clothes lying around, the bed sheets a shamble. No way would he make love to her on soiled sheets.

He pushed opened the door, already trying to remember where he'd put the only other set of sheets he'd bought, and his mouth dropped open. The room was neat as a pin. The bed made, dirty clothes gone, and a tray with two glasses and a pitcher of something—probably blood on the bedside table. God bless whichever of his heart sisters was responsible.

"Gideon?" It was only then he realized he'd been standing there like a total idiot. Instead of answering he turned Kat in his arms, captured her lips for a deeper than sin kiss, and enjoyed the slow drag of her body against his until he set her feet on the floor—their lips still locked.

By then his rod throbbed with lust and he prayed he could slow it down just a bit. No way would he take Kat while he was so out of control or could he?

His wife, however, took the choice out of his

hands when she tugged his shirt loose from his pants and ran her hands up and down his chest. The little moans she emitted made his blood pulse in his veins and especially in his shaft.

As he watched her lavender eyes tinged red, and her hands found his arousal. Even through the material of the pants, he felt every caress of her hand. He pressed himself further into her grasp, but it wasn't enough.

"Kat, babe, hold on. Let me get my pants off." Her response was a deep-throated growl. It almost scared him until he remembered the woman he held wasn't the only vampire in the room, and that her creature nature would never outweigh her love for him.

Gideon answered her in kind. He firmly pulled her hands from his flesh, and backed her to the bed. He jerked away from her grasping hands. He wanted to see Kat, smell her scent, and then take what he wanted.

"Gideon, please..."

"Kat, give me a minute, I don't want to rip your dress. He held her hands with one of his and used his thighs to hold her still. One quick tug and the zipper ripped right out of the dress. Damn, he forgot about the super strength he had now. He hoped the dress wasn't sentimental to Hope and that Kat would forgive him.

But at the moment, he'd let that ride. There were more important things he wanted to do and explore. With a modicum of rush he stripped the dress off of his wife's yielding body. The sight greeting him caused his fangs to descend. The silky barely there bra and panties showcased his wife's luscious curves.

He pushed her gently back on the mattress and then moved over her.

"Gideon I want..."

"So do I, Kat, but I want my turn first. I don't think I can wait to see what's under these lacy things."

Katheryne giggled and then gave him a smile of glee. "Fine, but turn about's fair play. You just remember that, Mr. Hawks."

"I'm counting on it, wife." Gideon's hands trembled just a bit when he reached out and unfastened the front hook of her bra. Rosy peaks atop twin mounds of ivory flesh greeted his gaze. A feast and he was ravenous. Katheryne remained still as he took one crest into his mouth. His first taste rocked him to his shaft. He tongued the ripe nipple and then lightly nipped it with his teeth, careful to keep his incisors from hurting her.

When he came up for air, he murmured. "Lord, baby, do you know how beautiful you are?"

He caught Kat's lips before she could answer and welcomed the moan coming from the back of her throat as he plundered the hot depths of her mouth. His hands found and caressed the flesh he'd kissed before, her breasts more than enough to fill his hands.

Gideon ended the kiss with a light nip to her bottom lip before sliding down her body. His tongue licked every inch of flesh between her slender neck to her navel where the edge of her panties began.

His teeth tugged the material down, and Kat lifted her legs to help as he revealed the concave of her flesh. The silky hair covering her sex was so pale it looked like silver. As he pulled the material down her legs, he caressed the insides of her thighs with his mouth.

"Gideon, no fair. You're setting me on fire." Katheryne's words were a whispered moan.

"And soon I'll join you in the flames." His words were poetic, not at all like he normally would speak to a woman he made love to, but Kat was not just any woman, she was his to be cherished.

His hand found and parted the twin lips guarding the nub he sought. Already erect with Kat's need, he lightly pinched and then circled the tiny kernel with his thumb and forefinger.

Gideon used his other hand to find the opening to her center. Her desire weeped onto his fingers and he grinned on the inside. She wanted him and she would have him, but first he wanted to make her feel every inch a woman. To tempt her, take her to the edge, and bring her back before he took her completely.

One finger eased inside her center. Kat's hips left the mattress, sending his digit deeper inside her offering. Good, he wanted her to want him; it would make her first time easier.

"Gideon, please..."

"Soon, Kat, soon." Another finger followed the first and then a third until he stretched the tiny opening a bit more. He searched for and found the one spot he knew would make her go mad with need.

Kat's moans turned into a sharp scream as he pressed her inner cavern. Her hands sought and then grasped his wrists. She guided his hands to move harder, faster, until her body trembled so badly Gideon felt the vibrations. He also felt the clenching of her vaginal walls as her climax hit her hard. Its force squeezed his fingers like a vise.

When her body released, the flood of her satisfaction coated his fingers before he withdrew them. Kat's body finally stilled from the throes of ecstasy and her breathing slowed.

However, the fire burning him was heating up. He moved over her pliant form, and then used his knees to push her legs farther apart. He had to have her now.

Katheryne was still gasping from the incredible feeling of her first ever climax when her newly wed husband leaned back. She caught a glimpse of his sizable manhood. The trepidation she would normally feel on her wedding night, if she were back in another time, was missing. No maidenly protests, no covering her eyes, only a desire that continued to grow to have this man, make her his on all levels.

She not only wanted him to take her as a man did a woman but to take her as a vampire did his soulmate.

Gideon's eyes were a combination of melt-in-your-mouth brown and the tiniest bit of crimson. As she continued to gaze up at her husband, his pupils turned completely red. Oh yes, as a man he was totally magnificent, but as a fully aroused male vampire he took her breath.

"I want you." Slipped from her lips. And he obliged her. Slowly he pushed against her creating a tightness that was uncomfortable as well as tingling. She pushed back and his flesh slid further into her body. She moved again, and was rewarded by a growl that vibrated throughout her body.

"Kat, are you sure you're okay? I didn't hurt you?"

She smiled up at him. "No, you didn't hurt me at all. And besides, the first time is supposed to be different."

"Babe, you have no idea what it means to me to be your first."

Gideon's body came down on top of hers as he pumped his flesh again and again inside her. Katheryne's blood pulsed. She felt the beginning of another release streaming through her body. Her hips met his every movement, she welcomed every caress of his tongue against her breasts, and then when she felt she could stand no more, he broke through her wall of virginity. The combined pain and pleasure made her wild. She wanted more, she needed him, the dark side of Gideon. How she knew this, Katheryne had no idea, but it seemed her vampiric instinct was taking hold.

Her fingertips turned into claws, she felt her eyes go red, and then she felt the most mind exploding feeling. Gideon's fangs nipping her neck. She felt the rush of heat going from him to her, the ecstatic joining of their minds, hearts, and bodies. When he exploded with fulfillment, she was slammed with the same bone-weakening feeling in addition to her own. When he released her breast and swiped his tongue across the pinpricks, she pulled his head down. Her fangs descended in a rush of need and she bit the strong column of his throat.

The taste of his rich succulent blood wept throughout her body. She felt like they had always been one. She continued to suckle a bit more and then laved the wound with her tongue right before a second climax made her scream.

Moments later, she lay in Gideon's arms, their naked limbs entwined, and her head resting on his chest where his heart beat strongly in her ear. Lord she loved this man.

"Did you say something?" Gideon's question confused her. She had not spoken out loud, had she?

"No, why?"

"I could have sworn I heard you say you loved me." Gideon's voice vibrated against her collarbone.

"I wonder…" Was it possible? Miles had said something about soulmates being able to hear their partner's thoughts.

"Gideon can you hear me?"

"Yes, but I'd rather concentrate on kissing you." His words shot into her mind and she jumped. Did he know what he'd done?

Katheryne pulled free of his embrace and stilled his protests with one word. "Stop."

"What's wrong, baby?" Gideon sounded sated as well as confused.

"I want you to stay right here while I go into the bathroom. Then close your eyes and listen, okay?"

His brown eyes blinked but then he nodded his head. "If that's what you want, but I wanted to grab something to drink and then make love again."

"And you can and we will, but first, I want to try something." Katheryne scooted off the bed and ignored the "Whoo hoo," as her husband ogled her naked body. She didn't need eyes in the back of her head to know this; she could feel the heat from his gaze.

Once in the bathroom she closed the door and her eyes. *"Gideon what are you doing?"* She held her breath and waited.

"I'm waiting on my wife to come back to bed." Her heart thudded inside her chest. It worked. They could hear each other's thoughts. Now to try something different.

"Gideon," this time she spoke aloud. "I want you to tell me what I'm thinking, okay?"

The bedcovers rustled and she heard his sigh through the door. "Kat, why are we playing these games?"

"It's important, now please can you tell me what I'm thinking?" Kat thought of the carriage ride they'd taken.

"Yeah, you're thinking of me and you in that buggy..." As she waited on him to say more, the door jerked open.

"What just happened?" His eyes were wide and his gaze puzzled.

"I think my husband, we have just evolved into what a lot of vampire couples experience after taking each other's blood."

He came on into the bathroom. "Meaning what?"

"That you can read my mind and I can read yours. Isn't that great?" Katheryne literally bubbled with excitement.

"Well, yeah, I guess, but I don't think I want you reading my mind all the time. A guy's got to have a bit of privacy."

She laughed at the very offended male look on his face.

"I agree, so now I want you to try to read my mind." Katheryne thought of the morning they met and then abruptly shut down her thoughts.

"Hey what did you do? One minute I could hear what you were thinking the next it was gone." Her husband looked amazed.

"I blocked my thoughts, and you should be able to do that too." Katheryne took his hand. "Now, you think something."

As she closed her eyes and concentrated, she could feel the heat of his sensual thoughts beating through her mind and body. All the things he wanted to do to her and then poof nothing else.

"You did it! You did it, Gideon." Her happy squeak of joy was captured by a kiss from her husband.

When he released her lips, she stared at him for a moment before asking, "Are you okay with this part of our relationship?"

"Sure, now that I know you can't read everything unless I let you." His smug smile made her want to nip his lips. Instead she teleported them both downstairs, placed a bag of blood in his hands and took one for herself. Once they satisfied their blood hunger, she cut a thick slice of their wedding cake and put it on a plate, grabbed a bottle of champagne and two glasses. "You ready to go back to bed?"

The look in his eyes turned her knees to puddles of warm water. "More than ready."

****

For the next couple of days, Gideon had his wife to himself. Zacke had indeed scored him some off time, and he'd taken advantage of having Kat right where he wanted her.

They'd made love on almost every piece of furniture in the house, not to mention the kitchen counter, which afterward Kat had scrubbed several times over. The fact she completed that chore while bare-ass naked had ended up with them baptizing the surface again. It was only after the third time, Kat had ordered him to the bedroom. He'd grabbed the last bottle of champagne from their wedding, a couple of slices of cold pizza, and a DVD he'd brought from his old place.

They'd spent the rest of the night in between bouts of making love watching old scary movies and laughing at the screen renderings of vampire and werewolves alike.

Right before dawn that morning, he received a call from Miles stating they needed to start his training before he had to report back to work.

"What did Miles want?" Kat's soft question caressed his earlobe sending a wave of desire to his already over-worked shaft.

"Sure you don't just want to read my mind?" He teased Katheryne about her penchant to do so every chance she'd gotten in the last forty-eight hours.

"No fair. You did your share of reading mine." Her open-mouthed protest did not go unrewarded. Gideon pulled her into his arms and kissed her lips before taking the time and pleasure to nip his way down her neck to her breasts.

"Enough, stop, that tickles." Kat pushed at his chest, and even though he barely felt her touch, he allowed her to break his hold.

"Now tell me what Miles said, please." Her breathless tone did nothing to rid him of his desire for her, but they did need to talk.

"He said we should start my Vampire 101 training tonight. And that Zacke said I had just a couple more nights off before Captain Myers came hunting me." His sigh was heartfelt. Never in a thousand years would he have thought he'd want to just hibernate and never go back to work, but Kat made him want all sorts of things.

"Well then, I suggest we make the best of our time before dawn. There are a few more things I want to learn about you, Detective." Kat's fingers strolled up his chest, tangled in his hair, and then she tugged gently. "Coming husband?"

"I hope so, wife."

Chapter Twenty-One

Gideon stood poised on the roof of his house. He faced the backyard where there were no streetlights to show a full-grown vampire fixing to be stupid. Although his darling and extremely concerned wife told him there was nothing to flying, and his brothers in arms, Miles and Zacke, who along with Hawk were coaching him in the fine art of Vampire 101, he still wasn't happy with the idea of busting his ass or any other important part of his body on the ground.

"Come on, Gideon, at the rate you're going we'll be out here all night." Miles laughter-tinged voice called from below. Gideon opened his eyes and looked down at his mentor and antagonist. "Shut the hell up, Miles. Give me a minute. I don't like heights."

"Honey, it's not that bad, just imagine you're flinging yourself into a pile of clouds then concentrate on moving toward the sky."

He wanted so badly to snarl at Kat, but didn't dare. He liked making love too much to have to sleep on the couch.

"I know babe, but it's my first time, so be patient." Gideon smiled down at her, knowing she could see him in the dark just like he could see everything just as clear as day. It was a perk he liked. And it could come in handy when chasing perps.

When the vamp boys and Zacke started harmonizing a popular song using the word virgin, he knew he couldn't wait much longer. Okay, concentrate on heading toward the sky. Gideon closed his eyes, tucked his arms in close to his body as he'd seen the rest of the group do, and then pitched his body forward. The sensation of air brushing his face, and the dryness he felt in his eyes when he opened then, were just a few of the sensations he experienced. Terror, however, was the utmost feeling, and it became stronger as the ground rushed up and slapped him in a hard hug of earth.

"Gideon! Are you all right?" Kat's soft tones soothed his fractured ego for a moment, before he heard the combined guffaws of the men. No way was he going to let them gourd him into losing his temper. One day, when he'd learn all he needed to know, he was going to have to show those boys what it feels like to mess with a Georgia redneck vampire.

"I'm fine, sugar. Now give me a kiss, and I'll go try it again." Kat's lips against his was just what he needed to rev up his courage—not to mention the motor between his legs.

The laughter became louder. They'd read his mind. Hell, he'd have to be more careful.

Gideon patted Kat's hand, and then stood. He waved off Miles who had flown him to the roof in the first place. No time like the present. He closed his eyes, bent his knees, and concentrated on the roof. He jumped and felt the air against his body. His feet connected with the roof's shingles and Gideon opened his eyes to look down in triumph at the gawking group below. Not sure if getting to the roof was just luck, he decided to try it again.

This time when he closed his eyes, he thought of circling the huge backyard just above the tree lines. A second later, he leapt off the roof. Instead of feeling the cruel ground, his body took him upward. Gideon opened his eyes to a view of tree branches, indigo night sky, and the realism he was actually flying.

With a vampire for a partner for years, he'd seen Zacke do the phantom of the skies act more than once but this was something else, different, and fun. He focused on a circle and began to navigate the circumference of the yard. He playfully dived bombed his sweet wife whose lovely mouth was still open in surprise, and he moaned the fact he wasn't in bed with her instead of playing super vamp.

Only one way to fix that, he needed to ace this and other lessons so he could do what he wanted. He flew a few more circles and then decided to try a trick that had fascinated him ever since he'd seen Zacke and then Miles and Hawk do it.

Gideon closed his eyes, thought of a thin stream of vapor, and then almost lost his concentration when he felt his body begin to thin and then dissolve. He prayed with all his might he'd be able to reassemble his molecules.

Katheryne stood in awe watching her husband flirt with danger, but she was so proud of him as were the men waiting with her. Their exclamations and excited mumblings were still going on as Gideon's body morphed into a streak of twirling smoke. She held her breath as the ribbon dived toward where she stood, and then gave a sigh of relief when a second later her husband, with all his body parts attached, grinned at her before catching her lips in a kiss that made her toes and the area between her legs tingle.

Before she could enjoy the sensation, all three men bombarded Gideon.

"Way to go, grasshopper. How'd you know what to do?" Miles question carried awe as well as pride in his pupil.

Her husband pulled away, gave her a wink, and then turned around to face the group standing almost on top of him.

"Thanks, Miles. I didn't know I could do any of

it, but I thought about how Zacke and you guys always just closed your eyes. I wanted to see if it would work for me." Gideon grinned.

"I think he's jumped way over your teaching syllabus, Miles." Hawk held out his hand, and Gideon shook it.

"Gideon, you were something else, partner." Zacke's smile was genuine but it seemed a bit sad to Katheryne. The detective pulled her husband into a bear hug and once released he accepted a slap on the back from Miles.

"So what's next?" He shot her a wistful look as he waited.

****

A couple of hours before dawn, she watched as her brilliant and oh so handsome husband learned to teleport. Essentially he'd already mastered the breaking down of molecules when he turned into vapor but this was a bit different. He needed to be able to go from one place to another and reassemble when he got there.

Gideon's milk-chocolate eyes were closed; the dark lashes brushing his tanned cheeks. His slightly crooked nose wrinkled for a moment before his lips thinned into a line of determination.

One minute he was there, the next gone. Before she could wonder where he went, a pair of familiar arms wrapped around her waist just as they had earlier that night. Katheryne leaned back into his embrace and felt the solid wall of his muscular chest, the comforting cradle of his hips, and the unmistakable hardness of his arousal.

"So, do I pass?" Gideon's words were spoken just above her ear, and sent shivers of desire running amuck along her nerve endings.

"Yeah, you did. Good job, guess I'll have to come up with something besides grasshopper for your name." Miles beamed from ear to ear.

"Call me brother, that'll work." Gideon kept his arm around Katheryne as he moved toward the men. He shook each of their hands again, and then spoke. "Now, if you don't mind, I'm going to take my wife upstairs. I suggest you two get home to your own women. Hawk, my friend, thank you!"

Hawk smiled back but for some reason, Katheryne felt like something was bothering the gentle giant. His shoulders weren't as straight as usual, and his amber gaze looked dull.

Before she could ask him if anything was wrong or say her own goodbyes, Katheryne felt the rush of energy right before she was teleported to their bedroom.

Once there instead of stripping her naked and making love to her, Gideon surprised Katheryne. He folded her into his arms, carried her to bed, and just sat on the edge of the bed staring at her.

"Kat, I'm not sure I'd told you enough how much you mean to me. I know I apologized for blasting at you over me being changed into a vampire..." His words trailed off. Just as she opened her mouth to speak, he caressed her face.

"I want you to know that the more I think about it, the more grateful I am you wouldn't let me just...stay dead. I see all the things I can do now, skills that could save another's life, catch the bad guys, and keep the people I love safe. That's a miracle..." Again his words trailed off.

"I know that Zacke thought being a fangy guy kept him from having a soul. I don't think that way. Your soul is a part of you no matter what unless you give it up to the Devil. I was raised in a good old country church where we went to services every Sunday. I know right from wrong, and I know that no matter how much you shout you're a good guy, the good guys are sometimes worse than sinners."

This time when he stopped, she touched his

arm. "What happened to make you believe that?" She held her breath praying he would trust her with that part of his life.

"My uncle was on the deacon board at our church. To the public he was the salt of the earth, someone you came to with a problem, and the first one to raise his hand to help the needy." Gideon's growl startled Katheryne.

"The problem was he also had no problem in raising his hand to strike my sweet cousin Maddy. At first I didn't realize the bruises she carried weren't from a fall until I happened to see him hit her one night. I tried to tell my folks but they thought I was making it up. It wasn't until I was older that I could go to him and threaten him with the same type of treatment he'd been handing out to Maddy if he didn't stop. By then I was a good size teenager. I guess he didn't want to take a chance on me beating the shit out of him or telling the church board, but at least he stopped."

"Oh Gideon I'm so sorry. How's Maddy now?" Katheryne wiped away a tear.

"Gone, she moved away from here as soon as she could. We kept in touch for a few years, but I think she was just too ashamed and wanted to forget all about her life here."

His words hurt Katheryne's heart as much as she knew it hurt her husband. He had such a kind heart, the same heart that had ached for Maddy was what brought him to her side the morning they met, and despite how some things had turned out, she would be forever grateful for that one small act of kindness.

To show him she cared, she kissed the hand that held hers and followed it up with a gentle kiss to his lips. She wanted him to know she loved him, and it wasn't all about the sexual gratification she knew they could always find, but to let him know she cherished him for whom he was.

Her actions, however, sparked a more heated response from her husband—one that she did not hesitate to return.

Chapter Twenty-Two

Gideon awoke with a hunger for blood and a pulsating need for Kat. They'd made love several times over until the dawn claimed them in sleep. He would satisfy first one hunger and then the other. His hand reached out and pulled the sheet covering Kat's breasts free, his other hand was poised to touch the bountiful offering when his new vampiric hearing picked up the sound of a car pulling into the driveway. Zacke. He'd know that motor anywhere. Gideon glanced at the bedside clock, it was barely six. The sun had just gone down. Since they were both going into work tonight, something was up. Otherwise, his partner would have waited until they got to the station.

Gideon glanced down at his sleeping beauty, and regretfully covered her soft vamp-cooled body with the sheet. Perhaps it was for the best; Kat might be a bit tender after the last time he'd taken her. He eased from the bed, and tugged on a pair of jeans not bothering with a shirt. Even though the house was cool due to the season, he didn't feel the cold like he always had before. He decided to utilize one of his new skills and teleported to the front door. Zacke was just raising his hand to ring the doorbell when Gideon swung it open.

"Hey bro, I wasn't expecting you. And remind me to get a key made for you that way you can come on in."

"Thanks. Uh, I don't suppose you have any coffee on, do you?" Zacke sounded tired. And something was definitely up with the way his partner avoided eye contact.

"No, but I can make some. Come on." Gideon headed back through the house. Once in the kitchen he pulled out the makings for coffee and programmed the coffee maker. The smell of chicory and almonds tantalized his nose. Since the champagne had stayed down on their wedding night as did the wine and beer while he and Kat were holed up for their honeymoon, he planned on drinking a cup himself.

Once they both had a cup of the fresh brew, and Gideon had taken a quick sip, he questioned Zacke. "Okay, you wouldn't have come over here for just a cup of coffee. What's going on?"

Zacke took a sip from his cup before placing it on the table. "We've got another body."

Gideon's fangs scored his bottom lip, and he concentrated to get them to retract. Another woman dead. Another needless death. Still, Zacke was hiding something. He guessed he could try to read his mind, but wouldn't. Over the last decade, his friend and partner had very seldom read his thoughts, and Gideon owed him the same courtesy.

"All right, that's not surprising. I hate it, but that's not what's got you over here when you could be at home enjoying dinner with Miranda and the twins. What's up?"

"The woman killed was the one you gave money to." Zacke's tone was sad and angry.

But nothing like the red-hot rage that swept over Gideon. The snarl he gave was vicious, the cup in his hand shattered, and he forcibly shot out of his seat. Where he was going he didn't know, but a soft hand on his arm stopped him.

"Gideon." Kat's voice cut through some of the rage and impotency he felt, but it wasn't enough to keep him from snarling. "Let go."

"No, my love. I'll never let you go." She caressed

the muscle in his arm where it bunched as he clenched his fists.

"How did you know?" Gideon's gaze torched Katheryne with its intensity.

"Your rage woke me. Now, come sit down and tell me what's wrong." Kat tugged him forward and the fact he'd allowed her to do so spoke volumes to her heart. He needed her as much as she needed him, like she needed the blood that sustained her. If she had to do without one or the other, Gideon would always be her choice to keep.

"Morning Zacke. Can I get you anything to eat? I know that Miranda and Hope stocked some regular food for us just in case we felt like nibbling."

"No, I'm fine, Kat. Thank you. I told Miranda I'd be back in a bit. She's holding dinner." He brushed a strand of coal black hair out of his eyes. The deep blue gaze was not as brilliant as usual. It had to be something to do with their job.

"So what's happened?" She perched on Gideon's lap and kept a firm grip on his hand. If she weren't mistaken his rage would ignite again.

"Another body was discovered. The killer continues to evade us. There's not one piece of evidence to point us in the right direction. No DNA, nothing." Gideon's voice shook.

"What else?" Katheryne hated to push him but he needed to get it out, to get beyond the rage and then he could find the killer.

"The woman killed..." He looked at Zacke.

"Last night probably. Her body was found about midday. They called me right before sunset. They want us in as soon as possible." Zacke fell silent.

"The woman was the one I told her we would find the killer. Dammit, Kat, she had kids." Gideon's eyes glowed red, but Katheryne didn't chastise him for his anger. She knew it was founded on sorrow.

"You'll find him. I know you will, and then you

will make it safer for these women." She caressed his face, and rejoiced when he placed a kiss on her hand.

Katheryne turned back to Zacke. "So there are no leads at all? I think that's what you call them."

"None, except, all the women killed had a flower branded into their chest." Zacke looked at Gideon who just looked grim.

"What type of flower?" Katheryne asked the question to keep Zacke talking, in an effort to give her husband a bit more time to gain a foothold on his rage and grief.

"It's strange, I haven't seen anything like it in years. It's a *fleur de lis*." Zacke took a sip of coffee, and Katheryne fought the chill that shot up her spine.

"How big was the symbol?" She despised the fact her tone had gone husky, but fear crawled into her body and her throat was not immune.

"I...I guess about the size of the tip of my ring finger." Zacke looked toward Gideon.

"Yeah, I'd say that's about right. It looked almost like what you'd see on a ring." Gideon caught her chin and turned Katheryne to face him.

"What is it, babe?"

"Nothing, why?" She wasn't really lying, she didn't know for certain if...

Gideon looked her in the eyes. "I'm a cop and I know when someone's hedging. When we started talking about the brand, I could feel your body stiffen. I could also—"

"Please tell me you did not read my mind?" She wanted to be outraged at the thought but all she felt was hurt.

"No, I didn't. But what are you hiding away you don't want me to know?" His tone was gentle and inquisitive, not harsh like it could have been. Katheryne loved Gideon so much she hated to tell him about her past or at least all of her past.

"I...uh..." She stopped and at that point, Zacke stood up.

"Maybe I should leave you two to discuss this alone."

"No, Zacke, please stay. You already know Gabriella turned me, but not the circumstances leading up to it." Katheryne eased off Gideon's lap. "I need to walk while I tell this, and I also think we both need to feed before I do. Is that okay?"

"Sure, whatever you need, Kat." Gideon stood to his feet and went to the refrigerator. He pulled out two bags of blood and handed Kat one. Instead of mixing her meal with juice as she normally did, she just put the bag to her mouth. Her incisors came down and did the rest. She looked around the brightly painted kitchen. Yellow daisies wove a pattern through out a moss colored background on the walls. The appliances were jet black and matched the granite counter top. Window shades covered the small window over the sink and the backdoor, and a set of faux wood vertical blinds were drawn over the repaired bay window. She finished the blood, and tossed the bag into the trashcan, before pulling the blinds back. The night sky was pitch-black. Not even a sliver of moon highlighted the backyard.

"Kat? You ready to talk?"

She turned slowly around and then walked to the table. Instead of sitting, she brushed at the wood veneer. "Yes, I'm ready, but I have to tell you it's not a pretty story."

"Whenever Gabriella was involved it was never pretty, Kat. You were a victim, and both Gideon and I know this, so just tell the story." Zacke's gaze filled with kindness, and she truly wanted to cry, to run away, to tell them she knew nothing that could help them, and to let the past stay buried, but she couldn't.

"He's right, love, you were an innocent at the hands of a monster." Gideon's eyes blazed red before he once again reined in his anger.

"A long time ago, and yes, I am a good bit older than you are, Gideon, I was just a little girl. My parents were wonderful, they loved me, and everyday was an adventure." Katheryne sighed. "Of course, that's how a child feels or should. When I was ten my parents died, and my Uncle Scott came to stay at Alastair Hall. My mother was English, and my papa was Scottish. At first my uncle ignored me, but when I got older, he began to look at me in a way that made my skin crawl."

Gideon snarled and Zacke looked like he wanted to tear someone apart also. "It's okay, remember that was ages ago. Well, something or someone changed his mind; it could have been the woman he married after inheriting my family's estate. The next thing I know at the age of ten and four, I was paraded at different gatherings and balls in the area. Lauded as Lady Katheryne Elizabeth Alastair. Beautiful and a virgin to boot." She looked at her husband. "Zacke can tell you virginity was a prize when a nobleman sought a wife. They might fornicate on the side, but their wives had to be pure." Again she sighed. Lord she wished the tale was already told.

Katheryne welcomed the warmth of Gideon's caress at her waist. It was the slightest of touches but it made her feel safe. She could do this. She had to; in case her belief that Marcel had come back was correct.

"This went on for at least two years. No one offered for me, but I made sure no one wanted me. I'd cross my eyes, drool, stutter, anything I could to stop them from making a marriage proposal."

"Why Kat?" Zacke's gaze was puzzled. "If you were married then you'd be away from your uncle."

"Yes, I would have, but the men who he conned into coming to the hall were drunkards, philanderers, and even worse. I couldn't bear the thought of belonging to any one of them. Rumors at that time were they traded women back and forth like they were possessions." Another growl came from her husband. She rubbed his arm and then kissed him on the cheek. "It's okay, I'm fine, it didn't happen."

Katheryne had often wondered if being some man's toy would have been preferable to being turned into a vampire.

"But, babe if you'd married one of them, then Gabriella wouldn't have turned you."

"You're right, Gideon, but then again, if she had not, then I would not have lived long enough to meet you. And that would have been a tragedy." She turned away from the sheen of moisture her words brought to his eyes and blinked away the dampness in her own.

"After awhile my uncle got tired of having me around. I was no good for anything, so he kicked me out with nothing but the clothes on my back. I was glad to be rid of him, but it was hard finding work that did not have me plying a trade on my backside. I worked as a tavern wench, a maid, and several other honorable jobs, until one night Gabriella or 'Lady Sanspree' as she like to be called stopped at the Laird's house I was serving. She was all niceness and ladylike but something about her frightened me even then."

Kat cleared her throat to get rid of the knot of terror the vampiress still brought into her mind. "I was asked to serve as a lady's maid for her, I did, and she treated me kindly. I know kindness is not something you would expect from her, but she had a reason. She liked my talent with her hair, and she wanted me to leave with her. I truly did not want to go, but I feared the consequences if I turned down her offer. It wasn't until I was packed and waiting outside, I realized I'd packed one of the Laird's books by accident. I didn't want to be hung as a thief, so I went back inside the castle. I could smell the blood before I saw the bodies. The carnage was horrific. Gabriella had no reason to kill that family. Mother, father, children all dead by her hand. As I tried to decide to run for my life, she just dropped down from out of nowhere in front of me."

Katheryne's shoulders shook with the terror of the past. "Well, she gave me a choice to go with her or die. I went with her."

"If you need to stop then do so, Kat." Zacke's voice was stiff with what was probably remembrance of the bitch that had changed both their lives and so many others.

"No, I need to tell you the rest of it. After we arrived at her home, she kept me busy doing her hair, anything she wanted. However, the one thing she didn't do was drink my blood. She told me to stay away from her chamber during the day if I wanted to live. I did. Then she began to throw parties. Night after night men would arrive. She'd take them to bed and sometimes they would leave at dawn when I awoke or she would feast on their blood and then have one of the male servants drag the bodies away. One night she invited a Frenchman named Marcel Charmant."

Her husband's body stiffened and again she touched his arm. As she caught his gaze, she sent him thoughts of love and understanding. "The more Marcel looked at me, the more Gabriella made sure I stayed out of sight when he visited. One night, he caught me and Gabriella caught him." Katheryne patted Gideon's hand but then moved away from the table. She needed to distance herself from him when she spoke of her shame.

"After making sure I had not propositioned him, Gabriella offered him a taste of my blood. I don't know why, maybe she thought he'd leave me alone after that. He was brutal as he tore open a small gash in my throat. Marcel only drank for a bit, Gabriella stopped him, but it took several days for it to heal."

Zacke's phone rang and she was glad when he answered. She needed a moment to gather the courage to tell the rest.

"I'll be home soon. Go ahead and feed the twins. Love you." Gideon's partner closed his phone and then gave Katheryne a slight nod. She dared not look at her husband. She didn't want to know his thoughts—not yet.

"After that I avoided him like any plague. I would hide in the privacy hole just to keep him away from me." Katheryne laughed mirthlessly. "Of course the stench was such I had to bathe before Gabriella woke up so as not to offend her sensibilities."

Zacke snorted, but she knew he wasn't laughing. Neither was her husband as she glanced his way. His brown gaze had gone all red, his fangs peeked out from his upper lip, and he looked ready to kill.

She needed to wrap this up quickly. "Hiding worked for several months, but one night he arrived early. He caught me in the front hallway. He tore my throat again, and fondled my breasts." Katheryne could not bear the pitying look Zacke sent her way. She should have been stronger, fought Marcel harder.

"Gabriella interrupted him before he could rape me. She attacked him and threw him out of the castle. Then she turned on me. I won't go into details because you already know, Zacke, and Gideon, I love you too much to tell you of my death but there is still more you need to know."

"Kat, stop." Gideon's voice trembled as he spoke.

She wanted to go to him but she felt tainted with the memories of Marcel's attack, Gabriella's torture.

"There is one more thing." She turned to Zacke. "I don't know if it's possible. I pray God it's not, but when Marcel was touching me I noticed a ring on his finger. It was silver and at the tip there was a fleur de lis." Katheryne watched Zacke's face and then Gideon's. Both looked astonished, then Zacke's countenance stiffened with what she assumed could only be disgust. Gideon looked like an avenging highlander from her way younger days.

"You think it's possible, Zacke?"

"Kat, what year were you turned?" The detective asked, without answering Gideon.

"It was somewhere around 1630. Why is that important?"

"Because, I remember hearing about a man who made his living peddling flesh. And if I'm not mistaken his last name was Charmant. I never met him, didn't really want to." Zacke's lips turned up in a mirror image of Gideon's without the fangs.

"So it is possible, this piece of shit is still around?" Her husband looked positively overjoyed.

Kat placed a hand on his chest. "No, Gideon. If it is Marcel behind these murders, he is too experienced as a vampire, too strong for you to fight. Please promise me you'll leave him alone." Her last sentence was a plea.

"Kat, this is not open for discussion. If Marcel is alive and here in Savannah, it is my job to find him and stop him any way I can." Gideon knew he sounded harsh—he couldn't help it. Women had died, possibly, because of this man—the mere fact he'd touched his wife, hurt her, taken her blood, made Gideon want to tear the vampire open from his fanged mouth to his ass.

"Please, listen to me..." His lovely Kat's lips closed as he held up his hand.

"Baby, I can't let this lie."

"Zacke, please talk some sense into him." Katheryne's eyes glistened red with tears and probably fear. He could read her mind to know for sure, but he wasn't certain he could handle the hurt she tried to hide from him. However, both that and her fear was nothing compared to his. The thought of the bastard still being able to get to Katheryne terrified Gideon.

"Kat, I have to agree with Gideon. Charmant must be stopped if he is our killer. And you know you want that too. I know when I learned Gabriella wasn't dead, like I'd hoped, until the day I met my death, she would plague me and all I loved. If indeed he is here, he may already have targeted you." Zacke exchanged a glance with Gideon.

"Oh no. You think he's the one who shot Gideon. But why? How could he even know about him?" Kat's tone trembled and Gideon wanted to take her in his arms, but not until he could better control his thoughts and passion. He wanted to take his beautiful wife upstairs, make love to her like there was no tomorrow, and keep her safe from the vermin who'd hurt her before.

Zacke stood, walked to the sink and rinsed out the coffee cup. "I think if he's as infatuated with you as he used to be, then he will know where you are and who you're close to—so I think it's entirely possible, Charmant may have shot Gideon to keep him from you."

"He's right, Kat. Take it from me, no man or vampire in his right mind would ever let you go willingly." Gideon held his hand out to her, and once she caught it, he spoke to Zacke. "Let yourself out brother, I'll be at the station in a while."

"Take all the time you need, I'm going to call Miles and Hawk to see if they've ever run up on Charmant personally."

****

Marcel snarled and welcomed the trickle of blood on his lip. Again his beloved was locked in the arms of another. He would not tolerate the newly made vampire much longer. No one should touch Katheryne but him. He'd paid his dues to have her. When Gabriella turned him out, she'd laughed in his face, threatened to gut him and then take his head. Not content to stop there, she'd had him blackballed from his clubs, and from certain financial institutions, almost making him destitute. Yes, he'd earned the right to Katheryne and he would take her—whether she was willing or not, it did not matter. As he watched the lights go off in the upstairs bedroom, he berated himself for not choosing to take a head shot. Then the interfering Detective Hawks would be dead.

Chapter Twenty-Three

Gideon waited until the door closed, used a mind thought to lock it, and then teleported himself and Kat upstairs. He needed the closeness lovemaking brought, the bonding of hearts, bodies, and souls to sooth the tempest in his mind.

Before he knew it, he had her up against the bedroom wall, the short robe she'd thrown on was tossed aside, and his hands were full of her curves. He suckled her neck and then moved to follow a line straight to her breasts. He welcomed her moan as he bit and then soothed her ache with his tongue. Then he shifted gears, dropped to his knees and found the place he most sought.

Katheryne let out a small cry, and Gideon loved how he could make her moan with his touch. Some of his anger dissipated, but he still couldn't get out of his mind how Marcel had touched his woman.

He tasted the sweet warm essence of desire of his wife's love. He welcomed the way her hands gripped his hair, and how she bucked her hips closer for him to dine deeper. When her climax hit, it was all he could do to hold her still as he finished loving her.

"Gideon!" Kat screamed his name and before the last note hit the air, he stood to his feet, unzipped his jeans, and set her on his aching rod. Iron hard and weeping for a deeper connection he barely gave her time to wrap her arms around his neck before he thrust hard and fast into her wet depths.

Over and over he marked his territory, rejoicing in the fact that Marcel had never taken her this way.

Still if he got his way the vampire would die a horrible death for touching her at all.

Kat's cries began again as he felt his own climax nearing, but there was one thing he had to do first. He tongued and then bit her breasts one at a time. His movement shot his wife over the edge, and he felt the tendrils of lust spiral higher. He pulled her even closer and then when he exploded with his climax he nipped her neck with his fangs. Her blood was an aphrodisiac that made him thrust harder.

He licked the bite and then allowed his world to spiral out of control taking him to the edge of ecstasy and beyond. Once his breathing calmed he picked Kat up in his arms and walked to the bed where he deposited her softly on its surface. His wife opened her eyes, and her gaze was sated with satisfaction. "Come here, please." Kat's soft voice mesmerized him.

Gideon did as she asked and lay down beside her. She snuggled next to him, and he stroked her damp back with his hand.

"Do you know how much I love you, Gideon?" Her question surprised him. Of course he did, but maybe it was a woman thing.

"I know if you love me as much as I love you then what we have will never die." He breathed the words against her ear.

"Then that is more than enough." She smiled at him and then batted away the hand he placed on her breast. "Enough, I think I need a nap."

"Nope, you need to get up and get moving. I don't like leaving you here alone, not with that son-of-a—"

"Gideon." Kat's shocked tone reached him and he smiled. Although several centuries older than him, his wife was an old-fashioned lady.

"Well, I can't go to Miranda's or Hope's. It would be too dangerous if it is Marcel. And if he has been following me, I don't want to lead him to either of them or the children." Kat's tone was sad, and he hated that the man still had the power to affect her.

"Okay, well then I'm going to get Miles over here and get him to put a safety spell on this place. He and Zacke both have used those in the past, and I'd feel a whole lot better."

"All right, but I need to get a shower before we have company." Kat eased away from him, and Gideon immediately felt the cold. He wanted to keep her by his side.

"Okay, you shower and I'll teleport to Miles and Hope's."

"You just want to practice your skills." Kat laughed and his insides turned liquid. Lord she had no idea what she did to him.

"Yes, I do, Gideon. Just like you know what you do to me. Now remember to guard your thoughts around Miles and Hope." Kat's teasing smile and her delectable naked buttocks was the last glimpse he had before she closed the bathroom door.

****

Gideon teleported into a meeting in progress between his vampire brothers and Zacke. "Hey I thought we were doing this at the station."

"Once I called Miles, he wanted to know if we could meet earlier. Hope's going out and he couldn't leave Sammie. We just got started to so pull up a chair." Zacke shot him a grin. "And besides, I thought you'd be a bit longer."

"Cute, I can do what I want and make an impression without spending all night doing it." He shot back.

"Yeah, but it's the all nighter's that are so rewarding." Miles smile looked as if he were thinking of one in particular.

"Okay, if we can stop talking about your sex lives, I'd like to find out more about this Charmant."

Hawk's normally even tone was just a tad off, and Gideon wondered what was up with that, but he kept his mouth shut.

"Okay, did Zacke tell you about this guy's history with Kat?" He pulled up a chair to the kitchen table where someone, he assumed Miles or Hawk had placed a laptop.

"Yeah, sounds like a nasty piece of work." Miles chimed in.

"Needs to be staked if you ask me." Hawk as always didn't mince words.

"I'm with you." Gideon looked toward Zacke. "Did you find anything on the internet?"

"Fixing to do a search now." Zacke keyed in some letters, and Gideon waited to see what popped.

"Interesting." Zacke's blue gaze as he studied the screen didn't waver."

"What?" Gideon barked.

"Keep your shirt on, partner. There are several hits and I'm trying to see which one fits what we need." Zacke's tone was mild but firm. "Okay, it says here there was a Charmant family residing in France in the late fifteen hundreds. I'm going to see if it pops up a picture of the estate or any of the family members."

By now, the entire room was completely silent.

"Hell, look at this." Zacke slid back a bit from the table and allowed the rest of the room's occupants a chance to look at the website.

"Damn, I'd hoped he was dead. I never knew his name but he was a piece of offal." Miles' snarl echoed throughout the room. A second growl came from Hawk. "He's not only a piece of offal but should have his nuts cut out."

"I agree, so how did you two run into him?" Zacke eyed Gideon who made a halfway attempt to keep from growling himself.

"It was way after we were turned. Remember,

we thought you were dead. We knew we had to get out of Scotland and England for a bit until we got our vampiric skills honed." Miles grinned at Hawk but then the seriousness of the situation wiped the smile off his lips.

"Charmant was one of a group of noblemen who hosted a party we got invited to. Damn Frogs were all decked out in lace, sporting jewelry from their necks to shoes. And this Marcel wore more than the rest. He had a hoity toity attitude that rankled big time with me." Hawk's lip curled like he wanted to spit.

Gideon waved at Miranda who moved through the kitchen to the fridge, popped a plate of food in the microwave, and when the timer dinged, pulled it out and set it in front of Zacke. "Eat, while they talk." She gave him and the other two vamps a look. "There's blood in the fridge, help yourself."

"So what happened when you ran into him?" Zacke took a bite of meatloaf that smelled terrific to Gideon. He really hated giving up some of his mortal vices.

"Well, Charmant paraded out a bunch of girls, really, they didn't look grown to me, and the others started mauling them. The kids look scared to death. Miles took one look at what was happening, took our host aside and told him if he didn't send those girls back to their parents, he'd wake up one morning staked through the heart, minus his head." Hawk laughed.

"Yeah, the little chicken shit didn't like it, but I wasn't playing. I hate to see anyone, especially women and children hurt." Miles' eyes went a deep jade. "He started herding those girls out and into carriages. Hawk stayed there, but I followed to make sure they got home."

"After you left, the party broke up but Charmant let it be known he didn't like to be crossed. I pretty much told him to bring it on, but he teleported away. I left shortly after." Hawk sighed. "I guess hindsight's whatever, I should have killed him."

"No way you could have known. I'm surprised the bastard isn't already dead by someone's hand." Zacke looked over at Gideon as he forked a good bite of mash potatoes and gravy into mouth.

"Gideon, are you hungry?" Zacke asked after he'd swallowed his food.

"Why yes, I am, thank you for asking. I don't think I've had anything since the ball except blood and liquids and maybe a small slice of cake and pizza." Gideon leaned closer. "You think it'd make me sick if I ate some real food?"

"I don't know. Hope eats some foods, and so does Kat. Only one way to find out. Miranda?" Zacke smiled when she hollered back, "What?"

Gideon couldn't keep a grin off his face. Married life was the best gift a man could have.

"Could you come in here a minute?"

And a few minutes later, Gideon had a heaping mound of food in front of him. He eyed the offering as if it were a million bucks. He picked up the fork and scooped up a bite of the meat and potatoes. The wonderful scent filled his nostrils as he popped it into his mouth. Just as he chewed the food, and prepared to swallow, Kat teleported into the room. His eyes feasted on the mounds of flesh pushing against and above the scoop neck, crimson, sweater she wore with her jeans, until he realized the other men were staring just as hard.

It took him a moment to register their gazes were pinned to the twin bright red blotches highlighting her cleavage. Damn! He'd forgotten about marking her. The food that had tasted so good went down the wrong way, and he almost choked, but managed to avoid death by strangulation as he jumped up, grabbed Kat by the arm, and teleported the hell out of there.

****

Kat didn't know what was wrong with Gideon, but he had some explaining to do. After her shower, she'd waited and waited for him to come back. When he didn't she'd gotten dressed and decided to pop in to see what they had found out about Marcel. Now her sexier than heck husband with fire in his eyes stood there like he wanted to blow a gasket. A phrase she'd heard Miranda and Hope use before.

"What is the matter with you? That was so incredibly rude, even for you, Gideon." Kat sounded like a shrew and didn't care.

"Well, excuse me, for not wanting my wife running around showing off her boobs and hickeys to my friends." Gideon hemmed her in against the bedroom door. After a lifetime of being told what to do and having men act like they were omnipotent, she wasn't pleased her husband was acting like a Neanderthal.

"Are you insane? There is nothing wrong with this sweater. Miranda gave it to me, and she wouldn't give me something shameless." Kat literally spit out her words.

Gideon sighed, ran a hand through his beautiful hair, and then reached out to run a hand over the top of her breasts. Kat looked down and then saw a raspberry shape on first one breast and then the other. Her mouth fell open.

"Now do you understand?" He asked.

"No, what are these and how did they get there?"

Her muscular and extremely handsome vampire husband's ears turned red. He cleared his throat, looked at her, and then looked away.

"Gideon?"

"Well, they're what some people call passion marks, I just call 'em hickeys. I kinda got carried

212

away, but I didn't like the idea of Marcel touching your breasts."

Lord she wanted to be angry with him, should be, but he looked so miserable, Katheryne didn't have the heart to tear into him. Of course she was going to make him pay for this in other ways as soon as he got home from work.

"Fine, but next time, warn me please. I've never had a uh, uh, hickey before." Kat stumbled over the modern slang.

"I will, I promise. Now can you put on something less revealing if you're coming back to Zacke's with me?" He smiled but his gaze was filled with a plea.

"Of course, silly. Now, tell me what you found out about Marcel." Katheryne moved to the dresser and pulled out a sweater with a high neck. She stripped and had her arms in the sleeves when she felt Gideon's hands cup her breasts.

"Baby, I'm truly sorry. I would never embarrass you that way on purpose."

She turned and kissed the underside of his chin when he leaned forward. "I know, and you're off the hook for now. Since I now know about these love bites, I will have to make sure you place them where they can't be seen." Katheryne gave him a saucy look and then pulled free. "Now do what you have to and let me get ready to go back to Miranda's. But the first untoward look from any of your friends, I'm going to raise holy heck." She used an expression she'd heard on a television sitcom.

"And I won't blame you. Hurry up, Miranda just fixed me a plate of food, and I want to see if I can eat it." Gideon's expression resembled that of a little boy's.

Katheryne laughed and then stepped into his arms. "Okay, let's go."

Chapter Twenty-Four

An hour later, armed with recipes and even groceries from Miranda's freezer, Katheryne teleported home. She wasn't sure how it worked, but with the safety spell Miles had placed on the house, it seemed that she, Gideon, or their friends could come and go as they pleased without sending an alert to Miles. The vampire had promised to teach both Gideon and herself how to weave a safety spell or did he call it a prayer.

She placed the perishables in the refrigerator, grabbed a bag of blood, and then sat down to make some sense out of Miranda's directions for southern cooking.

Her poor husband had to leave before he'd had time to eat. Their captain wanted to talk to him and Zacke. And Gideon learned a new trick, one she needed to try. How to mind think his clothes on. She wondered if it worked in reverse. After all turn about would be fair play. Gideon was always taking her clothes off but hardly ever let her return the favor.

Katheryne refocused her attention to the recipes. If she followed the directions exactly then maybe she could have him a plate of food prepared when he arrived home in the morning. She stood up to search the cabinets for cooking ware and a chill crossed her shoulders. Her gaze was drawn to the bay window. Even with the glass covered, she felt exposed.

She faced away from the window and pulled out what she needed to cook. Katheryne just hoped she wouldn't burn down the house. Fire and a vampire did not mix.

A couple of hours later, she had all the ingredients prepped and would just need to put them in the oven and cook the mash potatoes Miranda was certain she could make by hand. She still had a pecan pie to tackle, but she just couldn't keep her eyes open any longer. It'd been a long time since dusk and telling the story of her life had taken a lot out of her. Not to mention her husband's energetic lovemaking. Maybe she would take a short nap while she waited for Gideon to come home.

She teleported to their bedroom, and even knowing a locked door would not keep Marcel out if he broke through the safety spell, she locked it anyway. Not wanting to lie down, she sat up and pressed her back against the headboard.

****

Gideon swept Savannah's Red Light district from far above the city. He could get use to flying, and he loved being able to hone in with his vampire vision. It made looking for Marcel easier or it would have if Charmant didn't have the same skills.

His first stop after leaving Captain Myers office with a burning tirade in his ears of how he should be out searching for the *Fleur de Lis* killer, a name given to Marcel by the cities he'd hit north of the Mason-Dixon Line. It would have been nice if they'd put out an all points bulletin letting the lower half of the states know.

He'd also stopped and talked to several groups of street women. Some took his warning to heart, but others looked at him like he'd lost his mind. Of course, he knew if some of them stayed off the streets a night or two, then they would not be able to feed their kids.

Damn, the last woman killed had children. He needed to find out who had them now and help them out if he could. Gideon would also like to donate some money to help with the funeral services. If no family came forward, Lisa Dawn, her street name, would be laid to rest in an obscure plot at one of the city's cemeteries.

He felt a creeping sensation across his vertebrae and flipped around in mid-air. Nothing or no one was there. Could have been his imagination, or possibility the approach of dawn. Not taking any chances he closed his eyes and welcomed the feel of his body turning into a stream of vapor. He twirled and swirled as he headed for the station. Zacke should already be there, he was going to call some of the PD's up north, and see if he could find out more about the crimes committed.

Gideon decided to do a pass over his house. The lights in the kitchen and bedroom were on, and he felt the presence of his sleeping wife slumped against the pillows on their bed. It had been a long and drawn out night. So many events packed into fourteen hours, and he couldn't wait to get home to hold Kat in his arms.

The station soon came into view. He landed as Zacke used to behind the station. Once his body reverted to physical molecules instead of vapor, he made his way through the building and walked into Zacke's office.

"Hey, you find out anything?" Gideon slid into the chair facing the desk while he awaited Zacke's answer.

"Two of the detectives that worked the *Fleur de Lis* killer case were on duty at two different PD's. One in Maine and one in Michigan. They said and I quote 'the son-of-a-bitch got off on killing and if you find him they want a crack at him' end of quote. Other than that, they had no forensic evidence that might help us." Zacke sighed. "Guess we're back to pounding the streets and hope we find him before he kills again."

"Damn. I was hoping for better news. I stopped by and warned as many of the women on the streets as I could. You can guess how some of them took my well-meaning intentions." Gideon propped his booted feet on Zacke's desk. "Lord I'm tired."

"Dawn's fast on our heels. Probably why you're so fatigued." His partner rooted around a desk drawer and handed Gideon a bottle of water. "It's not the nourishment you need, but it'll wet your throat until you get home."

"So what's on the agenda for tonight?" He took a swig of the water.

"I think at this point we need to fan out in different parts of the district."

Gideon opened his mouth but before he could speak, Zacke continued. "I know you've been busting your butt searching tonight, but if it is Marcel, and I'd bet my shield he is our killer, then as a vampire, he's going to know even more tricks than you do."

He opened his mouth again and again Zacke beat him to it. "He's older, Gideon, by a lot. He's at least as old as me, Miles, and Hawk are, and he could be as old as Gabriella. And I've never been able to find out her exact age. He is skilled in deceitfulness, something you have no clue about."

The pencil Zacke was holding snapped in half. "You're honest like no one I've ever known in this century. You're loyal, kind, and care about people. You don't have the mindset to go against Charmant and win—not by yourself. I want to call in Hawk, he's fought other vampires, and he is excellent with a sword. Again something you aren't. He can also frequent certain clubs that Marcel might visit, while you would just look like a sore thumb. You've got cop written all over you even in plainclothes."

Gideon couldn't argue that point, and at the moment, he was too tired to say much of anything.

"Okay, I get it, I stick out like a cat in a roomful of dogs. So, you want to meet here, and who is going to watch the women? I don't like the idea that while we're out hunting him, he knows where my house is and maybe yours and Miles."

Zacke lost some of the tan color out of his face. "Hell, you're right. If he knew how to get to your house, then he had to follow one of us there. I can't believe he'd be that lucky otherwise."

"I know it goes against the grain for you to ask for help, but get Miles to put a safety spell on your place. He did mine, until he can teach me how to do it myself." Gideon stood.

"I can show you how if you like. I may no longer be a vampire but I haven't forgotten the safety prayers." Zacke looked a bit put out, but Gideon didn't understand why. His partner had achieved his dreams to become a mortal again.

"Hey, that's a great idea. We can do it tonight, and I say we meet at your house and Miles can do his thing. Okay?" When Zacke nodded, Gideon strode to the door, but turned back around. Zacke was fiddling with a paperweight on his desk, and didn't look up. "Hey, you okay?"

His partner looked up and met Gideon's gaze. "Yeah, I'm fine. Get home before dawn. The sun can cause a nasty burn if you're not careful."

****

Outside once more, he teleported home and to their bedroom. The bed was empty of the armful he sought, but as he looked around to pinpoint where Kat was, a heavenly scent assaulted his nostrils. A second later, he stood in the kitchen staring at his wife's sexy backside as she removed something from the lower rack of the oven.

Kat turned around and he couldn't decide whether to kiss her or just stare in amazement at the man-sized meatloaf she placed on the counter.

"Hey, I thought I felt you get home. You hungry?" Kat gave him an impish smile.

"At the moment, I'm not sure what I'm hungry for more—you or the food." Gideon literally drooled as his wife blew him a kiss.

"Well why don't you eat first and then we'll satisfy your male hunger." Kat placed an ample helping of the same food Miranda had offered him the night before on a plate and poured him a glass of something.

"What's in the glass?" He grabbed his fork as he waited for her to answer.

"Sweet tea and blood." She laughed when he turned up his nose. "Come on, try it, it's really not bad. There's enough sugar in the tea to disguise the blood.

Gideon wasn't sure if it was her confidant look or her subliminal "I dare you" but he did as Kat asked. His first taste surprised him, no semblance of blood at all. He gulped down half the glass and then grinned at his wife.

"Remind me to not doubt you in the future." He blew her a kiss and then attacked his food. Kat sat down and managed to swipe a bite from his plate every now and then. He watched the expression in her eyes as she tasted real home cooking.

After chasing down meatloaf and a biscuit with his drink, he asked her, "So what do you think of the food?"

"It's different. I think I could get used to it, though I think I'll see if it makes you sick before I eat as much as you do." Her laughter made his heart clench with gladness. God above he loved his wife.

"Good idea. Now," he patted his mouth with a napkin and stood up, "what about feeding my other hunger?"

"Go on up. I'll be there in a few minutes, I want to rinse these and put them in the dishwasher." She started gathering up his plate and glass. "I cooked enough you should have plenty for tonight, but if I don't put it in the refrigerator it could go sour."

"All right, I'll be waiting." Gideon waggled his eyebrows and then teleported to the bedroom. He stifled a yawn, pulled off his clothes, and made for the shower. After flying around all night, he probably could use some soap and water before bedding his wife.

A few minutes later, he strolled back into the bedroom prepared to do just that, but Kat wasn't there. He concentrated and heard the sounds of rattling pans and stuff in the kitchen. Okay, he'd just lie down for a bit, no problem. Kat would be up soon.

****

Katheryne hurried up the steps as fast as she could go. She'd taken a lot longer to finish her chores, but while putting up the food, she decided to make the pecan pie Miranda said Gideon would love. She opened the door to the bedroom and then stopped.

Gideon clothed made her heart beat faster, but naked he was a portrait of masculinity that would rival any Greek God. He lay on his back, in the center of the bed, his arms crossed at the chest. Dark blond hair fanned out on the black pillowcases. His chest was broad, with just a little bit of hair from right under his nipples, narrowing in a straight line to a part she favored most highly. A part that even in sleep was imposing. As she continued to stare at him, his manhood thickened and stood to attention. Did he know she gazed at him?

A smile graced his lips, and she wondered if he was dreaming about her, about them? The sun was coming up fast, and she made sure the shade was pulled all the way to the bottom. It seemed the food her vampire husband had consumed had turned him into a sleeping prince.

As much as she'd like to utilize the hardness of his shaft, she decided this would be a good time to do some laundry as Miranda called it—for when he awakened she knew her husband would satisfy his physical hunger before he even fed his blood lust.

She plundered through the clothesbasket in the bathroom, and after looking over the jeans her husband was so fond of, she pondered the idea of going shopping. Gideon needed some pants without the seams looking like they were coming out. She certainly didn't want her husband's male parts dangling for any other woman to see.

Katheryne backtracked and changed into clean clothes. Jeans with a sweater as well as a pair of sunglasses, she'd borrowed from her husband, should be fine for a quick trip to the mall.

Several minutes later, she sighed. The mall wasn't open yet. So now what? She could wait outside but didn't want to just stand in the bright morning sun. She thought for a minute. Miranda would be at work so she would just go visit with her for a bit.

Katheryne made sure no one was around and teleported to a back lot where employees parked their cars. She made haste as she headed for the entrance. She could feel the heat of the golden rays beating down on top of her head.

She caught up with Miranda just as the physician got to her office. "Miranda."

Miranda looked back over her shoulder, her expression startled, and then smiled. "Hi. I didn't expect to see you here...now."

Kat knew she referred to it being after sunrise.

"Well, about that...can I come in, and I'll explain."

"Sure thing. I might even be able to scrounge up some coffee if you want any." Miranda looked a bit tired as she ushered Kat into the room.

"No, I'm fine. I was going to go shopping for some new jeans for Gideon, but the mall isn't open yet." Katheryne took a seat.

"Yeah, it would be nice if they opened a bit early for those of us who have to get out early, but there are a few twenty-four hour places you might check." Miranda dropped her briefcase on the desk and slumped in her chair. "How did Gideon like your dinner?"

"He loved it, thank you so much! And after looking at me like I'd lost my mind, he drank the tea, also. I think I shocked him. And I made the pecan pie and popped it into the refrigerator for tonight." Kat watched Miranda's face. Her features carried more than fatigue, she looked like something was troubling her.

"Are you all right? Is everything okay?" At Miranda's questing look, Kat continued. "You don't seem yourself, what's going on?"

"Men are what's going on. My husband, your husband, Hope's and even Hawk are all planning to hit the streets with periodic check-ins on us women folk. I'm sick of it. I don't want my husband anywhere near this Marcel person." Miranda's blue gaze filled with tears.

Katheryne felt guilt riding her back. If it wasn't for her, Marcel wouldn't be in Savannah, the women he'd killed would be alive, and her darling Gideon would not be a vampire. For some reason, she couldn't decide if that would be a good or bad thing. Tears burned the back of her eyes, but she refused to let them fall. Life was hard, she couldn't change what had happened, but maybe she could help stop it before anything worse befell her husband and friends.

"Don't worry, Miranda, that won't happen. I'll just leave Savannah, and Marcel will follow me. It's simple, then when he gets tired of hunting me, I'll come back. It might be a few years, but it's okay. I don't want anything to happen to any of you." Katheryne stood and headed for the office door.

"Kat! Wait! That's not what I meant. Please, you can't leave. It would crush Gideon, not to mention you're one of my dearest friends. I don't want you to go." Miranda stood up and rushed around the desk. She threw her arms around Katheryne's shoulders. "Please, promise me you won't go anywhere."

What should she do? Tell her she wouldn't and then leave anyway? Did she want to leave? No! She loved her husband. Maybe he would come with her. Katheryne returned Miranda's hug but didn't answer her right away. Did she have the right to take Gideon away from the town he'd been born in, his friends, his job? No. So what choice did she have? None, and truly after hearing that voice in her head, she knew Marcel would not stop at anything to get her to comply with his wishes. Still she didn't want to run from her problems, and she especially didn't want to leave her husband.

"Stop crying, Miranda, please. I won't leave." When Miranda's head jerked up, and a smile adorned her lips, Katheryne wondered if her friend had put one over on her, if that was what it was called.

"Not right now. Wait, I mean I have to leave to go shopping, but I promise not to leave Savannah just yet." She gently removed Miranda's arms. "Now please, do not mention this to anyone."

When Miranda opened her mouth, Katheryne forestalled her. "I mean it. If you tell Gideon or anyone I *will* leave. I don't want anyone else hurt. I don't want you worried, and I don't want to have to worry about everyone I care about, so please."

"Okay, I'll keep it to myself." Miranda went back to her chair. "Please just promise that you'll let me know if and when you do leave."

"That I *can* promise. Now, I'll see you later." She waved her hand, and then left without looking back. There were drawbacks to having friends, but since she'd never had any until coming to this century, she simply couldn't wish for it to be any other way.

****

Marcel had gotten lucky. He'd watched and waited for the detective to go home, and then when he had given up hope of seeing even a glimpse of his elusive Katheryne, she'd left the house. So flummoxed at this extremely unexpected luck, she'd almost gotten away from him before he tracked her scent to the hospital. The taking of her blood so many years ago enabled him to follow her once he was close enough.

She'd spoken with the other detective's doctor wife, and then he'd stayed far enough behind her she could not detect him. Now he was content to wait until she finished her shopping. There would be plenty of time to approach, talk with Katheryne, and then take her away.

Chapter Twenty-Five

Katheryne hooked her arm around several shopping bags, smiled at the clerk, and left the store with a light step. She shouldn't allow the thought of Marcel to get to her. He would love to know he had that power over her, and she would not allow that to happen.

"Katheryne." The voice came from directly behind her, and caused the hair on her arms to stand straight up. My God in Heaven, he'd found her.

"Yes, I found you. Why would you think I wouldn't? We have a blood tie, and you belong to me."

She forced her body to turn around and face the vampire who would haunt her to her dying day. Then she slammed her mind shut. He could read her thoughts.

"Naughty *ma petite chat*. I love to read your thoughts." His oily tone made her skin crawl but then anger raised its head.

"Don't call me Cat." Keeping her mind steeled against his intrusion, she vowed she'd see him dead before she allowed him to call her even a semblance of Gideon's name for her.

"There is no need to be angry. It's time to put our past grievances behind us. I forgive you for leaving me."

"You forgive me? You're insane, Marcel. Gabriella kicked you out after you mauled me. Then she attacked me and turned me into a creature like you and her. For God's sake, she tore my throat out.

There is nothing for you to forgive, but I will never forgive what you did to my husband." Katheryne's fury was full-blown, so much so, she knew her eyes were blazing red behind her dark glasses.

"Your husband? That vampire-newcomer is not worthy to be your husband. It is I who searched for you through the years, even centuries, and only I am worthy of a woman such as yourself." Marcel placed his hand on Katheryne's arm. She used the hand not carrying the bags to slap it away.

"Stay away from me, Marcel. I know what you did to those women. That is a death sentence here in Savannah. You won't care for it either. My understanding is they will inject you with a lethal doze of some type of drug. After you die, they will drain the blood from your body and fill it with embalming fluid. You can't live without blood." Katheryne sneered the last part of her sentence.

"My goodness, the little chat has grown claws. Well, I have news for you *Kat*, you will loose everyone you hold dear in this accursed century. I will make sure of it if you don't come with me." Again he reached for her arm.

"I told you I'm not going anywhere with you, and don't try the mind thought action on me again. Leave me alone." Katheryne snatched her arm away, but found she couldn't move her body after that. She stood there frozen in fear and at Marcel's mercy. Would he teleport her away? Could she fight him? And what would happen if she did?

His hand on her arm caused her body to go weak. She could feel the beginning of the teleportation process starting. Her heart and mind screamed even as her lips stayed locked together.

As she waited for what would be a death sentence to commence she heard as from a distance.

"Ma'am is this man bothering you?" The police officer's question had Marcel turning toward him, and the spell he'd put her under weakened. Katheryne tried stepping back and when that worked, she spoke.

"No officer, I am fine. Thank you." She didn't look at Marcel but ducked back into the store she'd exited from earlier, found the Lady's room, and then teleported home. Miles' safety spell should keep Marcel out—if not, she would stake him and take his head herself, before she allowed him to touch her again or to harm Gideon.

****

Gideon awoke to find Kat almost bear-hugging him in their bed. Her cheeks were a bit pale, and she had on street clothes. There were tear marks on her face. Something had upset his wife between the time he'd fallen asleep and now.

He caressed her face; his thumb touched the still damp moisture on one lash. What had happened? He closed his eyes and with his hand still on her face, he tried to concentrate on her thoughts. At first it was a hazy pattern of words—leave, away, and protect were the main three, and a red flag of warning reared its head.

Gideon tried harder to break through the almost impenetrable lock Kat had over her thoughts. He couldn't. Since they had shared their blood on their wedding night, he'd not often taken advantage of that vampiric gift. Both he and Kat wanted their marriage to be as normal as a mortal's.

She stirred next to him, but did not awaken. His inner clock told him sundown was close. He could wait until then to ask her what was wrong. In the meantime, he'd shower and get ready for work. Then after their talk if she wanted to make love they would, but Gideon had a sneaking suspicion that was not going to happen.

****

An hour later, he'd finished two bags of blood

and wolfed down a cold meatloaf sandwich. Since eating that morning had proven he could still indulge his mortal liking for real food, he saw no need not to enjoy the delicious meal his wife had prepared. Gideon now held a knife in his hand, ready to cut a piece of beckoning pie when his hearing picked up Kat's awakening.

As he listened to her stretch, then heard the bedcovers rustle as she got up, Gideon concentrated again on her mind thoughts.

Gideon must never know. I have to keep him safe. I will do anything I have to in order to make sure Marcel never touches him or anyone else I love.

The knife clattered to the kitchen counter. Why was she thinking of Marcel? Of course, Kat had every right to worry, something he prayed would stop once he killed the vampire, but he didn't care for the panicked note accompanying her thoughts.

Why, why did I go out? I should have waited to go shopping. Why didn't I go somewhere else? Of course it probably wouldn't have mattered. Marcel must have followed me.

Gideon's vision turned a brilliant red. Rage exploded in the back of his skull, followed by a desire to dismember Charmant. Before he could enjoy that thought, a question popped into his head. That morning when he'd lain down it was almost sunrise and Kat had been in the kitchen. No way she could have gone out and then gotten back before the sun did its thing.

How on earth had she been able to walk outside in broad daylight? On the heels of that thought came could he do it?

A soft sound at the door signaled his wife had found him.

"Evening my sweet husband." Her gentle tone had him turning and facing her. All signs of distress had been cleansed from her face. Her smile was a bit thin, but the love shining in her beautiful lavender gaze was not faked.

How should he handle what he knew? Toss it out and see what she said or ease into the subject. He welcomed the arms sliding around his waist, the almost possessive grip she bestowed on him, but couldn't help but wonder if it was due to what she'd concealed from him.

"Evening darling." Gideon dropped a kiss on the top of her head. Best to proceed as if he knew nothing and in order to do that, he needed to block his thoughts.

"I sorta went ahead and ate. I was fixing to have a piece of pecan pie when you came down." No need to let her know he'd heard the stirring of her awakening.

"I might try a small bite. So was the food okay warmed up?" Kat ended her bear hug and stepped back. After going to the drawers lining the counter, she pulled one open and grabbed a couple of forks.

"Actually, I just ate a cold meatloaf sandwich." He chuckled at her look of horror. "Honey in the south, that's a staple when it comes to left over meatloaf or fried green tomatoes. I don't suppose Miranda gave you the recipe for those, huh?"

Kat picked up the knife he'd dropped and began to slice off a huge slab of dessert. Even as the questions continued to revolve inside his head, his nose with its keener sense of smell reacted to the sweet treat, and his stomach began a happy dance.

"No she didn't, but I'm sure she will if I ask. Now come, sit down and enjoy." Kat took the saucer with its divine offering, placed it at his spot on the table, and took a seat opposite him.

He allowed her to spear the first bite of pie and then took a hefty bite of his own. Gideon savored the delectable sweet, all the time pondering how to approach the topic of Marcel.

"Gideon..." Kat's tongue reached out to swipe at a crumb, and he almost jumped. He wanted to make love to her now, but first things first.

"Yes, Kat." He banked down his lust and took another taste of dessert.

"I was thinking, maybe we should go on a honeymoon. You know like I read about in some of the magazines?" Kat looked at him with such an earnest plea, he almost said yes before realizing this was probably a ploy to keep him away from Marcel.

"Gee babe, I'd love to..." His words trailed off at the jubilant expression on her face and then he mentally squared his shoulders. He was a cop, dammit, and needed to question her to find out what was going on.

"But at the moment, no way can I take off from work. You know with me being missing from action because of the transformation and everything, and these prostitute murders, not to mention Marcel..." He paused to see how that one word would affect Kat.

Her face whitened and her eyes grew wide. He couldn't let her off the hook. Too much was at risk.

"What's wrong, Kat?" He eased the question out there in an inquiring tone and hoped she wouldn't pick up on his anxiety.

"Nothing. I just have a lot on my mind." Her evasiveness didn't help. He'd have to pull it out of her bit by bit. He scarfed down another bite before speaking.

"What happened to you this morning, you never came to bed." He purposely kept his gaze on his plate before quickly glancing up. He caught the startled look in her eyes.

"I uh, I uh..."

"What is it, Kat? You can talk to me." He reached across the table and took her hand in his.

"I went shopping. You needed some new jeans."

Her words carried the mark of truth in them. He concentrated but could not break through her mind barrier.

"Hey thanks, I knew I was getting low but planned to pick up some this week. So, care to tell me how you can be out when the sun's up?" This time Gideon didn't try to disguise his interest. What he wasn't expecting was her sigh of relief.

"Oh that... well since I was first transformed, I've tried staying up later and later past sunrise. Then when I didn't turn into a pile of dust, I decided to see if I could go out in the sun." Kat leaned forward, seemingly warming to her subject.

"I love the sun, Gideon. It was right after dawn when the glorious rays would touch the garden in my old home and turn the flowers into dazzling faery damsels. Colors exploded, greenery looked like a beautiful carpet, and I felt peace like I was the only one in the world." Kat sighed. "I didn't want to lose that feeling, so I would at first stick my foot out the door. The sun burned just a bit but it healed by the time I woke that night. I continued to test the sun's rays on all of my body until I could step out into the dawn. And the length of time I could spend in the sun began to grow." She sent him a bewitching smile.

"It restored my peace over being transformed into a vampire. Not even Gabriella knew I could do this. She only stayed around for a few months after she changed me, not caring how I got the blood I needed, and then disappeared."

"So when I found you lying in that alley with sunrise almost on top of us, you knew you would be safe." He really wanted to know her answer.

Kat looked away for a moment before returning his gaze. "Actually, when you found me, I planned to allow the sun to end my life."

Gideon gasped aloud. "Why and how would that

be possible if you can be out in the sun?"

"Oh Gideon, at that time I didn't know you. I was tired; I hadn't taken blood in several weeks. My body was weak, I just didn't care." She squeezed his hand, but it didn't dispel the chill coating his already cool body.

"What changed your mind?"

"You did when you came to my rescue." Katheryne smiled. "Never in my centuries of living had anyone but my parents been so kind."

He lifted a hand and caressed her face. "I'm glad. I can't imagine never having met you. Now, why would the sun kill you?"

"Well all the times I've been out after sunrise, I've taken precautions, and I was never directly in the sun for long. So I hoped by going to sleep and allowing my body to bear the full force of the rays I would just turn into ashes." She gave him what could only be an apologetic look. He didn't know what to think about her revelation; it scared the shit out of him. What if he'd come along later or hadn't found her at all?

Gideon allowed some of the fear he felt to manifest itself in a stern tone. "I want you to promise me no matter how bad things could be in the future, you will never put yourself in harm's way again."

A glimmer of peace entered her gaze. "I promise, but you have to promise the same. Marcel is dangerous."

"Kat, you know as good as I do, I have to try and catch him. It's my job." He didn't snarl the words but he wanted her to understand he would not bow out of what needed to be done.

"I know, but just promise me you will be extra careful." The catch in Kat's voice almost undid Gideon.

"I promise and now let's talk about how I can

program my body to stay out after sunrise. It would make it easier if I had to be out late. I know Zacke can or could do it for a bit, but he had to wear a lot of clothing to keep the sun's rays from cooking his flesh."

"Oh, I'm sure you can, and maybe we can even learn how to stay out all day if we needed to. It's just trying to focus your mind on not sleeping." The little giggle she gave told him she was relieved. He hated to burst that bubble, but he had no choice.

"And focusing your mind comes in handy when you're trying to keep your thoughts of Marcel finding you from me." He kept a grip on the hand she tried to jerk back. Her cheeks turned pink and then paled.

"How did you know?" Her whispered question sounded despondent, resigned, and hopeless.

"I woke up and found you next to me. You'd been crying. I only got a few words from your mind. You're good at blocking your thoughts even in sleep. The rest I got after you awakened before you shuttered your thoughts again." Gideon hated he caused the look of panic and fear on Kat's face, but again, there was no help for it, not if he wanted to dig out the truth.

"I'm sorry." Kat's tone was low.

"I know, but what I don't know is why you felt you had to protect me? To keep back the fact Marcel found you." Gideon needed to know her reasoning.

"Because Marcel is evil. He threatened you and the rest of my new family. Gideon, there are children whose lives could be at stake. I knew if I told you you'd react this way. You can't go after him, he will kill you."

"Not if I kill him first. Now listen up, Kat, we're going to call a meeting, and I want you to tell us exactly what Charmant looks like now, what he's confessed to, and then you will stay with the other women."

Right on time her mouth opened but he jumped in before she could protest.

"Hope will help, and between you two and Miranda's tendency to be a bear when it comes to her children, ya'll should be okay."

Finally she nodded her head. "What are you going to do?"

"I'm going to Zacke's and make sure they know Marcel can move around in daylight." Gideon didn't want to waste time on getting a shower, so he closed his eyes, thought of being clean with his hair washed, and fully dressed in clean clothes. He opened his eyes and was amazed to find it'd worked.

"You coming with me?" He hoped Kat would, because he didn't want to leave her alone, although he felt the safety spell would keep Marcel out. The thought the man had accosted her, threatened her, and planned to steal her away made his incisors ache.

He grabbed a bag of blood, drained it dry, and then asked again. "Well, are you coming?"

"Yes, not because I'm scared to stay here, but I'm frightened you will do something stupid." Kat's eyes flashed red before she schooled her features against her upset. "Go ahead and teleport to Zacke's. I want to change clothes and feed and then I'll follow you."

At his questioning glance, she replied. "I'll be there in less than fifteen minutes."

He kissed her hard on the mouth, and she welcomed the connection. It seemed her husband had become proficient at a variety of things, reading her mind being one of them. She'd have to be careful in the future. But for the moment, Katheryne was happy she didn't have to lie to Gideon. And just maybe there would be a way to stop Marcel without anyone getting killed.

Even as she kissed him back, she wondered if

she was just dreaming the impossible.

Gideon released her lips and then poof he was gone. Katheryne teleported upstairs to get changed and then satisfied her blood hunger before teleporting to the Kensington's.

Zacke, Miles, Hawk, as well as her husband sat at the kitchen table. Miranda and Hope stood at the counter talking quietly.

Looks of concern, sympathy, determination from the others, and a heated gaze of love from Gideon greeted her arrival.

"Have a seat, Kat. We want your input into what you think Marcel will do next." Zacke motioned to an empty chair next to him. She did as he asked.

"I don't think he has an agenda, Zacke, except for me leaving with him." She refused to look at her husband but heard his growl.

"Well then we need to set a trap to keep that from happening." Miles tossed in before patting her on the back.

"Yes, that would be great, but I know Marcel, he won't leave without me. He is tenacious. He will do anything he can to get me, and he won't care whom he hurts to accomplish his goal."

A sharp intake of breath came from Miranda. Katheryne turned toward her. "Don't worry before I let him harm any of you, I'll leave. That's what I tried to tell you this morning before Marcel found me. Now, I know it's the only thing I can do." Katheryne fought the tears trying to take hold.

"No. You won't leave. *We'll* leave if necessary. I won't have my wife out there by herself." Gideon's voice was rough, determined, but she heard the ache he felt also. These were his people, family, his job he would be giving up. She couldn't allow it.

"No, Gideon, nothing will be resolved that way. He would just come after you. I won't have your death on my conscience." Before Katheryne could say anything more, the other men gave her a stare she could not misinterpret.

"First off, Kat, we don't abandon family. We've all been through a lot together, Gabriella's attack on Savannah and us, Hope's manager stealing and then trying to kill her. We take care of our own. You're part of our family, and Gideon we could never do without you." Zacke paused, before continuing. "Now, let's see if we can find a viable solution to this problem. All of us together."

The next few moments were spent discussing different scenarios of drawing Marcel out. At the end of the meeting and with her husband's loud protests, it was decided Katheryne at her insistence would be the bait. Miles and Hawk would shadow her every move as she walked the streets of Savannah as a lady of the night.

****

Marcel laughed even as the anger he felt about his failed attempt to take Katheryne that morning still raged. His beloved traipsed back and forth in the Red Light district, and he wondered if they really believed he would not recognize Katheryne, even dressed in the repugnant clothes of a whore? Her beautiful silver mane of hair hidden by a garish red wig could not disguise the fact she was a lady, and the vampires following her were not as secretive in their pursuits as they thought. Foolish imbeciles. Although aged, they were not as old as he was, and their angst at Katheryne's situation literally inundated the night. Both Dunbar and Sherwood, lords of old, had forgotten to school their thoughts.

Yes, they were amusing, but he wasn't interested in them, and not even Katheryne's new husband. He wanted to know more about Detective Kensington. His name bred remembrance in Marcel's mind. He would swear by all unholy the man had once been a vampire, but now he wondered if by some unexpected circumstance something had changed.

He would leave the two bumbling vampires to their guard duty while he did some research on Zacke Kensington. If the man indeed was mortal it would make capturing Katheryne much easier.

Chapter Twenty-Six

Gideon clenched and unclenched his clawed fingers into fists as he waited for Kat to get home. He'd been strictly ordered to not go near the district. An order he'd been solely tempted to disobey, and only a severe talking to by Zacke had made him focus his mind on trying to find Marcel's hiding place. If they could pinpoint where he slept during the day, then the vampire could be dispensed with immediately upon awakening from his death sleep. His partner's honorable disposition would not allow for staking the bastard while he slept.

But Gideon didn't feel that way, he'd stake the man in his sleep, in the daylight, anytime he could if it would keep Kat safe, but Zacke's reasoning had always been sound. So, for now he would honor his partner's wishes.

The night had been long and nothing on Marcel's whereabouts had turned up. Gideon had spoken to a few of the women on the streets who were parading their wares near a downtown hotel. None of them had seen Marcel that night but did know about him. Gossip among their sisterhood indicated the vampire had approached a few of them over the last week, but word had passed on the street to be careful of any stranger. Most of the women were only taking care of their regular clients.

A fact that could be a blessing or a curse. Marcel would have to feed his thirst to keep up his strength. At least, Gideon hoped so. If Charmant was old enough he could dispense with feeding for long lengths of time and that would not be good for any of them. Disgusted, sick at heart, and scared shitless the creature wanted his Kat, Gideon got up and retrieved a bag of blood. He would go ahead and eat and by then his wife should be home.

He wanted to try her technique of being able to stay up past dawn and to see if he could keep from getting toasted if he stepped foot out the door.

A slight disturbance in the air signified his wife's return. The moment she materialized inside the kitchen, he tossed the empty bag into the sink and pulled her into his arms.

"Hey babe, you okay?" He nuzzled the question against her neck but then drew back. The subtle fragrance of lavender Kat habitually wore had been replaced with a nose wrenching and cloying scent of something he didn't like.

"What kinda crap are you wearing?"

"What are you talking about? You already know I had to dress this way." Kat looked confused.

"Baby, I'm not talking about the seductive skirt and hardly there top you've got on, though I do like it on you here, not on the street, but that nasty perfume you've got coating your neck."

"Oh that…" Kat laughed. "It's a little something Miranda and Hope mixed up to keep johns from approaching me. You don't like it?" Her lips turned up in a pout, but her eyes twinkled as she awaited his answer.

"That explains the whiff of garlic and onions I could smell last night. Well did it work?" He prayed it had, and although he knew his vampire brothers wouldn't allow any man to hit on Kat, he still would prefer no one approach her at all.

"Yes, it did. I even got asked to leave a restaurant when I went in to get a cup of coffee." Kat grinned. "Are you happy?"

Gideon closed the distance he'd put between them after noticing the smell. "I'll be happy once I wash this stuff off you." He braced himself against the odor, pulled Kat into his arms, and then teleported them the bedroom.

He blocked the smell from his nostrils and took his time unhooking the bustier his wife wore. The crimson color made her moonbeam hair glow even softer. He loved how she looked, fragile but seductive as hell. His hands stripped off the garment and then found solace in the succulent mounds of flesh marred slightly by the punishing stays.

Gideon kissed his way to the short leather skirt hugging her hips and thighs before he tossed it to the floor also. His eyes widened at the picture Kat made standing before him in a pair of thigh-high stockings and mile-high heels. God above she was the sexiest thing he'd ever seen. The tiny scrap of material hiding her lush center only fired his blood more. He took the band between his teeth and ripped the red offering away. His mouth found and suckled the welcoming fount of Kat's desire. So wet, so ready for him to take, but first he wanted to soap her up, rinse her off, and then use his body as a towel.

"Gideon—"

He cut off her moan as he traveled back up her body to her lips. While still tasting the tempting cavern of her mouth, he back-walked her into the bathroom. He released her long enough to turn on and regulate the shower's temperature before ripping off his own clothes.

Kat's attempt to help him move faster only tangled their hands. He pushed her gently under the cascading waterfall and then joined her.

He poured shampoo into his hands, soaped her hair, and then covered her face with his hand as he rinsed it out. He continued to clean every part of her body, paying close attention to the neck he wanted to suckle later, her breasts, and the valley between her legs.

The moans coming from her sensual lips only made him hotter, harder, and he rushed through his task. He needed to take her, to make her his again, to block out the endless night of worry and rage.

Kat's grip on his waist tightened as he lifted her to ride his hard shaft. He raised her up and down and then braced her back against the tile as her heated sheath clenched and tightened around his flesh—taking his breath.

The moment he felt the first tremors of his climax strike, Kat nipped his throat with her fangs. He welcomed the sharp bite and then the sensuous thrill of her feeding.

Tighter and tighter the spirals of lust swirled. Kat released his neck, and her eyes rolled back as she screamed out her release.

He allowed his head to drop forward, found the pulse beat in her neck and bit down hard. Her scream turned into a moan once again as he fed her what he was experiencing. Their combined climb toward orgasm pushed him to the edge and the colors behind his lids bled dark as the force of the climax hit him hard. His legs trembled as he kept his grip on Kat, and tried to keep from pitching them both to the stall floor. He licked his love bite and then caught her lips with his. The kiss went far beyond the last ebbs of ecstasy.

Katheryne's hand trembled as she took her husband's when he led her from the bathroom. Her body still damp with water droplets and their released passion. She felt the bed against her weak body, and then welcomed the feel of Gideon's arms around her after he pulled the coverlet over their entwined limbs.

"Woman, you're going to be the death of me." Gideon's words were whispered and though she knew he meant something else, she couldn't help but shiver at that morbid thought. Her mind became tangled with the night's events, out on the street to ply her wears to lure Marcel out; Katheryne had quickly realized that men were the same no matter what century. Sex was uppermost on their minds, regardless if they had a wife and family at home. Their thoughts were an open book and she found it was not one she wanted to read.

"Kat?"

So involved in her own thoughts, she almost missed his sleepily uttered word.

"Go to sleep my husband. You need to rest." Katheryne intended to stay awake, to find a way to draw Marcel out, away from those she cared about. Then she would kill him.

"You need to sleep too." His words were a bit disjointed since he'd spoke into his pillow. A moment later, a snore greeted her ears before he was out completely. Kat lay there for a few minutes longer, savoring the aftermath of their lovemaking, thinking of a life without Marcel, and one filled with Gideon and maybe children? She hoped that was possible, but Miranda would be the one to ask. As her mind leapt from one subject to another, she found her eyelids to be unmovable as they closed on their own. Her last thought was of Gideon and how she'd die to keep him safe.

****

"No! It's too dangerous." Gideon roared, and Katheryne didn't care for it not at all.

"And being on the street acting like I want to go to bed with any man who might approach me is safe?" She poked Gideon in the chest with her finger, regardless of their guests who stared at both her and her irate and totally clueless husband.

"That's not the same thing, Kat, and stop poking me with your finger. It's irritating."

For some reason their guests thought his

statement was funny. She had no idea why, but an inkling came when she heard Miles whisper to Hawk, "She must have gotten that habit from Miranda."

"I heard that," came from both Katheryne and Miranda with accompanying glares.

"And, if you would not act like a horse's ass, I wouldn't poke you."

"Katheryne Elizabeth Alastair Hawks, watch your mouth." Gideon's shocked gaze and Katheryne's giggles helped dispel the tension in the room.

"It's not funny. You shouldn't talk like that." Her husband, although he fought a smile, did not back down.

"And why not?" She couldn't wait to hear his answer. Sometimes he acted more archaic than the men she'd known way back when.

"Cause, it just don't sound nice coming from a lady."

As she looked from him to the others in the room, the men were all nodding in agreement, but Miranda and Hope were giving her high-fives.

"Gideon, grow up." The moment the words left her mouth, she regretted them, but the man had gotten on her last nerve. For the past three nights, she'd been out in that same little outfit trying to get Marcel to come to her. No luck. She was tired of wasting time. She knew in her heart, the vampire was just waiting for the chance to make good on his threat to hurt Gideon or her friends.

No matter how much she'd pleaded with her husband he remained adamant that no way could she go out in broad daylight without someone watching her back. And since he couldn't go he didn't want her to go at all.

"Fine, it's not ladylike but at the moment I don't feel like a lady. I feel disgusted and tired. Nothing we've done so far has gotten Marcel to come out in the open. We have to do something."

"Kat." Zacke's soft tone did not help her nerves. All she needed was another male explaining why she couldn't do what needed to be done.

"Yes." She turned to face her husband's partner.

"I know you want to help catch Marcel, but to put you out there when we can't all be there is not safe. I don't have the powers I use to have or I'd say let's do it in a heartbeat, and even though Miles and Hawk could do it, they can't stay out indefinitely and neither can you." He stopped and then continued, "Or can you?"

Katheryne sighed. "No, I can only be out a couple of hours at a time, but it can be at different times of the day. What if I switch those times up, then Miles and Hawk could take turns."

"No, I still don't want you to do it. You got away from him last time, it might not happen again." Gideon sounded tired, she knew he wasn't sleeping as heavy as a vampire should, and she blamed herself. Her upset on their not being able to find Marcel, the worry he would strike while her vampire friends slept, or attack her mortal friends had caused her to be listless. She wasn't feeding on a regular schedule, and not even Gideon's sweet and skillful lovemaking could pull her out of the depression assaulting her spirit.

"He didn't just let me go, I took off after a police officer asked me if I needed help, then I teleported away." She spit out the words not caring if it made the situation worse. Her husband needed to know she could take care of herself.

"You what?"

"I teleported away. Gideon he's after me. I want it to stay that way. I don't want him coming after you or anyone else in this room. I want him to stop killing those helpless women because he can't have me. Do you know how this is tearing me apart?"

Katheryne walked away from her mate and began setting serving dishes on the table. The arrival of their guests had interrupted that small task, and the food would be cold if they didn't eat soon.

"I'll give you a hand, Kat." Miranda grabbed a casserole dish as did Hope. In a matter of moments the meal she'd cooked before going to bed sat alongside the dinnerware and glasses.

"Okay, everyone, let's eat." Kat waited until everyone was seated before seating herself. She couldn't bear to look at Gideon, his thoughts were beating in her head and heart so hard it made breathing almost impossible. She hated this, hated the fact she'd upset him, but she hated the thought of losing him more. If only he could understand how she felt.

"I do. I'm sorry." The balm of his words caused her to turn her head. The crooked smile he sent her way made her want to snatch him up and flee with him to the farthest most point of the world. Instead she settled on blowing him a kiss and sending him her own thoughts. *"I'm sorry too. I love you."*

Food was passed around and for a while, silence prevailed only to be disturbed when Gideon spoke. "So why don't we use me as bait. The bastard wants me dead anyway."

****

Marcel strolled from the library, his steps light, the full moon highlighting the street. A sensual look, a mind thought, and he'd had all the information he needed about Detective Kensington. The desk clerk had brought him every newspaper article, and shown him how to look for back issues on a computer, and then he'd feasted on her blood. Not enough to kill her, but enough that she would wake from her daze wondering why she felt sexually sated.

He made his way down to the riverfront. It was

too early for his beloved Katheryne to be out in her garish outfit, and although he loved watching her and the two bumbling vampire guards run around in circles trying to draw him out, he was getting tired of the game.

And after what he'd found out tonight, he had what he needed to pull her to him without an argument. Sir Zachary Kensington as he'd been known while serving King James was no longer a vampire. Of course the papers didn't tell him that, but after reading of his exploits along with Katheryne's upstart husband, he'd put together the facts.

After a serious illness, which coincided with Gabriella's death, the detective had been seen at all stages of daylight, out eating food, and he'd sired children. Not unheard of for an aged vampire, but the fact he'd not taken part in training his partner in the art of vampirism (an amusing scene he'd watched from afar) and the fact he'd begun to show more lines in his face from age signified somehow the man was indeed a mortal once again.

Marcel could and would use this information for his own good. Besides, it would be titillating to see how Katheryne would react to his soon to be launched plan.

Chapter Twenty-Seven

Gideon left the station the next morning and decided to walk home instead of teleporting. He needed the brisk fall air, the quiet of the pre-dawn to settle his thoughts. He'd finally gotten Kat to see reason, and to forget about going out as bait. Now, if he could just find Charmant.

He unlocked, eased open the kitchen door, and promptly stumbled over something lying at the threshold. Damn, he should have seen the obstruction and probably would have if his mind wasn't focused on killing Marcel. The package, he'd managed to almost trip over and kick a few feet across the kitchen, was about the size of a shoebox, not wrapped, but taped together.

It was addressed to him without a return address. How did it wind up inside the house? Fear made his hands tremble as he ripped the lid off and then gazed in shock as several pictures of his wife, in various stages of dress, and all inside their home stared up at him. Underneath the pictures lay a pair of silver handcuffs. Something about silver and vampires pinged in his mind, as he grabbed the pencil from his back pocket and lifted them out of the box. A sheet of paper was the last item inside the box.

Katheryne is mine, I will come for her, and no spell as you see can keep me out.
MC

A whoosh of air sounded behind him, and Gideon bared his fangs and extended his claws. He turned ready to attack.

"Hold, Gideon. It's us." A very pale Miles with an equally porcelain-faced Zacke stood in the middle of the kitchen.

Hawk materialized a second later.

"I assume this is not a social visit." He eyed all the men before his gaze lit on Zacke.

"Dammit, no." It was the curse on Zacke's lips that turned Gideon's blood even colder than it should be.

"I assume you received a package?" He prayed they hadn't but didn't hold out much hope.

"Hell yeah, right in my house." Miles stalked around the kitchen like an avenging warrior. "*How* is what I don't understand."

"Me either, but Marcel left a package here and said no spell could keep him out." Gideon grabbed bags of blood from the fridge, and handed them out to his vampire brethren, before programming the coffee maker for Zacke. He tried to keep his thoughts neutral; he didn't want Kat rushing downstairs.

Zacke, visibly shaken, took the mug from Gideon when the machine ran its cycle. Miles didn't look much better, and Hawk had a murderous glint in his eyes.

Gideon waited until the other two had slapped their breakfast to their teeth, and then did the same. Marcel was turning the flames up a notch, and there'd be hell to pay either way—whether they caught him or not.

"Okay, my package had pictures of Kat, and silver handcuffs. Any one want to tell me about those?" Gideon shoved the box into the middle of the table.

"Silver is like poison to vampires. I know the movies say werewolves have a problem with it, but for some reason the silver when it cuts us, it makes the wound harder to heal." Hawk spit out.

"So, I assume he plans to take Kat and put those

on her or me if I find him before he cuts off my head." Gideon again tried to still his runaway heartbeat. All he needed was his wife to be aware of this conversation and then all hell *would* break loose.

"I'd say that's about right. I can only think he's trying to scare me off by leaving pictures of Hope and Sammie—" Miles broke off as a shudder rolled over his body, before his eyes turned a deep jade, and his fangs erupted. The growl coming from his throat scared the shit out of Gideon, although he felt the same way.

"Did he leave anything at your place, Hawk?"

"No, but I wouldn't expect him to, I don't have a wife or children." His words were hollow and something about his attitude made Gideon wary, but now wasn't the time to have a heart to heart. He turned to Zacke, and dreaded the question he needed to ask.

"What did he leave you, Zacke?"

His partner's face creased in lines of despair. "Pictures of Miranda at work, home, the children with the babysitter. I don't know what to do. I can't protect them, not anymore. I'm human, dammit, and this sonofabitch is stalking my family."

Gideon knew how he felt, and it had to be ten times worse with the children involved. At least Miles had vampiric strength, but he wondered if that would be enough for any of them.

"Okay, okay, we need to think this through and regroup. Miles what if you bring Sammie to Zacke and Miranda's, that way all the kids are together. Then I'll bring Kat, and she and Hope can help guard them. You can stay too. I'll keep a watch on my house and Hawk can do the same for yours if that's okay."

"No, I'll be standing guard at my house. I want the little cockroach to come calling so I can send him to hell. Hawk would be better anyway. He's not as emotionally involved." Miles' face twisted into a horrible caricature of his usual lordly features. He was scared shitless and so was Gideon.

"Fine by me, what about the rest of you?"

"Works for me, Gideon." Hawk glanced around the room and the look Gideon had spotted earlier was still there. "Zacke?" Gideon prompted his partner who still looked shell-shocked.

"Yes, I'm okay with that... I just wish..."

"I know partner, but we'll all work together to keep the women and children safe." Gideon paused before blurting out, "Maybe I should just leave with Kat."

"It won't do any good, he'll follow you and if he's enraged enough, he's liable to come after our families anyway." Miles inserted.

So softly he barely heard the pads of her feet, Kat crept into the kitchen. "I'm sorry, I'm so sorry. I should never have come here. I tried to tell Miranda that, but she told me I shouldn't leave. Now, Marcel's found a way to break through the safety spells. Please forgive me." She pitched herself into Gideon's arms, and he held her so tightly he heard her breath hitch. Why hadn't he guarded his thoughts better? He released his grip a bit and then raised her chin so he could look into her eyes.

"You did nothing wrong. You were a victim as was Zacke, Miles, and Hawk. Gabriella's legacy binds you all together with blood, and you're bound to me because of it. We'll find Marcel and take him down. Never doubt that. I just want you to stay out of harm's way."

At her questioning look, he spoke again. "You're going to Zacke's and together you, Hope, and Hawk will guard Miranda, Zacke, and the children. Between the three of you, you should be fine." God above, he hoped so.

"What about you? You are just newly turned; you're no match for Marcel. And how did he break the spells?" She turned to look at Miles who had been certain no one could get through.

"I don't know. He must be a lot older than we thought he was, maybe even more aged than Gabriella when she died." Miles tried to smile at Kat and for that Gideon was grateful.

"Gideon's right, you didn't do anything wrong. We're a family, as he said, bound by blood." Miles' voice trembled as he finished his sentence.

"Okay, everyone, it's a plan. Kat go get some clothes together. I don't know how long you'll have to be at Miranda's but I don't want you teleporting back here for any reason, hear me?" Gideon bit off the growl he wanted to use to reinforce his words.

"And where will you be?" Kat's entreaty was despondent, but her eyes were now dry as she awaited his answer. "Here, hoping Marcel shows his ugly face. I have to do something, he's not going to stop stalking you. He's killed others, leaving behind orphaned children, and there's no telling how many more we don't know about.

Katheryne knew Gideon was right, but she didn't have to like it, and she certainly didn't want to leave home and allow her husband to fight a demon from her past.

"Kat, it's not up for discussion. I know how you feel." Gideon's gaze was determined, and when she looked closer, she could see the faint etching of fear staring back at her. Was it her fear reflected in his eyes or his? Either way, she didn't want to add to his burden.

"Fine, but if you get killed, I'll...I'll...kill you again myself." She knew her words were crazy, but it brought a smile to her husband's lips, and just a bit of a chuckle from the other men.

"Now go get ready, I want you out of here before

the sun comes up." Gideon swatted her lightly on the bottom and turned his attention back to the men in the room.

Katheryne wanted to stay and listen but knew it would only distract Gideon. He'd been so careful about trying to keep his thoughts hidden; she'd almost missed the desperate meeting of the four men who were anchors in her life.

She teleported to their bedroom, threw clothes haphazardly into the bag Miranda had given her weeks ago, grabbed some toiletries, and then returned to the kitchen. Gideon was alone.

"So what happens now?" She prayed he'd changed his mind about her leaving.

"Now, I'm going to teleport with you to Miranda's. Zacke wanted a few minutes to talk to Miranda, and Miles needed to speak to Hope also. Hawk is doing a quick flyby over all our houses, and then he'll go to ground for the day. He'll be over when he awakens."

"Gideon what about when you're asleep? Marcel can be up after sunrise. Someone needs to watch your back." Katheryne grabbed his arm.

"Watch my back? You've been watching too much television my wife. I'll be fine. I promise. I'm going to booby trap the bedroom, and sleep with my gun." Gideon smiled but his usual bright gleam seemed tired.

"A gun won't stop Marcel." Katheryne wanted to hit him. Gideon was going to wind up dead, and she couldn't face the prospect of life without him.

"Shhh, baby. Seriously, I don't think Marcel will attack during the day. He wants a confrontation, I'm thinking, and if I'm asleep he won't get that satisfaction. So come on. I want you tucked in asleep so I can get some rest. You need yours too." Gideon caught her close and the next moment they were at the Kensington's.

Gideon did as he always did, gave Miranda a hug, and then turned to his friend and partner. Katheryne just stood there. Her presence was a reminder that a mad vampire was stalking her friends. A danger to their children. What could she say to Miranda?

Thank God she didn't have to say anything. Miranda opened her arms, and Katheryne ran straight into them. They cried and then patted one another on the back before turning to their husbands.

"So where shall we have our slumber party?" This came from Miranda, and Katheryne knew her calm tone was an effort to prevent the four-year old twins, and Hope's small daughter from being aware of what was going on. Katheryne knew all three children had exhibited at some time or other a skill for doing vampire tricks. These were not ordinary offspring, and they would have to be careful in what they said and did.

Zacke spoke up. "I think the living room would be best. That way we can protect them from anything that goes bump in the night." He held his hands up and playfully growled at the two little girls and his son who squealed and ducked their heads.

"I think you're right, let's go troops." Gideon grabbed Braden and Sammie, while Zacke picked up Brierana. Katheryne as well as the two moms stood and just stared at one another.

"So how bad is it, Kat?" Hope looked worried but not nearly as much as Miranda.

"Pretty bad. Did your husband's tell you anything?" Kat hated to cause a rift between these women and their mates, but they had a right to know.

"Only that Marcel Charmant is gunning for you, and using us as ploys in his plan." Hope's fangs flashed out before she controlled them.

"And that we're all to stay together to make sure the children are safe. Is that right, Kat?" Miranda's blue-eyed gaze was steady but she could hear how fast her heart was beating.

Not sure if she was doing the right thing or not, Katheryne responded. "Yes, but it's also to keep us women safe. Each one of our husband's received a package with pictures of all of us in different stages of dress or undress."

Miranda's mouth fell open but she didn't utter a word. Hope, however, growled her displeasure.

"And pictures of the children also." As she watched, Miranda did a total turn around. Gone was the misty-eyed, worried wife—in her place stood a woman with fire in her eyes, shoulders straight, and a look that almost sent shivers down Katheryne's spine.

"Oh hell no. That piece of scum is not touching one hair on any of these children's heads. I'll kill him myself."

Hope's green-eyed gaze turned into a sharper green, and the nails on her hands grew two inches and curved into claws.

"No, you can have what's left after I get finished with him."

"Kat, you told them." Gideon's tone was not so much accusing as disappointed as he entered the kitchen. Too bad.

"Yes, I did. I'd want to know if it were one of our children in danger." She expected an argument, what she got was a deep and sensual kiss that ended way too soon.

"I love you, babe." He eased his arm around her waist and held her closer to him. She savored the feel of his body next to hers. She just prayed that come sunset that night or sunrise in the morning, he'd still be alive.

"I love you too. So you're leaving?"

"Yes, I need to get back to our house. I'll be here as soon as the sun sets, okay?" Gideon looked like he thought she'd argue, but she didn't want to send him off that way.

"Okay, just promise me you'll be careful." Katheryne caressed his face, and then stepped back, and Gideon was gone.

Zacke came into the kitchen. "I think under the circumstances we need to let both our babysitters know we won't need them for a few days."

Katheryne noticed the haggard expression he'd worn earlier was now gone. The calm, assured, take charge warrior was back.

"I'll call and leave a message for Captain Myers that Gideon and I will be pursuing a promising lead in the prostitute murders and won't be coming by the station tonight." He turned to his wife. "I know this is going to sound strange under the circumstances but are we set up with enough food and blood?"

"Yes to both. And I'll see about getting some breakfast on the table. We all need to eat. Hope when's the last time you fed? Kat?"

"Last night." They both answered.

"Okay, so chow down on some blood while I whip up some pancakes, bacon, and eggs. When you're finished, ya'll can set the table and get the children ready to eat." Miranda's movements were concise as if she were trying to make sure her body parts worked. Yes, she was worried, and Kat couldn't blame her. Marcel had a lot to answer for. The plan to lure him to her had failed and now her friends and their families were in danger. But she'd do anything necessary to keep him from hurting them—anything.

An hour later, Zacke, Miranda, and Hope were entertaining the children and Katheryne headed to the living room. They planned to bed down there until sunset. Despite the worry and frustration of not knowing when Marcel would strike and whom he would hit first, she fell asleep almost immediately after her head hit the sofa cushion.

****

Gideon watched as Kat made soft little noises with her mouth when he pressed tiny kisses against her face. He had awakened earlier than usual and teleported to the Kensington's. Zacke looked a bit frazzled with three kids running around, but Miranda seemed in her element. Her features were smooth once more and not pinched with worry. He chatted with them a few minutes before finding his wife. Hope was just stirring when he walked into the room and then she teleported out, probably for a quick chat with Miles.

"Gideon if you don't stop teasing me, I'm going to hit you." Kat's sleepy voice was music to his ears. Even though they slept like the dead during the day, he'd grown accustom to having her by his side when he awoke.

"I'd rather you gave me a kiss before I have to leave again." His voice was low, his body heated with need, but it would have to wait. Time was running out to find Marcel before the vampire struck out in his rage at losing Kat.

She did as he asked and the kiss that started sweet ended in a bone-melting pull on his senses. He forced himself to release her delectable lips, and stepped back.

"Come on and walk me to the door. I need to get back home."

"Can't you wait a bit?" Katheryne didn't sound like she expected his answer would be an affirmative, and she was right. He couldn't afford to waste any time.

"Baby, you know I can't. Now, stay inside, Hawk should be arriving soon. He may be doing another fly by and hopefully before this night's over, Marcel will be a bad memory." God in Heaven, he hoped so.

Kat did as he asked, and Gideon said his goodbyes. A moment later he was home and looking at Miles who teleported in.

"How's everything at your place?" Gideon gestured toward the fridge.

"I already fed, but thanks. Nothing out of the ordinary, but I'm prepared for any and everything." Miles looked pensive. "Why is it when we find our mates shit happens and we have to fight like hell to keep them safe?"

"I don't know, but if you find out I'll pay you for the answer." Gideon sat in one of the chairs and felt the absence of his wife. He missed her. Yeah, they'd only been married a few days and this was suppose to be their honeymoon. Nights filled with lovemaking, not worries about a vampire who should have been staked centuries before.

"I'm going to head back to the house." Miles smiled just a bit. "Looks like you got some beauty sleep. I slept a bit, but it's hard to sleep without Hope and Sammie there. Reminds me of too many nights I spent alone before I found Hope."

"I know what you mean. I'm surprised I slept at all. Guess it's a good thing though. If we run into Marcel or he brings it to us, we'll need all the help we can get. I'm glad Hawk's going to be at Zacke's."

"Yeah, me too. Stay safe, bro." Miles lifted his hand and then disappeared.

The night stretched endlessly before him, and Gideon decided to grab a deck of cards from the upstairs closet and play solitaire. He settled in and after several games was finally winning. The last card he needed to make it a sweep beckoned. His hand reached for the King of Spades when he heard a thump out back.

The cards scattered as he jumped up and hit the

kitchen running.

He yanked the door open in time to see Marcel—
or at least he assumed it was the French bastard—
leap toward the indigo night sky.

Chapter Twenty-Eight

Gideon didn't think twice before he did the same. His forward momentum took him straight up toward the skyline where he almost hit a descending Miles.

"Where'd he go?" Miles looked like Gideon felt. Ready to kill.

"Straight up is all I saw. The jerk-face had the gall to be in my backyard." Gideon saw blood as he realized how easy it was for the vampire to come and go as he pleased.

"Let's do a fly by over Zacke's. I don't trust that slimy French frog." Miles took off and Gideon followed him. They kept their conversation to a minimum as they flew side by side, their gazes searching the surrounding area above and below.

They reached the Kensington's home and landed near the porch. Gideon concentrated, as did Miles, but did not hear anything but the sounds of children laughing and women talking as they cooked dinner. Zacke was in his study and all seemed right. Yet, he didn't get a sense of Hawk.

He turned to Miles to ask if he'd heard from him and at that moment, Marcel appeared across the street. Before Gideon or Miles could reach him, he launched himself skyward once more. His laughter rode a chill down to the small of Gideon's back.

Marcel's taunting chuckle sent Gideon skyward in a blast of red-hot fury. He forgot about being a detective, all he saw was crimson and in the center was the object of his hatred. The vampire had destroyed his wife's peace, been the cause of her death at the hands of Gabriella, and now threatened her again. He would pay and it would not be pretty.

Gideon sensed Miles coming up behind him. *"Bro, you need to go back and make sure Marcel doesn't double back."*

"No, I'm sticking with you. It's going to take our combined strength to bring Charmant down. He has the speed of several vampires, and I'm thinking he's fed on more than bagged blood." Miles sounded worried and disgusted. Gideon knew he used to do the same but never hurt a woman when he fed. And after he met Hope, the woman he saved when she was just a child, he'd stopped feeding from the hoof.

"Fine by me, but Marcel's mine." Gideon wasn't in the mood to argue and was grateful when Miles only grunted.

The clouds overhead darkened as he followed the trail of particle dust Marcel left. The night air hung pregnant with rain, and he hoped it held off until daybreak. He wasn't sure he could fly in possible torrents of water. And he wasn't sure why the creature was leaving them a trail to follow. It didn't sit right with Gideon. Why lead them away from the city—from Kat?

Gideon stopped so quickly Miles slammed into him. They both grappled for their balance before hanging motionless in the air.

"What the hell are you doing, Gideon?" Miles looked confused as well as incensed.

"It's a trick. Think about it, why would Marcel lead us away from Kat in the first place? It makes no sense." Gideon couldn't believe he hadn't seen Marcel's ploy sooner.

"Ah, hell, the women—" Miles eyes rolled back in their sockets, and he plummeted toward the ground far below.

Gideon reached out to stop his fall and wham! Something smacked him in the back of his head.

Stars exploded in front of his eyes, and his vision blurred. He dropped like a rock, gravitation pulling him toward the hard packed earth.

The impact rattled his brain as well as his entire body. He tried to shake it off, to climb to his feet. Miles' body was a crumpled heap, and he couldn't tell how badly his friend was injured. Gideon's knees barely held him as he tried to stand. He heard the not at all amusing sound of Marcel's laughter, before he felt the sickening reverberation of something hard against his temple. His last thought before lights out was how could the vampire be invisible?

****

Kat helped with the after dinner chores and wished she could sneak out to see her husband. She hadn't heard a word, not even a mind thought, since he'd left earlier. Not exactly sure how close they had to be for a soulmate to talk on that more intimate line, she'd finally decided it was the distance keeping her from touching his mind or her hearing him.

"Okay, it's time for bed. Brier, Braden, Sammie, come on. We're going to make a big bed in the living room." Miranda produced a lackluster smile as she tried to herd the kids into the area Kat & Hope had straightened up earlier.

"Can we make a tent out of sheets and sleep under it?" This came from Braden, but before Miranda could answer him, his sister started to cry.

"What is it, Brier? Don't you want to play camp out?" Miranda dropped to her knees and rubbed the little girl's back.

"I want my bear, the one Uncle Miles gave me." The blue-eyed mixture of both her parents rubbed at the tears running down her face.

Kat watched in awe as a patient Miranda shushed Brier's twin when he poked fun at her by laughing, and in the same motion pulled the little girl into her embrace. "Okay, Brierkins where did

261

you leave him?"

"Outside. Can I go get Mr. Bear?"

Miranda looked at Kat before responding. "No baby, Mr. Bear will be fine. I'll get him for you in the morning." Kat hated her own problems were causing chaos. She felt like crying right along with Brier.

"Now come on, scoot, we'll play for a bit and then have a story.

Hope called from the doorway. "I'll be in soon to get Sammie settled. I'm going to start a load of wash. She goes through clothes like I go through chocolate." Her comment brought laughter and a needed release of tension for the moment.

The phone rang, Miranda picked it up, and mouthed to Kat it was for Zacke. She then pointed toward the study and made the universal sign for walking with her fingers. Kat nodded her head and then pointed toward the stairs. "I'll be right back."

She wanted to try and contact Gideon again. She could call his cell but it would be more effective the other way. Cell service, she'd been told, could be spotty in areas outside of Savannah. Although, the little girl's tears had miraculously disappeared as soon a Miranda left the room, the upper floor would be quieter. Kat teleported to the upstairs landing, closed her eyes, and concentrated. Nothing. She tried again. She couldn't' pick up anything from Gideon.

As she debated whether to try again, she heard a soft snick like a door closing. A split second later a child's shrill cry assaulted the night, only to be cut off immediately. Before she could teleport downstairs she heard the door crash backward and the sound of something hitting the floor.

Marcel! He was here.

Instead of teleporting, unclear as to where he might be, Kat tiptoed down the steps, through the deserted living room, past the now open study door, and into the kitchen. Stunned she stopped in her tracks.

Hope lay on the kitchen floor blood seeping from a large gash near her temple. Miranda stood motionless, her face white as the curtains hanging in the window. Zacke stood right behind her, his hands fisted together, but she could smell his fear and rage.

And Marcel stood at the back door with a knife under Brier's chin. The other children were standing near him, whether they had been coaxed or coerced, she didn't know. What she did know was it had to stop now.

"Marcel, let the little one go. She's done you no harm." Kat tried to keep her tone reasonable, all the while sending out a mental SOS to Gideon.

"Katheryne, you have put me to a lot of trouble. I don't like that, and just so you know, your husband and the other vampire won't be coming to help."

At her startled cry and lunge forward, he tightened his grip on Brier.

"Steady Kat, please." She stopped immediately upon hearing Zacke's voice. He was right, she did not need to antagonize Marcel, and that would be all she ended up doing. He was stronger then any of any of them. Look at what he'd done to Hope, Miles, and Gideon...her heart bled at the thought he might be dead.

"Never fear my dear. I didn't kill him." Marcel actually smiled. Before she could rationalize his complacent mood, he spoke again. "I want him alive to see that you belong to me."

The shudder that wracked her body was involuntary. She tried to still her thoughts. Marcel did not need a reminder of how much his touch repulsed her. She needed to diffuse the situation and get Brier out of his grip.

"Thank you for not killing him. Now, please let

go of Brier and I'll come with you." She heard
Miranda's quick intake of breath and then Zacke
spoke. "No, Kat, you…" His words trailed off. She
knew he was horrified and felt as helpless as she
did, but bottom line, the children's lives as well as
his, Miranda's and Hope's were all at stake.

"You think to soften me up by being compliant.
Well, that won't work. I know you detest me, but
that will change." Marcel smiled, showing off slightly
yellow fangs.

"Yes, it will, but if you harm that child, I will
never ever come to you willingly. You will have to
beat and rape me to get me to do what you want."
Katheryne growled and allowed him to see her own
fangs.

"Having you fight me could be amusing, but very
well. I won't harm the child, but maybe I'll take her
with us." His leer sent shivers down Kat's spine.
Before she could say anything, Miranda lunged for
Marcel. A blur of movement so quick she could
barely see it, and Miranda crumpled at the
vampire's feet. Her hands clutching her stomach as
she tried to hold her insides together.

Marcel laughed and held the blood covered knife
up like a prized trophy. Zacke's face turned white,
his features frozen with horror, and then he went for
the hand holding the knife.

The vampire let go of Brier, and Kat grabbed
her and the other two children and pushed them
toward the den. "Hide." She whispered and then
turned back to see Zacke in deadly mortal combat
with the vampire. At first it looked like his shock
induced adrenaline was giving him an edge, but then
Marcel twisted the knife until it was pressed against
his chest.

Kat didn't see when he rammed the blade home,
but she saw Zacke's body stiffen, his head slump
forward, and then heard the horrendous noise his

body made when it slammed to the floor.

"You lied, you said you wouldn't hurt anyone if I went with you." She screamed her accusation.

"No. I said I wouldn't hurt the child, and I didn't. Now come with me before I change my mind." Marcel held his hand out, and Katheryne stepped back. She knew her eyes were wide with horror, the shock of the past few minutes. The senseless deaths of her friends.

She stepped closer to Zacke and Miranda's bodies and knelt down. She brushed at the blood red tears falling on the floor. Then she noticed a slight rise in Zacke's chest. She looked at Miranda and realized although her eyes were now closed, she still breathed also. A miracle with all the blood she'd lost, but that wouldn't last long if she didn't get help.

"Fine, but let me call someone." She pleaded.

Marcel shook his head, and again held out his hand.

"Please, Marcel, there are children here." Katheryne prayed he would listen.

"And they will have someone as soon as this vampire," he pointed to Hope's unconscious form, "wakes up. Not to mention, I'm sure your husband and his friend will show up sooner or later." He sneered and Katheryne wanted to rip it off his face. However the word friend made her think also of Hawk. Where was he? Why hadn't he arrived?

A rough and cruel hand grasped her hair, jerked her to her feet, and tilted her head back. Marcel's fangs were now very close to her throat. She stilled her face not to show her fear, and blocked her thoughts so he would not sense her horror, but when he bit down, crushing the skin, his incisors locking on and holding her captive, she involuntary screamed the one name she shouldn't. "Gideon!"

Chapter Twenty-Nine

Kat's scream echoed in his subconscious and jarred Gideon back to his senses. He looked around—she wasn't there! He shook his head, a mistake, for the ground he lay on blurred in a dizzying haze. Gideon counted to ten and tried to breathe in slowly and deeply. The scene in front of him kaleidoscoped into a clear image and the memory of what had happened.

Miles lay still, but if he concentrated hard enough he could hear a heartbeat. Thank God, Marcel had not taken either one of their heads. And since he hadn't there was a reason, and it had to be Kat. Her frantic cry pinged his still rattled brain. She was in trouble and that meant the vampire had breached the safe guards of Zacke's home.

Gideon crawled to where Miles lay and gingerly shook his friend. The movement hurt his aching head and caused Miles to groan before rearing up in a fighting stance—fangs and claws evident.

"Whoa bro. Save those for Marcel. Come on, we've got to get to Zacke's. Something's wrong." He slowly got to his knees, and then stood. Gideon stretched his hand down to help Miles, but his friend waved it off.

"I can't reach Hope. She's not answering my mind thoughts." Miles sounded anguished and had every right to be. If Hope wasn't answering, his child could be in trouble also. Not to mention Zacke and his family. Gideon closed his eyes and tried to connect with Kat. A blank wall greeted his attempt.

"Kat's not answering either. I thought I heard

her scream my name, but now I'm not sure." Gideon checked his watch. It had only been around seven or so when they started chasing Marcel. Now it was a little after eight. Too much time had passed.

Miles shook his head. "I don't think I can fly, we'll have to teleport. Can you do it after being hit?"

"How'd you know that, you were out when I came tumbling out of the sky?"

"You've got blood running down your face, which means whatever Marcel hit you with did a number on your healing powers." Miles looked concerned, but then his eyes turned back toward the city lights in the distance.

"I can teleport. Let's go." Gideon closed his eyes and willed the process to take effect. The usual dizziness intensified, probably from the blows to his head. When he felt his body reassemble itself, he stood at Zacke's kitchen entrance.

The door stood wide open, and the scene he faced turned every molecular atom in his body to ice cubes. Hope was on her knees, a haphazardly tied bandage around her forehead, her hands covered in Miranda's blood.

Miles dropped to the floor by her side. "What happened?"

At first, he wasn't sure if Hope heard her husband, but as Gideon knelt by Zacke's body, she responded. "I'm not sure. Marcel just walked in the back door with Brier. He had a knife at her throat and when I tried to jump him, he knocked me out."

Gideon stared at the wound in Zacke's chest. He checked for a pulse and breathed a sigh of relief when he found one. He caught the towel Hope tossed him and stuffed it between Zacke's shirt and skin. His heart wept at the sight of his partner's lifeblood staining the material.

Hope pressed another towel from the pile next to her to Miranda's wounds. "When I woke up I found them like this. All the children," she looked at her husband, "including Sammie are safe, but scared shitless."

"What about Kat?" Gideon dreaded the answer she would give.

"I'm sorry, Gideon, I don't know. Brier kept saying it was all her fault but I didn't see Kat." Hope's attempt to staunch Miranda's blood flow wasn't working.

"Gideon..." Zacke's whisper was low, and as he watched Zacke opened his eyes, and tried to sit up. His gaze ravaged by pain and despair.

"Zacke save your strength." Gideon's hand trembled as he gently put a hand out to press him back down. Zacke allowed it, and then spoke again.

"Kat tried to save all of us. She promised to go with Marcel if he didn't hurt Brier. But that promise didn't include me or Miranda." Zacke coughed, caught his breath, and Gideon flinched at the blood dotting his lips.

"Hang on buddy, we'll get you to the hospital." He couldn't fathom what Zacke told him. His wife at the hands of that merciless killer. He wanted to go after her but Marcel had shown unless he wanted to be found, they'd be pissing in the dark in their search for him. Right now, he needed to try to help his friends.

"Don't worry about me, Miranda needs help. He gutted her like a fish, Gideon." Zacke's features distorted; his gaze held a horror Gideon did not want to contemplate.

He looked over at Hope who shook her head. Tears rolled down her face as she kept her blood-covered hands against Miranda's belly.

"How's she doing, Gideon?" Zacke's question caused another fit of coughing and when his body was still once more, he lay ashen.

"Partner, I've never lied to you, and I ain't gonna

start now." He caught Zacke's trembling hand in his. "Miranda's dying. There's nothing Hope can do, and you know she learned from the best." He didn't have to say the best was Miranda.

A chorus of crying came from the doorway to the den. Gideon looked up. God above—the children.

Zacke clutched his arm, a grip surprisingly strong despite his grievous injury. "Don't let them see anymore than they already have."

Miles stood up, stumbled to the children, and grabbed Sammie in a quick hug, before doing the same to Brier and Braden.

"You have to turn Miranda. It's the only way. I know I'm dying. The twins need their mother. Promise me you'll do it, Gideon." Zacke's eyes glistened with tears. Gideon knew he was hurting physically and it cut to the essence of his soul, but how could they change her?

"Zacke, Hope's injured, and Marcel did a number on me and Miles. I'm not sure we can pull a change off." Gideon looked at Hope who looked as horrified as he felt.

"Hawk can do it." Zacke's eyes closed for a moment, and Gideon checked to make sure he was still breathing. Yes, Hawk could help, but dammit, Hawk wasn't here. He should have been, and then just maybe none of this would have happened. Kat would be safe, and Zacke and Miranda wouldn't be dying in front of his eyes. And then it hit him, even if they failed, they had to try.

"Okay, bro, we'll take care of it." Gideon patted his partner's shoulder in a helpless gesture.

"Take care of what?" Miles asked. He knelt down by Gideon this time.

"Zacke wants us to change Miranda." His gaze locked with Miles'. "It's the only way she has any chance of surviving."

Miles in turn looked at Hope who nodded her

head. "Zacke, you know it might not work. Her wound is worse than yours, let us try to change you first." Miles' statement was a plea.

The loss of Zacke after centuries of being his friend would devastate Miles, and Gideon couldn't contemplate having anyone else as a partner, brother, friend. No one could take Zacke's place. Yet, he loved Miranda also.

"No, if you change me first, there won't be enough time to save her. You will need to drain almost all my blood. It will take too long. I need you to do this, Gideon—our blood—what's not pouring out on the floor—will strengthen you also. Then you will have to give us blood. If there's not enough in the house, then contact Mac at the hospital, Miranda's aide, he'll know what to do."

Gideon's horror at the prospect must have shown.

"I know, my friend, but you have to go after Marcel. Kat sacrificed herself for my child. And another thing, if Miranda and I don't make it, I want you to raise the twins." Zacke coughed up more blood and then closed his eyes.

God above, how was he supposed to raise kids when he might not even have a wife? "Zacke, I may not be able to save Kat." The thought caused his heart to spasm. He couldn't think about not having her by his side, and he definitely couldn't contemplate centuries of being alone not after he'd found his soulmate.

"You will. I have confidence in you, my friend. And if worse comes to worse, you will have Miles and Hope to help." Zacke looked at the other two vampires. "You need to start now. No more delays."

Miles looked at Gideon. "It would go easier if there were three of us to do the change. Hope will have to keep Zacke alive until we've transformed Miranda. Where is Hawk?"

The blood scented air in the kitchen stirred. Gideon prayed it wasn't Marcel. Although he wanted his ass dead, no way could they fight him and change Zacke and Miranda before it was too late.

Hawk materialized in the room. "I'm here." His face was flushed, as his amber eyes took in the bloodstained kitchen and the man and woman dying in front of them.

"Where the hell have you been?" Gideon didn't realize he'd moved until Miles grabbed his fist before it connected with Hawk's jaw.

"I...I..." Hawk's voice trailed off.

"It doesn't matter where he's been, Gideon. We can't change what's happened, and time's wasting. We need to start the change now." Miles tugged Gideon over to Miranda. "You drink first, you'd going to need all the blood you can get to stop Marcel."

Gideon actually felt his eyes roll back in his head. He couldn't drink Miranda's blood. The thought was horrific.

"Yes, you can. You drank from all of us when Marcel shot you. Now start. We have to save Miranda and then Zacke."

He squatted by a woman who was like his sister. He looked at Hope who nodded and then he pulled Miranda into his arms. He might not like what he was doing, but he loved her enough he would do it as tenderly and respectably as possible. He waited for his incisors to drop and when they didn't he leaned down and sniffed her blood soaked clothing. Yes! Now, how to start.

"Take her hand in yours and suckle from her wrist." Hope's quiet words focused him on the task, and he did as she suggested. The blood tasted sweet just like Miranda's personality. He also detected a bit of chocolate. A woman after his own heart. As the blood filled his mouth, and then worked it's way throughout his body, he felt a resurrection of strength. He looked around the room. Hope sat next to Zacke, holding his hand and whispering so softly even Gideon couldn't hear her.

Finally when he couldn't drink another drop, he waved Miles over. The other vampire sat next to Gideon and took Miranda from him. Gideon wiped his lips with the back of his sleeve and finally looked at Hawk.

The man or vampire he'd also called brother, over the last half decade or so, looked like he'd been to hell and back. As much as he wanted to kill him for not being here earlier to stop the carnage and to keep Marcel from stealing Kat, he just didn't have the emotional or physical strength to light into him.

He moved over to Zacke. Hawk also moved closer to their brother in arms before speaking, "I know I don't deserve an answer but I'd like to know what happened."

"Marcel's what happened. Somehow he got his hands on Brier and used her as a shield and a threat to get Kat to go with him. He slaughtered Zacke and Miranda but why I don't know." Gideon took a deep breath and then sighed. "You're not the only one who should have been here. Marcel lured us out of the city and before we could turn back, he attacked—knocked us both right out of the sky. I swear he was invisible. I never saw him."

"It's possible. There are some aged vampires that can make themselves disappear and still be able to act physically. Not like when we're in vapor form." Hawk shook his head. "Do you think either one of them will make it?"

"Truth? I don't know. Marcel knocked Hope out also, so we're not even sure how long Zacke and Miranda lay here bleeding before Hope woke up and we arrived. I know when we tagged his ass across the street from here it was only about 7:00 or so. When we came to in the woods, over an hour had passed."

"Gideon?" Zacke's whisper was so threadbare he had to lean down to hear his next words. "How is she?"

"She's still alive for the moment." He looked at Miles who now raised grief-stricken eyes. His skin a rosier hue than before, his lips stained red. "It's done. Time to give her our blood."

Zacke clutched Gideon's arms, his fingers pale and almost shriveled with the blood lost. "Take some of mine. If I die, I want her to have a part of me with her...please."

Gideon didn't waste time arguing. He took the syringe Hope fished out of Miranda's medical bag, inserted it into Zacke's arm, and pulled back the plunger. The blood flow was slow—Zacke had lost too much blood.

"I've got it, partner." He removed the needle, handed the plunger to Miles, who promptly shot it straight into Miranda's heart.

"Okay, now we're going to bring her back. You rest Zacke, and don't you die, dammit." Gideon's voice trembled, but he wasn't ashamed. This man had saved his ass over the years, and the very real chance Zacke would not be alive when Miranda's change was complete, haunted him.

Miles opened a gash in his arm and began to dribble it into Miranda's corpselike body. When she immediately began to drink, Gideon was shocked as were the others. She took to the blood like it was one of her diet colas. Faster, she imbibed until Miles pulled his arm away.

"Your next, Gideon." Miles motioned Gideon over, and they watched amazed as Miranda took up where she'd left off. Hawk gave his blood next and against all their arguments, Hope did the same. After she was finished, she swayed a bit, but managed to get to her feet. "I'm going to try to get the children to sleep." She left leaving an expanse of silence except for the faint rattle in Zacke's lungs.

Time blurred after that for Gideon, and they went through the same sequence of actions for Zacke. The minutes ticked by. Zacke's inhalations were so scant; Gideon feared they'd already lost him.

Both he and Miles tried to get Zacke to drink from their wrists, but his partner wouldn't or couldn't. At this stage of the game, it didn't matter either way. They had to get the blood into Zacke or he would die.

God he felt so useless. His wife was in the hands of a killer. His best friend might not make it, and he sat here like a snake in a bog. *Think Gideon, think.* What could they do to get him to drink?

When the idea hit him, he couldn't believe how simple the answer was but it would take all of them to help Zacke survive.

Hope walked back into the kitchen. Her face a testimony of the children's anxiety and fear.

"Hope, how many syringes do you have?" He knew he sounded like he'd lost his mind, but he didn't care. His plan had to work.

Chapter Thirty

Katheryne kept her eyes closed. It was past dawn. Over twelve hours since Marcel had attacked her friends and locked her in this cage. The silver-coated bars burned when she brushed against them, so she'd curled up in a tight ball facing the bed Marcel slept on. She didn't want to turn her back on the vampire.

After they'd arrived at this place, he'd pushed her inside and left her alone. To say she was surprised didn't describe her reaction, although she'd done her best to keep it from Marcel. He'd leered at her a bit, postured like he was God's gift to womankind, and then disappeared.

Some women, and she knew there had been many females in Marcel's several lifetimes, would think him handsome. When she'd known him centuries before, she'd made every effort to never to look at his face. Gabriella would have taken that as a sign of interest. When he'd accosted her outside the shop and then during his attack at Miranda's she'd barely paid any attention to his face. However she had not been able to avoid looking at his features since he'd kidnapped her.

How she wished she could scar the lightly tanned skin, poke out the silver eyes, break the Greek god nose, and rip off his lips.

After that, she'd chop off his legs so he wouldn't be so tall, tear out the hair on his broad chest, break all his fangs, and then castrate him like a gelding.

And she would if she got the chance. Katheryne planned to fight him until her last dying breath. No way would she make it easy on him to rape her body, and hell would freeze before she allowed him to kill Gideon.

Gideon! Oh how she needed to know if he was okay. While Marcel had been out she'd tried to connect to her husband again, but she couldn't and then Marcel had returned. She'd kept her mind on clothes, books, and trivial matters. Katheryne didn't want him picking up on any thoughts of the man she loved and the friends she called family.

Although there were no windows in her prison, she could feel the sun's journey across the sky. It was almost midday. Gideon would probably be asleep. She prayed he was for that would mean he was alive.

****

Katheryne woke when she heard the rattle of a lock. She forced lids heavy with sleeplessness to open. Marcel stood at the door of the cell.

His gloved hands worked a key into its counterpart. A second later, she heard a click. She sat up and scooted as far to the rear of her cage as she could without touching the bars.

"Well my dear, I'd hope a good day's sleep would put you in a better frame of mind. That you would welcome me with a smile, that your lips would speak the words that you have changed your mind about being here. I see I expected too much." Marcel tossed the lock aside, and tugged open the door.

Katheryne could not move back any more. If she did the bars would burn her back, leave her with painful wounds even if they did not scar. She tried to avoid the hand grabbing at the front of her sweater, but his grip was tight, cruel as he wrenched her forward. Marcel dragged her over the threshold of the cage, her knees barely protected by the denim jeans she wore.

Once free of the silver she gripped his hands

trying to get him to release her. His chuckle only made her more fearful. Marcel could torture, kill her, bring her back to the undead, and torture her again. In between, he would take great pleasure in raping her until she begged for mercy. Somehow she had to stop him.

"You can't, ma petite. I am much stronger than you are, and rape is just a word. You will enjoy what I do to your body."

Katheryne was appalled she'd allowed him to read her thoughts. She shut her mind down completely and glared at Marcel.

"Your anger wounds me, but fear not, I will survive. Too bad, you might not." He pushed away her grappling hands and then with a flick of his wrist a surge of power hit her in the chest. The blow sent her slamming into a metal locker.

Stunned Katheryne shook her head. Before she could run toward the only door in the room, Marcel was on her. His hands, now minus the gloves but tipped with claws, ripped at her flesh. She bit back a shriek of pain as he punctured the skin above her sweater's scooped neck.

She fought to free herself, but his hold tightened.

"There is no use fighting me. You cannot possibly escape." He released her so abruptly she fell backward. Her butt hit the floor and her elbow plowed into the cabinet.

"However, I've decided I would rather punish you in front of your husband." Marcel's fanged smile so malicious and evil, sent shudders down her spine.

"And just for fun, I think I'll take his head and mount it over the bed so you can see it every time I take you.

His words stoked a fire of fear so strongly in Katheryne that she flung herself at Marcel. His first blow stung her face, the second opened a cut in her cheek, and the third threw her into a world of darkness.

****

Gideon's body came to life just as the sun dove toward the horizon. He stretched, wondered why he was so stiff, and then he remembered. He covered the distance between the downstairs sofa and the master bedroom in two seconds flat.

He started to open Zacke and Miranda's door to see if they had awakened from the transformation but stopped when he heard Hawk speaking.

"Zacke, I'm so sorry man. It's my fault. I should have been here with you not trying to satisfy my own gratification." Hawk's words were low and filled with pain.

Gideon eased the door open just enough so he could see Hawk sitting by Zacke's side of the bed. Zacke lay still, the effects of the change had ravaged his body, and they were still worried he might not survive. Miranda's well being, even though she'd accepted their blood like a trooper, was also still up for grabs. She'd awakened once running a fever and doubled over in a fetal position. He assumed from the cramps of the change. After they eased, she'd sipped from a bag of blood before resting again. For several hours, those same events occurred over and over until Miranda had fallen into a somewhat relaxed slumber.

So focused on Zacke, he almost missed Hawk's next words.

"You see, I'm jealous of what you have with Miranda, what Miles has with Hope, and now Gideon with Kat. I felt left out. I know that's a lame reason to feed off the hoof and then take the woman to bed, but I didn't mean to oversleep." Hawk reached out toward the man lying so motionless. "I didn't even realize I felt that way until recently, and it's become harder and harder to be a part of a group of soulmates when I'm by myself."

As Gideon watched, he spotted the blood red tears coursing down Hawk's face spotting the white linen covering Zack's body.

Should he say something or just leave?

He turned to go but heard Zacke's weak voice. "You didn't purposely cause the events that happened. Forgive yourself, Hawk. It will make life easier than living with regrets."

"Zacke! We weren't sure..." Hawk's tone was a match to Gideon's feelings. Astonishment that their friend had awakened.

"That I would survive? Well, I wasn't sure if I would either." Zacke's reply was whispered.

Gideon moved into the room, nodded to Hawk, and approached the bed. "Man, you had us going. Glad to see you're back amongst the living!"

"Me too, partner. How's Miranda?" Zacke looked fearful.

"She's fine, bro. Took to taking blood like a snake on a rat, although she did have a bit of a hard time with the change. She's sleeping right next to you."

Zacke turned and faced his wife whose timely opening of her eyes caused his partner to smile. "My love, I thought I'd lost you forever."

Gideon looked away from the light caress husband and wife gave one another, lifted his thumb toward the doorway, and followed Hawk out into the hall.

"Gideon..."

"It's okay, Hawk. I heard what you told Zacke. What's done is done. At least Zacke and Miranda will be all right. As for Kat..." Tears blurred his vision. What if he couldn't find her?

"I'll do anything I can to help get her back, I promise." Hawk laid a hand on his shoulder, and Gideon nodded.

"At the moment I can only hope Marcel will contact me. Otherwise, I have no idea where to even start looking."

Gideon started down the hallway and then made his way downstairs to the kitchen. He felt Hawk on his heels. He pulled a bag of nourishment from the fridge. "You want one."

"No, I fed a while ago." Hawk met Gideon's gaze.

"Good. We're all going to need our strength if and when Marcel gets in touch." He took a cup from the cabinet, split the bag open and poured some of the liquid into the container, before lifting it to his lips. He repeated this again and then again until the bag was empty. He could have just slapped it to his fangs, but he needed the structure of focusing on not spilling a drop to keep from yelling.

Once finished, he tossed the bag in the trash. A second later, Miles and Hope entered the kitchen. "Hey we looked in on Zacke and Miranda. They're doing good."

"Yeah, Hawk and I were just up there. So how did ya'll sleep?" Gideon knew Hope had spent the day in the twins' room sharing a sleeping bag with Braden, Zacke's son, her daughter bunking with Brier.

"Not bad. Brier had a couple of nightmares, but Sammie and Braden slept the day through. Considering their sleeping schedule is off, I'm glad they did." Hope and Miles both took the bags Hawk offered and drank their breakfast standing up.

Once finished, Hope looked at the men. "We need to get something started for the kids and get them back on some type of schedule, but with Miranda and Zacke now having to sleep through the day, I'm assuming that will be the norm, I'm not sure how to do it."

"We'll figure it out as we go. Let's fix some food, get the kids up, bathed, and dressed, and go from there." Miles locked his arms around his wife's waist. "It'll all work out." He kissed the top of her head before looking at Gideon. "So where do we start in getting Kat back."

"Yeah, I want a piece of Marcel myself. My head still hurts where he hit me, not to mention scaring those kids almost to death." Hope's fangs were bared, and Gideon bit his lips to keep from misting up like a girl. His friends were one of a kind. Willing to risk all to help, but he couldn't let them do it. The past night's events had shown just how precious life was, and he would not take a chance on something like that happening again. The children had to be taken care of no matter what.

"*We* don't, I do." At their open-mouthed protests Gideon continued. "Look, I love you all. I mean that, but you have obligations. Last night proved none of us is infallible. The children have to have security. And that can't happen if you all are out fighting with me. I will handle this alone."

"Then you're going to need this." Zacke and Miranda's arrival had gone unnoticed by him and by the looks of it the rest of the crew in the room.

"Here." Zacke handed Gideon a sword over four feet long.

"Zacke?" Gideon took the hilt and swore as he almost dropped it.

"Careful, the blade's silver. It'll burn like hell fire if you touch it." Zacke grinned as he kept his arm around Miranda.

"So anyone want to fill us in on what happened after we went nitey night?" Their host escorted his wife to the table and then caught the blood Miles tossed their way.

"Nothing to tell, once you two went down for the count." Gideon took notice of how Miranda's face was still a bit pale as was Zacke's. The blood they were consuming should help. Yet, he couldn't help but wonder how they would mentally endure the events of the last twenty-four hours.

Zacke took Miranda's empty bag as well as his own and handed them off to Hope. "Nothing from Marcel?"

"No." Gideon replied.

"I'm sorry, Gideon. I feel—"

"Don't you dare say responsible, Zacke." Gideon interrupted his partner. "No one could have known Marcel would strike the way he did. Kat did only what she could do. She's..."

"Fantastic, beautiful, worthy of being your soulmate?" Hawk spoke up.

"Yeah, that and more. I just wish Marcel would contact me." Gideon looked at the faces of all the family he had left in the world except for Kat. "I..."

"We know what you mean. It's hard when it's your wife in danger." Miles nuzzled Hope's neck.

"Hey, we feel the same way about our husbands." For the first time Miranda spoke. "It's not easy knowing as mortals or vampires you are out there, subject to some maniac serial killer or a vampire with revenge on his agenda."

"Miranda's right. We worry too. So, sometimes it would be better if you all stopped treating us like china dolls and realize we can help too." Hope moved away from her husband's arms. "Gideon, Kat is a strong woman. I didn't see what she did last night, but it took courage."

"More than courage, Hope." Miranda looked at Gideon. "She stood toe to toe with Marcel and fought for Brier's life—offering herself in exchange. She tried to get us help after he stabbed me and Zacke. You have to get her back and you have to let us help in someway."

Miranda patted Zacke's hand when he caressed her face. Gideon looked at the woman who'd taken him into her home over the years, listened to him whine, and then helped the woman he loved. "Are you okay, Miranda? I know you never would have wished for this change."

For a moment, her blue gaze dimmed. "You're right, it's not something I would have willingly embraced just to do it, but my kids come first. I'm glad I can see them grow up, and now with my being a vampire, I have more control on protecting them, and my husband." She shot Zacke a grin.

"Woman, you've got that backward. No matter that you have your own fangs, it's still my place..." He trailed off when she placed a hand over his mouth.

"No, you've got it wrong. I've waited night after night when you were out on the job for a phone call telling me you were injured or dead. Now, I won't worry quite as much, but I still reserve the right to do all I can to protect my family." Miranda exchanged looks with Hope.

"She's right. For too long, you guys put us into the background. To be protected, and I think it's time you realized we are not just soulmates but helpmates." Hope turned to her husband. "I love you, Miles, but your archaic thinking makes me crazy."

"Hmph, why didn't you say anything?" Miles queried.

"Oh please, would you have listened if what happened last night hadn't happened?" Hope shot back.

"Probably not. I'm a bit of an ancient throwback, I guess." Miles' ears turned a bit pink.

"Ya think?" Hope and Miranda both laughed at their husbands' pained expressions, and Gideon was glad he wasn't in the line of fire.

"Okay, let's get started. Children first, then we'll talk about what to do about Kat." Miranda stood up and moved to the door.

"I'll start breakfast after I wake up the kids. I

want Brier and Braden as well as Sammie to see we're okay." Miranda looked at Zacke. "You coming?"

He grinned before answering, "Whatever you want, my love."

An hour later after all the chaos died down, Gideon teleported back to his house to shower and change clothes. He needed the time to think. Dark thoughts of a beaten, raped, and mutilated Kat crowded his mind. He wanted to shred anyone in sight, physically and verbally, and that couldn't happen. His friends meant well, and had every right to be celebrating the renewal of life for Zacke and Miranda. He was overjoyed also but he couldn't help but wonder how he would live without his soulmate if he couldn't get her back.

And if Marcel had tortured her, he would spend the rest of his lifetime helping her recover. Nothing and no one, not his job, his friends, and especially not his own life were more important than Kat.

He exited the bathroom and came to a stunned stop. An envelope that had not been there five minutes earlier lay in the center of the bed Kat had made before all this started.

His hands trembled as he picked it up, slid a finger under the sealed top, and pulled out a single sheet of paper.

Your wife misses you. Why not join us. I might even give you a chance to kiss her sweet-tasting lips before I kill you. I will expect you within the next hour and if you're not here, I will start the party without you.

Gideon noted the address, which was outside the city limits. Probably where Marcel had been holed up all along. A white-hot rage shook him, his fangs descended, and his nail tips became claws. He didn't care how old the vampire was, when the lights went down, and the last song was played, Kat would be coming home with him.

Chapter Thirty-One

Gideon arrived at the rendezvous only a minute before the hour curfew. He didn't want Marcel to sniff out his presence until the last moment. He'd come without any backup, a decision that had cost him time while he dealt with his friends' concern. All of whom were not happy.

Zacke had been the first one to cave, and he'd told Gideon about the sword he planned to use to cut off Marcel's head. It'd belonged to Zacke's ancestor, and was called "Death Giver." A name Gideon especially liked! It had also been Zacke's weapon of choice when fighting for King James. The rest of the group had helped him get his supplies together. A can of hairspray, a grill lighter, some twine, and dynamite. Lord, he hoped he got a chance to use all of them.

He carried the weapons, except for the sword that was holstered around his waist, in a leather pouch Zacke said he'd used centuries before on the battlefield.

Now time to face Marcel and rescue his heart.

Gideon opened the door of the old deserted mansion and followed Marcel's directions to the basement. He kept a sharp eye out for the vampire. He wouldn't put it past the other to jump him at any time.

Once he descended the many steps leading to the bowels of the house, he stopped before crossing into the wider expanse of the basement. His gaze sought and found Kat. Her face was puffy, and several cuts oozed blood. There was also a laceration on her throat. Dammit, Charmant had bitten Kat. She should have healed, but if he was right, the cage the sonofabitch had her locked in was made of silver. She lay in the middle of her prison, but as he watched, she stirred and looked his way. He winked at her before finding Marcel who stood on the other side of the room.

The vampire was a big SOB. Larger than Gideon remembered from the brief glimpses he'd gotten of the man. Eyes burning enough red fire that the black irises were almost obscured. A hank of wheat-colored hair was tied back in a ribbon, of all things, and the man was dressed in old-clothes that Gideon wouldn't wear for Halloween. The ring sparkling on Marcel's hand branded him their killer.

He would have a fight on his hands by the looks of the man's arms and upper body, not to mention his vampiric skills, but fight he would and he planned to win.

"Charmant, we have some unfinished business." Gideon's voice cut through the silent room.

"Yes we do, detective. Katheryne was meant to be mine centuries ago. Even she does not know her father promised her to me at birth. Alas, he changed his mind when he realized I was a vampire." Marcel looked toward Kat.

"A pity really that he and your mother had to die so young. I was hoping for more cooperation from your uncle. However, he felt you should be older, and I left for a few years to come back and find you were gone. I wasn't pleased at all, Katheryne."

Kat sat up in the cage, and glared at Marcel. "You killed my parents, didn't you? They never died in an accident."

"Oh but it was an accident. A deliciously contrived act." Charmant preened. "And now I have their daughter. What I wanted all along, except you married this piece of offensive backwoods offal."

"Oh please, Gideon's little finger is worth more than ten lifetimes of yours, Marcel. He is a good man." Kat's tone was an icy inflection, and considering the circumstances, Gideon was so proud of her he wanted to preen himself, but not yet.

"It doesn't matter what happened years ago, Charmant. Kat is mine. Now, did you bring me all this way to yack or to fight?" Gideon knew his words hit home when the vampire snarled and his eyes went solid red. Good, he wanted him mad. Then he would make mistakes. The first one in believing Gideon was only a dumb hick, newly turned vampire, who didn't know his ass from a hole in the ground. Too many times he'd been labeled a redneck and whereas the slurs no longer hurt, they had enabled him to become stronger over the years. Able to hold his temper when it counted. And tonight counted big time.

"There will be no fight. I will slaughter you without a thought." Marcel bit out the words and moved so quickly, Gideon barely jumped out of the way in time.

As the vampire hit the wall in his rage, Gideon pulled out the lighter and hairspray. The vampire turned and snarled, his fangs red—a reminder he'd taken some of his precious Kat's blood. A fact that almost made him lose control.

Gideon stood his ground as Marcel moved his way. At the last possible moment, he aimed the can at the vampire, pressed the button, and then flicked the lighter. A rush of flames met Charmant's attack. The vampire howled and grimaced before retreating.

"You do not fight like a gentleman." He whined.

"Hey, I'm a redneck and proud of it. I fight to win, so let's get this over with shall we?" Gideon knew he was taunting a monster but didn't care. He wanted Kat home with him before dawn.

His words ignited a deeper rage in Marcel or so

he gathered from the vampire's open-mouthed snarl. As Gideon watched, the creature seemed to fly toward him. He had no chance to bring up the hairspray to scorch him again before an open-handed slap knocked him backward. His face stung like the devil, and he could feel blood running down his cheek.

He could handle the pain, but Kat's moan of terror hurt worse than any injury. He cleared the blood from his eyes and focused on Marcel.

Katheryne wanted to close her eyes. She couldn't bear to see Marcel attack Gideon again. His precious and handsome face was marred by gashes on his left cheek and near his eye. Thank God Marcel's aim had been a bit off.

As she watched, her husband nodded his head at Marcel. "Good job, I hate being the only one to get licks in when I fight."

She wanted to shriek at him not to taunt the aged vampire. Her heart thudded, skipped, and beat like a bird's wings in flight.

Gideon stood relaxed or so it appeared to Kat. His mouth posed in a grin. Lord was he crazy?

"Well, I will try to oblige you, detective." Marcel flicked his hand, and Gideon was knocked back a few feet. The fact he wasn't slammed into the wall astonished Kat. Why?

"It seems I underestimated your power. Maybe you need a bit more of mine." Marcel again flicked his fingers, and this time her husband went sailing through the air narrowly missing being stabbed by the sword he wore.

He shook his head, stood to his feet, and then motioned to Marcel. "Is that all you've got?"

Her gasp was lost in the scream of rage flying from Marcel's lips. She watched, in horror, as the filing cabinet, lifted into the air and went hurtling toward her husband. Only at the last moment did

Gideon jump away. Kat's horror began to turn into anger. Why on earth was he doing this? Did he not realize Marcel could kill him?

"Again, is that all you have?" Gideon mocked Marcel's stance as the other vampire stood with one leg slightly bent and his arms across his chest.

"Actually, no it's not, but I think I am growing bored with you." Marcel strode to Kat's cage and despite his lack of gloves opened the lock and then the door. His handling was rough as he pulled her free and then literally threw her toward Gideon.

She didn't see her husband move but she felt his gentle arms as he caught her. A moment later, she was behind his massive frame.

Gideon could have shouted for joy. He never dreamed Marcel would just throw Kat at him. But now that she was out of the cage, and he stood between her and Marcel, he planned to up the action a bit. Again, he used the hairspray and lighter as a flamethrower forcing Marcel toward the empty cage. If he could get him close enough, he hoped to cage the vampire.

Yes, he was out of his league, but love was supposed to conquer all or so he'd heard. And his love for Kat far outweighed centuries of hate and possessiveness from Marcel.

Gideon continued to lob flame toward the vampire but he stayed out of range of the cage. He would have to come up with something else. What?

"Stay here." He told Kat without turning around, and then he moved toward Marcel. He needed to direct the game in order to play it out.

The vampire looked a bit worse for wear. His previously neat ponytail was loose, his pristine coat and vest marred by soot, and the smug look on his dirty face was now missing. He needed to get under Marcel's skin and stay there.

He got within four feet of Marcel before the

vampire moved. His blow was quick, painful, and made Gideon mad as hell. He should have seen it coming. His head reeled a bit but he ignored the feeling and shot back with a right to Marcel's smiling face.

The force of the blow caused pain to shoot through his hand and up his arm, but Marcel's look of surprise was worth it and more. He next delivered a roundhouse blow to the vampire's midsection and then a kick to the balls for good measure. When the vampire went down, Gideon was ecstatic. It seemed even as a vampire there were some parts of the anatomy that were more susceptible than others. He'd have to remember that in the future.

As Marcel fell at his feet, Gideon pulled Zacke's sword free. But it seemed bad sportsmanship to kill a man while he was holding his jewels, so he backed up a bit. "All right, I can cut your head off now or you can stand and fight me as a man, not a vampire. You were one, I take it, at some time or other."

Marcel looked up with pain ripe across his features. For a moment, Gideon thought he would choke on the rage he glimpsed in the other's eyes. Then he got the surprise of his life when Marcel bowed his head. "Fine, we will fight but it will be with swords."

Damn, he should have kept his gentlemanly mouth shut. How could he fight with a sword? He'd never had lessons. Still maybe all he had to do was stay out of Marcel's way and then get in a lucky blow. Nah, but he'd give it his best shot.

Marcel stood and a sword materialized in mid-air. So much for hoping the vampire would have to run out to get one. As the other made impressive strokes through the air, Gideon said a quick prayer, shot a smile at Kat, and then unsheathed "Death Giver."

Marcel struck first, his blade coming close to

Gideon's shoulder. A blow that would have severed his arm if he hadn't jumped back. He swung his sword and felt an instantaneous burst of energy pour through him. His arm didn't feel the weight of the blade; his movements were concise, almost as if directed by something or someone else.

He felt the blade when it pierced Marcel's flesh, the silver leaving behind an open and slightly smoking wound. Before he could rejoice and bring his weapon to bear a second time, Marcel blocked the blade. The vibration echoed all the way up his arm.

Marcel pushed forward, causing Gideon to back up. He tripped over something on the floor, but righted himself in time to block another blow. He needed to get a handle on this and fast. He stepped sideways, spun around and came up with *Death Giver* leading the way. The point of the sword pierced and then buried deep inside Marcel's chest.

The vampire gasped, grabbed the edge of the blade and tried to pull it out, but with Gideon forcing it in deeper, he couldn't free himself.

Marcel's face contorted, his eyes bled as the skin on his chest began to smoke and then caught fire. When the sparks touched the blade, Gideon pulled it backward. Marcel fell to his knees, and Gideon swung the sword with all his might. The vampire's head parted from his shoulders, hit the floor with a sickening thud, and rolled a few feet away.

It was done. Now, he needed to destroy the carcass and the head.

Kat stood frozen in place. Her heart finally came up from her feet and beat erratically inside her chest. She forced her legs to move forward until she was running to Gideon. She caught him around the waist and held on for dear life.

"Babe, I love you, but I've got to finish this. Stand back, please." Gideon set her gently away from him. He then sheathed the sword inside the holster belt, before pulling out some sticks from a bag.

He placed two under Marcel's decapitated body, two beside his grotesque looking head, and then more around the room. Gideon then took several lengths of some type of string, tied them to the white cords sticking out of the red sticks, and ran the entire thing to the exit.

"Come on babe, let's go home." Gideon's grin galvanized her into action. She ran to his side and together they ascended the steps. In the main portion of the house, her husband continued to unroll string until they stood outside and away from the house. He then took out the lighter he'd used before and touched it to the string that began to crackle and burn. They watched as the flames ate up the length until it disappeared inside the house.

Gideon dropped an arm around her waist, clutched her close, and as the house exploded, they teleported away. Their arrival at the Kensington's turned into a melee of noise as Gideon was congratulated, she was fussed over, and they both reassured their friends that Marcel was dead. It was only then that the realization she and Gideon were free to live and love for an eternity hit Katheryne.

One moment he was talking and the next she had him by the arm. "I want to go home, husband."

****

Gideon thrust into Kat's welcoming body and cherished the moment. They were alive, well, and together. He wanted to shout "thank you" to the heavens. His beautiful, perfect wife was safe.

As he pulled out and pushed forth again, Kat wiggled her hips, pulling him even closer into her wetness. He leaned forward, took first one and then the other luscious nipple in his mouth before taking her lips.

His sac drew tighter, his shaft harder, and his blood pumped faster as the spirals of lust roared for release. He eased his hand between their bodies and touched the core of Kat's desire.

"Gideon... I... Can't..." Kat's scream echoed throughout their bedroom, and acted as a catalyst for his own lust. He followed her to the height of desire and then as they crashed down to reality he held her close.

"Baby, I love you. I thought I'd lost you forever." His throat closed up as he said those words. The reality of how close to the truth it was still scared him shitless.

"And I thought you were going to die. You must never ever, and I mean this, take on another vampire of Marcel's status." Kat berated him all the time running a slender, soft hand up and down his chest.

"Okay, I promise to stay away from vampires stronger than I am, if you promise you won't be so damn heroic."

"You know I had to do it, Gideon. Marcel would have killed Brier." Kat's whisper was a plea for his understanding, he knew that, and answered in kind.

"I know, and I did what I had to do too, babe." He grinned at her chagrined look and yelped when she slapped his arm. "Hey, watch it, I bruise easily."

"Wimp."

"You've been hanging around Miranda and Hope too much." His remark was met by Kat's soft giggles and they soothed his heart, He prayed they could always be like this. Of course he'd love to have a bunch of kids with Kat, but odds were that might be impossible. Besides, he didn't need a bunch of smelly, snot nose kids under foot. Liar!

"Gideon quit mumbling. It's time to rest." Kat burrowed closer beneath his arm, and he rested his chin against the top of her head.

He closed his eyes and had almost drifted off when he heard the faintest of sounds. So soft, he thought he imagined it, but then the childish voice called again. "Daddy, I love you."

"Kat, did you hear that?" Gideon's heart beat so fast he thought he was having a heart attack.

"Hear what? I was asleep." Kat murmured softly.

Afraid he was losing his mind, he responded. "Nothing, sorry I woke you."

"No... problem." Kat's snores were the only thing he heard in the room. Probably the only thing he'd heard before. Lord knew he was tired from everything that had happened. Yes, just his imagination. No way could he have heard a child's voice. Gideon closed his eyes and allowed sleep to take him.

Across the room, a beam of light formed and then drifted closer to the bed. The ball of rainbow colors hovered over Gideon and a soft whisper stole through the room. "Through trials and tribulations you have come. Fighting foes to make the world a better place. To those who stand for right against evil, miracles can and do happen."

The globe then moved to Kat's body, twirled over her prone body three times, and then disappeared.

****

Several months later, Gideon walked into his house to a chorus of "Happy Birthday's" Katheryne glided forward and his surprise turned into joy. She walked with grace despite the large baby bump pressing against a silver mist maternity dress.

"Babe, you've been busy," he whispered in her ear as his hand caressed their unborn child.

"I wanted to surprise you. So much has happened in our lives in the past months, I didn't want you to think I'd forgotten your mortal birth date."

He kissed her lips, and then turned to his extended family.

Zacke was the first to slap him on the back, followed by Miles and Hawk. Miranda and Hope gave him hugs and kisses, while their children jumped up and down in excitement.

It was a moment he would treasure always for it was a culmination of the past and present.

"Come on, it's time to blow out your candles." Kat's sweet voice did what it always did to Gideon— melted his bones. He still couldn't fathom how he'd ended up with such a sexy, kind-hearted, and beautiful wife. Nor could he figure how they were going to be parents. It was highly unusual in the vampire world, but he was grateful for the miracle they shared.

"And what happens if I don't blow out all the candles? Does that mean my wish won't come true?" Gideon's question did not get the results he expected. Kat's face contorted in a grimace of pain.

"You okay?"

"I'm not sure, but I think I just had a contraction." Kat smiled at the look of horror on her husband's face. They had talked about this moment, he'd jokingly said he had everything under control, but she'd secretively wondered if that was the case. Now she knew.

"Okay, Okay, we need to go to the hospital." Gideon spun around and almost knocked over Miranda who carried the cake in her hands.

"Gideon!"

"I'm sorry, I'm sorry. Kat's in labor. We have to do something."

His words brought equal looks of terror from the other men, but Miranda and Hope's grins were so wide she feared they would split their lips.

"Gideon calm down. We don't have to go to the hospital. Remember? Miranda and Hope are going to deliver our baby. And it's not like it's going to happen right now. I just had one tiny little pain." Kat's sentence ended on a moan as a cramp ripped across her abdomen, doubling her over.

"Little, oh my God in heaven. Do something!" Gideon's yell only added to further chaos.

As Kat breathed through the contraction's end, Miranda grabbed Zacke's arm, whispered something in his ear as Hope did the same with Miles. Both men then turned and grabbed Gideon by the arms and hauled him outside. Hawk quickly followed them.

"Okay, looks like your little one is trying to come into the world at a much faster rate than our kids did." Miranda looped her arm around Kat's waist and helped her stand upright. Hope blinked out of the room for a moment and then returned with a medical bag.

"Okay, let's get this baby born." Both women gently helped Kat up the stairs to her and Gideon's bedroom. Once there, she settled on the bed, and tried to rest. She knew her labor could last a long time, she prayed it wouldn't. She wasn't at all sure her husband could handle the strain.

"You doing okay?" Hope asked as she spread a clean sheet under Kat's hips and then helped her to take off her dress and panties.

"I think so. Just wished—" Another contraction stopped Kat's words in mid-sentence.

"Well, looks as if we're going to be aunts rather quickly." Miranda helped raise Kat's legs until her knees were bent, and then after taking a quick look she grinned.

"Wow, not sure if it has anything to do with you both being vampires when you conceived but this baby is ready to make an appearance."

The next moments blurred as Kat pressed down with her hips, sucked in air through her pains, and then gave a sigh of relief as their baby came into the world.

A quarter of an hour later after both women had checked the little one's lungs and everything else, they helped Kat get cleaned up and ready to present the new addition to Gideon.

"Kat?" His query came from inside her mind. She was truly surprised he'd not tried contacting her before now, but the men must have kept him busy.

"I'm okay, our baby's okay. Come up and see for yourself." Kat's thought had just left her mind when Gideon materialized inside the room. The rest of the men followed on his footsteps.

Gideon found it hard to breathe as he crossed to Kat's side. His heart pounded like a sledgehammer out of control. His wife looked even more beautiful holding their child in her arms. He dropped a kiss on her welcoming lips before raising an eyebrow.

"Gideon, I'd like for you to meet your daughter."

His heart sped up even more. A girl. A deliciously, delicate, tiny, bundle of trouble.

As he looked into the bright blue of his daughter's eyes, reached out to touch the silver down on top of her head, he felt tears burn his eyes.

When he caught one of her flailing fingers in his overly large hands, he marveled at the wonder of this miracle of birth. Gideon shot a glance at his wife. "You did good, babe. More than good. I love you!"

He barely heard her "I love you too," when the baby smiled up at him. For the second time in his natural and now unnatural life he fell completely and utterly in love. Woe to anyone who ever hurt a hair on his baby's head. He'd hunt them down and make them pay for any and all sins.

"So what are you going to name her?" Miranda's question pulled him back to the present.

Although they had discussed several names

neither he nor Kat had decided on what they preferred. Now looking down at his daughter, he realized there was only one name she could have.

"Grace, we're going to call her Grace." For without the grace of good friends, the unbreakable vows of his and Kat's love, and the Almighty, she would never have been born.

A word about the author...

Faith started her journey to publication when she joined the Romance board at iVillage.com, where she became a community leader. She has written book reviews for *Bridges* magazine, MyShelf.com and Romantic Times Book Reviews. She also pens a column for a local magazine. Her dream of having her own work published is a blessing and an honor.

Faith resides in the South with her daughter Amanda, memories of her now-angel husband Rick, and a special zoo crew of furry babies.

Visit her at www.faithvsmith.com

Other books by Faith V. Smith:
Beware What You Wish
Kensington's Soul
Dunbar's Curse
Viking, Go Home
Semper Fi Magick

Coming soon from The Wild Rose Press:

IMMORTAL JUSTICE
Book 1 of The Immortal Executioners

To my readers...

Some of you have been with me before I ever became published, and some of you are new fans. Thank you so much for making me love my work. I appreciate each and every one of you!

Look for *Hawk's Salvation*, Hawk Sherwood's story of love, coming soon from The Wild Rose Press.

~Faith V. Smith

Thank you for purchasing
this Wild Rose Press publication.
For other wonderful stories of romance,
please visit our on-line bookstore at
www.thewildrosepress.com.

For questions or more information
contact us at
info@thewildrosepress.com.

The Wild Rose Press
www.TheWildRosePress.com

To visit with authors of The Wild Rose Press
join our yahoo loop at
http://groups.yahoo.com/group/thewildrosepress/